Just You

Also By Pamela Humphrey

Hill Country Secrets

Finding Claire

Finding Kate

Finding Treasure

The Chase

Other Books

The Blue Rebozo: A Novella

Researching Ramirez: On the Trail of the Jesus Ramirez Family

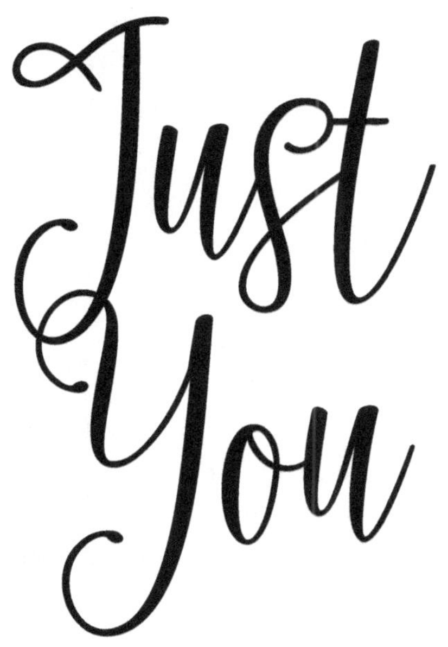

Just You

PAMELA HUMPHREY

Chapter One

Travis Bentley clicked the end of his pen as the call dragged on. Mr. Colter reviewed everything they'd covered in their two-hour phone conversation, despite the fact that Travis promised an email detailing all they'd discussed.

He glanced at the time. Kate would be arriving at any moment, and he didn't want to keep his daughter waiting. Having her back in his life—after searching for her for nearly thirty years—put her at the top of his priority list.

His personal assistant, Mari, poked her head in the door and smiled.

Kate had probably arrived, and Mari was checking on him.

Mr. Colter didn't show any sign of wrapping up the conversation. "Have you decided what you will get each family for Thanksgiving?"

"I'll have all that information in the email. You'll receive it tomorrow." Travis stood, itching to end the call.

Bret Colter had been a volunteer for Travis's charity for almost fifteen years, and while his help was appreciated, his long-windedness could be mildly frustrating. "Before lunch would be better for me. I know it's only April, but I want to make sure everything is ready in time for Thanksgiving."

"I can have it there sometime in the morning. Thanks so much for everything, Bret. My daughter just arrived, so I need to run."

"Give Kate a big hello from me. It's still shocking that she's back. And it's hard not calling her Claire."

"We're all glad she's home. Talk to you soon." Travis ended the call and saved files on his machine. When he walked out the office door, he'd be done for the day.

Named Claire at birth, his little girl had been kidnapped by his brother. A long and heart-wrenching story, it at least had a happy ending. She'd found her way home. Renamed Kate, she chose to keep that name. Travis didn't care what she called herself. His little girl was home.

Their relationship—stilted at first—had deepened in the three short months she'd been back. Now that she and her fiancé, Alex, were planning their wedding, Travis's excitement exploded. It was one more chance to spoil her and make up for the years she'd been gone.

Travis strolled to the waiting area outside his office.

As he walked through the door, Kate threw her arms around Mari. "Thank you. Are you sure?"

"Absolutely." Mari's smile made his heart beat faster.

They'd worked together for seven years, but in the last few months, his feelings about her had changed, not that he would—or could for that matter—do anything about it. He was her boss, and office relationships were complicated.

"Am I interrupting?" He wasn't sure what had prompted the scene, but it made him happy because it clearly made Kate happy.

He opened his arms as she stepped toward him.

Delight lit up her face. "Mari is going to help me with wedding plans."

"Really?" He turned his attention to Mari. "That's wonderful. Thank you."

"I'll try not to let it interfere with my job." Her short, brown curls bounced as she laughed. "Where's Alex tonight?"

"In the truck. His sister called just as we parked." Kate pulled a notebook out of her purse. "Organizing the information, keeping track of who I've spoken with—that's what's driving me crazy. And there are so many choices. I've written most of the stuff in here, but I've only been at this a week."

Travis stepped out of the way as the women huddled near the front desk.

"Let me have a look." Mari pulled her readers off the top of her head and slipped them on before flipping through the notebook. "You've been busy."

Kate pointed at dates jotted in the margin. "I'm hoping maybe July. Thankfully, there are still places with weekends open then."

Travis moved closer to Mari so that he could see but hesitated and stepped back. Leaning over her shoulder and smelling her shampoo weren't going to help him maintain a professional relationship, and the last thing he wanted was to make Mari uncomfortable in any way.

"Oh!" Kate grabbed Mari's arm. "Why don't you come to dinner with us? We were going to talk about the wedding. You don't mind, do you, Dad?"

Travis tried not to look as excited as he felt. "Of course not. Please join us."

"My evening plans consisted of cheesecake and Netflix, nothing I can't postpone." Mari rarely spoke about life outside the office, other than talking about her son, who was nearly out of the house. "Dinner sounds great."

"Perfect!" Kate closed the notebook and tucked it back in her purse. "I'm going to run back down to the truck. Alex and I will see you at the restaurant." She waved as the elevator door closed.

Mari spun to face Travis. "If I'm intruding, I don't have to go. She kind of put you on the spot."

"If I hadn't meant it, I wouldn't have said it." He smiled down at her, thankful for their easy rapport. "I think it's great that you'll be joining us and that you are helping Kate with wedding plans."

"With only a son, this may be the only wedding I help plan." She slipped her readers—or cheaters as she called them—to the top of her head, and they were swallowed by her curls.

Without shoes on, she stood eye-level with his chest. Attractive, she was younger than he was by at least fifteen years. For that reason alone, he kept a tight rein on his interest. At sixty-three, he didn't expect it would be reciprocated. The fact that he was her boss, only added another complicated layer of reasons.

She patted his arm. "Let me shut things down. I'll just be a minute."

He followed her into the office. "I really do appreciate you helping Kate. Without a mom around, she feels overwhelmed, and besides writing checks, I'm not much help." He leaned on the edge of the desk while she saved files, her fingers gliding across the keys. "But I will hire whoever and buy whatever y'all need. I don't know the first thing about planning a wedding, but budget isn't a concern."

She grinned, a tease playing in her brown eyes. "Who's more excited about this wedding? You or Kate?"

"Alex." Travis caught himself before he winked. "Honestly, please make sure Kate understands that. I'd buy the Alamo if I thought it would make her happy."

Mari laughed. "I'll remember that."

"Remember the Alamo." He rolled his eyes at his bomb of a joke. "Want to ride with me? It'll be fun." He jingled his keys.

After a moment's pause, she nodded. "You still driving that red Porsche?"

"I am."

"Only if you put the top down." She switched off lights as they made their way to the elevator.

While Travis loved having dinner with Kate and Alex, adding Mari to the mix promised an even better evening.

Before backing out of his reserved spot, he put the top down as requested. The weather couldn't have been more perfect for it.

Buckled into the passenger seat, she almost giggled when Travis zipped around a corner. He might've been showing off a bit, and her smile was the reward.

"Told you it'd be fun." Out of the office, he relaxed and worried less about who might see them or make assumptions.

Chapter Two

Mari stepped into the restaurant as Travis held open the door. Kate and Alex waited just inside.

A smiling hostess stepped up, cradling menus. "Four? Table or booth?"

"Booth." Kate glanced at Mari. "Is that okay?"

Surprised to be asked, she nodded. "Of course."

The waitress led them to a booth in the back corner. Alex and Kate slid into one side, which left the other side for Mari and Travis. She didn't miss the fact that he hugged the outside edge of the bench as close as possible. If she'd bumped him, he might have fallen off.

She set her purse between them.

The long table offered ample space for poring over details in the notebook. While they waited for their food to arrive, Kate and Mari talked about the wedding.

"We're thinking July. Right, Alex?" Kate held his hand as she talked.

"May works, too." His green eyes twinkled. "Sorry, yes. July is great."

Travis chuckled. "What type of venue are you thinking? There are so many great places in and around San Antonio."

Kate tapped her notebook. "Move this way so you can see my list. I'm thinking a place in the Hill Country. Are you familiar with any of these places?"

Travis glanced at the purse before sliding up next to it. Mari tried not to spend too much time admiring his profile. In his early sixties, he'd aged very well. His striking good looks, piercing blue eyes, and salt and pepper hair still turned heads.

He scanned the list. "I've been to a few of these over the years. They're all pretty nice."

"I've got prices for several places. I'd kinda like it to be all in one place—wedding and reception." Kate flipped through pages full of scribbled notes.

Mari found herself getting excited. "Have you visited any yet?"

"I saw three yesterday. They were okay, but I'm hoping I find something else. I'm going to two others on Monday. Think you would be able to go with me?" Kate drew arrows next to two on the list.

"I'd have to check with my boss." Mari glanced at Travis.

A delicious twinkle sparkled in his blue eyes. "He approves." He winked at Kate. "If I don't have any meetings, maybe I could tag along?"

"I'd love that." She bumped her shoulder against Alex. "You coming too?"

"Maybe." He shrugged, a teasing smile pulling at the corners of his mouth.

Mari feared that maybe dinner had been a mistake. She spent hours every day around Travis, but he was a different person outside the office. More relaxed and more charming, he made her wish he wasn't her boss. She'd definitely be messaging her friends when she got home later.

Travis straightened his utensils, lining up the bottom edges. "Take off whatever time you need to help Kate, but I won't allow you to use vacation days. Just mark yourself out of the office." Not known for dictating, he sounded almost humorous saying he wouldn't allow it.

They'd worked together long enough for her to point out his poor choice of wording. She raised her eyebrows. "Won't allow?"

"You know what I mean." He leaned back as the waitress slid plates of food onto the table.

Halfway through dinner, Mari's phone beeped. She fished it out of her purse. "It's my son."

Travis moved to stand up. "Need to slide out?"

"Oh no. It's just a text."

Carlos had texted: *Leaving later than planned but on the road now. Love you, Mom.*

She stared at her phone. How was her son old enough for college? Since she'd been widowed five years before, it had been just the two of them, and she wasn't ready for him to leave at the end of the summer. Closing a chapter of life was never easy.

She tapped out a reply: *Have a safe trip. Let me know what you find.*

He responded with a thumbs-up. *Here's hoping we find a decent apartment.*

Too many feelings flooded over her, and she stayed focused on her phone while she shoved them all back inside. Sitting at the table with her boss wasn't the place to unpack them.

"You okay?" His voice soft and tender, he focused those blue eyes on her.

Mari pasted on a smile. "Yes. Carlos is looking for an apartment. College. It makes me feel old." Laughing it off, she tucked her phone away and avoided meeting Travis's gaze.

He didn't look away.

She poked at her food before glancing at him. "I am okay. Really."

"Is he going to school nearby?" Travis picked up his fork.

Glad that Alex and Kate were absorbed in their own conversation, she sighed. "About an hour away. Between here and Austin."

"That's better than moving to another state, I guess."

"Very much so. I'm happy for him. I am. It's just … I'm not sure what happened to all the years."

Travis looked over at Kate, who smiled when she noticed. "I know exactly what you mean."

Overwhelmed by a sudden urge to hug the boss, Mari focused on her plate. "This is really delicious."

"It is good." He never moved back to the far edge of the bench.

During dessert Kate pulled out the notebook again. "This is my checklist. I printed it off the internet. Anything I'm missing?"

Mari put on her cheaters and scanned the items. "I don't think so, but I'd suggest hiring a wedding coordinator. I am more than happy to help, but getting someone who does this all the time will ensure things don't fall through the cracks."

"That's a great idea." Travis pushed his empty plate away from him.

Kate seemed more relaxed than when she first opened the notebook. "I'll find one this week."

∾

Tucked in bed, Mari messaged her friends: *Interesting night. Instead of cheesecake and Netflix, I had dinner with the boss, his daughter, and his soon-to-be son-in-law.*

Remi answered right away: *Oooh? A little office romance?*

No! Mari wanted to nip that thought in the bud. Travis was wonderful, good-looking, and charming; but he was her boss.

They'd worked together long enough to be friends, but the relationship had to stay professional.

She laughed at Charlie's response.

Why? To the point, Charlie rarely wasted words.

Mari couldn't resist teasing a bit: *Why no romance? I didn't expect that question from you.*

She'd met Charlie and Remi online nearly five years ago, after her husband, George, died in a car accident. At the time, they'd all recently been widowed, and sharing grief, a friendship blossomed. The three of them were undoubtedly kindred spirits, as they liked to call themselves. While Mari had casual friends who were local, those two, her closest friends, lived halfway across the country in opposite directions. Once a year they met up for a girls' weekend, and Mari couldn't wait until September when they'd descend on San Antonio for three days of fun. *Four and a half months.* She only had to wait four and a half months for late-night chats while sipping premixed margaritas.

Charlie was probably rolling her eyes as she typed: *Why would you have dinner with your boss? If it wasn't an office function—just seems odd.*

Remi always viewed life from one angle—a romantic one. *Who invited you?*

Mari slipped into her memories. Travis hadn't seemed bothered when Kate extended the invitation, but he'd kept a physical distance that he didn't in the office. That made him sound bad. Always the gentleman, he wasn't handsy or in any way inappropriate, but at dinner he'd been more guarded but only with Mari. Overall, he shed the businessman persona, laughed more, and became someone entirely charming.

She was glad her friends couldn't read her thoughts as she typed out her response: *His daughter asked me to join them. I'm going to help with wedding planning.*

Exciting! Weddings are so fun. Remi could find the bright side of a blackout.

Charlie responded: *It's kind of you to help her. Did Carlos find an apartment?*

Where is Superman when I need him? I want him to fly backward around the earth and give me years back. I'm not ready for him to move out. Mari fought tears as she typed. *I don't care that I'm old. I don't care that I'll be alone, but I care that I'll be without him. He won't need me anymore. No one will.*

She wiped her eyes and continued tapping away at the keyboard: *He left this evening while I was at dinner. They look at apartments tomorrow.*

Charlie replied first: *Want me to come out there? I have some leave time I can take.*

I can write anywhere! Maybe I'll stay out there and write cowboy romances or billionaire romances or maybe one about a billionaire cowboy. Give me five minutes to pack. Remi wrote romance novels for a living, which skewed her view of the world in a delightful and entertaining way.

I'm okay. Y'all don't need to hop on a plane. Mari shifted the laptop and leaned back against the pile of pillows. *I'm happy he's growing up.*

Want to talk about why you are taking it so hard? In her mid-fifties, Charlie had three children, who had all moved out years before.

Mari wasn't ready. *Not ready to unpack all that yet.*

Planning the wedding will help keep you busy. But message us A LOT. Remi had a vibrancy Mari craved.

I will. Mari shook her head, thinking of people who referred to online relationships as cheap imitations. She'd found true friendship thanks to the internet.

Charlie ended the conversation: *You better! Night all.*

Chapter Three

Travis glanced at the clock as he hit send on the email, hoping that Mr. Colter didn't take an early lunch. With more than half the day's task list crossed off, Travis had no reservations about leaving the office. When a knock sounded on the door his office shared with Mari's, he smiled, excited about the afternoon for more reasons than one.

"Come in."

Mari hooked her purse on her shoulder. "Ready?"

"Just one more second." He saved files, then shut off the machine. "Where are we headed?"

"A plantation in Kendall County and another venue just outside of San Antonio. But not in that order." She fished in her purse and pulled out keys. "They both look really nice from what I saw online."

He waited for her to look up, wanting to read the reaction in her brown eyes to his suggestion. "I'll need the addresses, or we could ride together—unless you'd rather not."

Surprise registered. "We can take your car." She grinned as she dropped her keys back in their spot.

He didn't hide his delight, but he did keep quiet about how he'd hoped she'd want to make the drive together. "Did Kate find a wedding coordinator?"

"Yes. And she's meeting us out there."

Remembering the receptionists sitting outside his office, Travis stopped before opening the door. "Take my keys. I need to do one quick thing, and I'll meet you at the car."

She shot him a puzzled look but didn't ask any questions.

Walking out together when the office was empty was one thing, leaving together at lunchtime could start rumors he wanted to avoid. He should have let her take her own car, except he wanted to be able to chat with her between venues.

After delaying three minutes, he stepped out of his office. "Fran, Erika, I'm headed out to meet Kate. If something urgent comes up, text me."

"Yes, sir." Fran flashed him a nervous grin. She'd worked in the position six months and still acted as if she was afraid of breaking something.

Erika nodded. "I think Mari is out for the afternoon."

"She is, so contact me on my cell if there's a problem." Travis stepped onto the elevator, leaving work behind and looking forward to the outing.

When he slid in behind the wheel, Mari handed him the keys. "The first place is just off the interstate west of here. I'll tell you where to exit."

He eased onto the highway, wondering if she'd guessed the reason for his delay. "So, tell me about the place we're seeing first."

"Looks beautiful. And it's not far from town, which is convenient. They have a gazebo and seating outside for the ceremony. The reception would be indoors."

"Cons?" Travis had learned to read between the lines when Mari gave him details.

"It's not very big. I'm not sure how many people Kate is planning to invite. She hasn't said, but the place seats one hundred, maybe one fifty."

"She asked me for a list last night, but I haven't sent it yet. I think mine will have more people than that place will hold."

"I'll mention something."

Travis didn't want to add stress to Kate's planning. "No, don't. This is Kate's wedding. Whatever she wants. I can narrow my list to five people if necessary."

"This is your exit. Go left under the bridge. The place is up on the left."

They parked, but Kate and Alex hadn't yet arrived. Mari stepped out and smiled. Dappled sunlight danced on the driveway, and birds chirped in the tree canopy. The venue had all the ingredients for a romantic day, but it was smaller than Travis had imagined.

Cars pulled in, and a woman walked out of the building. Travis hung back, watching as Mari greeted Kate and Alex, then met the wedding planner and the woman from the venue.

Appreciative of the extra time spent with Mari, Travis grappled with his thoughts. Because of the age difference, he'd assumed she wouldn't be interested, but there were moments last night that made him question that assumption. But as things were, since he was her boss, he couldn't open the door to a relationship. It risked making her uncomfortable if she felt differently, and it risked raised eyebrows from others at the company and in the corporate world in which he did business. So, he had to wait until life changed, choosing to enjoy the friendship as it was.

He tagged along as they toured the venue, and Alex fell in step beside Travis.

Alex tucked his hands in his pockets, eying Kate as he walked.

"Thought I should warn you—Kate is very excited that Mari is helping with the wedding planning."

Travis ignored the implication. "I'm glad she's helping. Between Mari and a wedding planner, Kate might be able to enjoy the process."

"She's happy for the help, but she's also happy that … never mind. What do you think of this place?"

"It's surprisingly quiet, considering how much is around here."

"We're thinking it's not going to hold enough people. That's what Kate was saying on the way over here."

"Maybe the next place will be the one." Travis smiled when Mari waved him over. "I'm wanted." He hoped that was true, in more ways than one.

Chapter Four

Mari guessed that maybe they'd found the perfect spot as Travis pulled up to the plantation. She loved the view from the hilltop location and couldn't wait to see inside the large house.

Vivian, the wedding coordinator, talked with Kate and Alex on the wrap-around porch. A woman stepped out to greet them.

Before getting out of the car, Mari made her prediction to Travis. "I think maybe she'll choose this place."

"How many does it seat?"

"Not sure, but I think five hundred."

"Ready to see it?" He climbed out and opened her door.

As they approached the group, the woman turned to face them. "Mr. and Mrs. Bentley, so glad you could join us. I'm Tessa."

Mari hoped her face didn't register her shock. "Oh, we aren't—I'm a friend helping Kate." She wasn't sure whether to be horrified someone had mistaken her for Travis's wife or to be depressed someone thought her old enough to be Kate's mother. Did she really look old enough to have a thirty-two-year-old daughter?

Tessa paled. "Please forgive me. I'm so sorry."

Kate jumped in, rescuing the group from any more awkwardness. "If we wanted to do the ceremony outside, is there a place for that?"

"Absolutely. Let me show you. It's beautiful." Tessa led them around the porch to the other side of the house. "And the grass is always that gorgeous green, no matter the season."

Travis tapped Mari on the arm, motioning for her to hang back. Once the others were out of earshot, he chuckled. "I'm sure she thought you were a step-mom—a newer, younger model."

"Right. I'm sure that's what it was." She winked for added effect. "Know any good therapists? Plastic surgeons?"

His eyes twinkled when he laughed.

How had she never noticed that before? And how could she go back to not noticing? Overwhelmed with attraction, she changed the subject. "You like this place?"

"I like what I see." He didn't even look around. "We should probably join them, so we can get the full tour."

Mari agreed, and they hurried to catch up.

As the group walked the grounds, taking in the details, Mari tried to focus on the information and not entirely on the man beside her.

After a half hour, Kate eased up next to her dad and slipped her arm through his. "What do you think, Dad?"

"I think it's perfect." His blue eyes held a mesmerizing gleam.

Tessa and Vivian stepped away to secure the reservation.

"You were right." He flashed a lopsided grin as Kate and Alex stole away to a corner.

Mari discovered that being right held more reward when that grin was part of the prize. "I am once in a while."

⌒

Just as Mari pushed open her front door, Remi messaged. And as typical, she included Charlie in the thread. *How'd it go today?*

Mari had mentioned she planned to visit venues, but she hadn't expected her friends to be waiting for details. And with the shift in her emotions, she needed to answer cautiously. *Went fine, if you ignore the time the lady thought I was the boss's wife, and by extension—the mother of a 32yo.*

Charlie was the first to respond. *What were you doing that she assumed you were married?*

We only got out of the car. Mari felt silly defending herself.

Remi chimed in: *You rode together? Who drove?*

He drove. Mari could almost hear the tsk tsk from Charlie.

You need to tell us what he drives. It's important. Remi wasn't letting up.

Mari braced for the ribbing. *A red convertible Porsche.*

So, what did you say to the lady? Charlie kept things on topic.

Mari recounted the rest of the story, including Travis's comment and her response.

You flirted! Remi followed her message with hearts.

Mari stared at the screen, a knot forming in her stomach. *No. It wasn't like that.*

It couldn't be like that. He was her boss, and flirting would have crossed all sort of unstated boundaries.

After a quick goodbye, she laid the phone aside and replayed the scene in her head. It wasn't flirting, was it? She'd behaved like she always did at the office. After working together for seven years, she and Travis had a rapport, so she'd thought nothing of his teasing. Although, she couldn't remember a time when he behaved quite like that at the office.

She shook her head, trying to sort out her thoughts. She didn't want to assume meaning where none was intended, but she also didn't want to send the wrong message or give Kate the impression that Mari had her sights set on Travis. The idea had never occurred to her. Thanks to the lady at the plantation, that idea now flashed like a lightbulb in Mari's head.

Helping with the wedding meant Mari would be spending time with Travis outside the office. She'd have to be extra careful with what she said and how she reacted.

～

By the end of the day on Wednesday, Mari was more relaxed about the situation. Travis acted as he always did at the office, and none of their interactions since that day on the porch would have been mistaken as flirting—not even by Remi.

As Mari checked her calendar, Travis strolled into her office. "Kate wondered if you were free Friday and Saturday night. She's narrowed down the rehearsal dinner places and wanted to get our opinions." He straightened the corners on a stack of paper. "Carlos is welcome to come along."

"Kate emailed me. I'm free, but Carlos has stuff going all weekend. It was kind of you to invite him."

"Good. Great. You've been such a big help. I know Kate appreciates it. I do, too." He continued to fiddle with the papers.

"I'm happy to help. It's not like I've done much, but I've enjoyed spending time with Kate." Picking up the papers, which needed to be filed, she stood, putting her eye-level with his chest. Mari hadn't noticed before how amazing he smelled. Not strong but very inviting, the scent wrapped around her and tugged at her.

He didn't move right away, which made fighting the urge to step closer and bury her nose in his shirt a little more difficult.

"I, uh—these need to be filed."

"Let me get out of your way." He stepped aside, but his gaze stayed riveted to her face. "I'm happy to pick you up both nights."

"I don't want to inconvenience you." She opened the file drawer, trying to remember which letter came after P in the alphabet.

"Not at all." Arms crossed, he leaned on the wall next to the filing cabinet. "If you'll just send me your address."

"I'll do that. Do you need me to order dinner for you tonight?"

Travis had been a widower more than a year, and she was almost certain he hadn't cooked a single meal for himself in all that time.

"Nah. I'll just grab something. You can take off."

"Okay then. I guess I'll see you in the morning."

"See you tomorrow." He wandered back into his office.

Mari pulled her purse out of the bottom drawer, wondering if there was anything she forgot to do. She tapped the top of her head to confirm that she had her glasses before walking out the door. Then she remembered. *Tomorrow's meeting! I didn't remind him.* She pushed open his door, knocking as she did.

Travis stepped back, his hand on the knob. "Oh, I was just going to see if I could catch you."

"Wha—" Her phone rang, her son's picture filling the screen. "Let me grab this."

"Sure." Travis did that leaning thing again.

She shifted, staring at the carpet. "Hey, Carlos."

"Just letting you know I'm making dinner. Should be ready soon. Hope you don't have to work late."

"Thanks for cooking. I shouldn't be too much longer." Mari slipped her phone back in her purse and focused on Travis again. "I'm sorry. What did you need?"

He shook his head. "It can wait. See you in the morning."

"Bye." She hurried out toward the elevator.

Halfway home, she remembered she'd forgotten to remind him, so when she pulled into her driveway, she texted him: *Just a reminder I have an appointment in the morning. I'll be late getting into the office.*

Good to know. Now I won't worry about you.

His text made her smile, then panic a little. Maybe she'd been spending too much time with him. Or maybe she was reading more into what he said, mistaking his casual friendly comment as almost flirtatious.

Chapter Five

Settled at his desk, Travis opened the takeout container. With the wedding date set, he could make plans for the rest of the summer—and beyond. Scrolling through symphony dates, he tried to decide which weekend would be best.

He opted for a Saturday a few weeks after the wedding.

After arranging for the tickets, he leaned back, imagining how he would extend the invitation. He hoped by then, the situation would be less complicated.

Watching Mari hesitate when she'd stood up in front of him, seeing the quick glance she shot him before pointing to the filing cabinet added another glimmer of hope that maybe he wasn't alone in his interest.

Seeing her walk into a room put a smile on his face. Single again, he hadn't planned on dating, but the more time he spent with Mari, the more time he wanted to spend with her—in the office, outside the office, anywhere.

But being her boss, he couldn't be impulsive or irresponsible.

Timing was everything. A few times in the last few days, he'd come close to saying too much.

Late Thursday afternoon, after most employees had gone home, Mari knocked as she walked into his office. "Anne called. She wanted to know if you had a few minutes to talk."

Travis nodded, wondering it might be about. Anne had worked for the company many years and had never requested a meeting on short notice. "Of course. Did she say if everything was okay?"

"She didn't say much. I'll be in my office if you need me."

Travis hated keeping Mari late but appreciated that she cared enough to stay. "Thanks."

When Anne walked into his office five minutes later, he could see from the tissue clenched in her hand that she wasn't as calm as she appeared.

"Everything okay, Anne?"

She sat, then jumped back up, pacing. "I'm moving. My daughter had a baby a few months ago. They live in Tennessee. After visiting last month, I decided that I need to be close to my grandbaby."

Travis stifled his laugh. When she walked in, he had been worried that something happened at the office to upset her. Glad that the situation was different, he smiled. "Congratulations on your grandbaby. I completely understand that you want to be close. You'll be missed. Have you told Roger?"

Anne had long been the personal assistant of Roger Talbot, one of the younger vice presidents. "Not yet. I'll tell him Monday morning."

"When are you leaving?" Travis hoped she'd at least stay two weeks. Replacing her wouldn't be easy.

"In a month. I don't want to leave you in a bind."

"I appreciate that." Travis crossed the room and opened the

door to Mari's office. "Mari, she won't tell Roger until Monday, but Anne is leaving us to go live near her grandbaby. On Monday, will you get with her to make sure we have a thorough job description?"

"Of course." Mari stood and hugged Anne.

"She's a baby girl—Luci. I've had to learn to use the video phone thing to see her every day." Anne wiped her eyes. "I promised myself I wouldn't cry. But fifteen years at the same company is a long time."

She stunned Travis when she wrapped him in a hug.

"We'll miss you, Anne. Send us a picture of that little one." He remembered Anne screening the interviewees for his personal assistant position years ago—when the only resume she didn't toss was Mari's.

"I would've told Roger today, but he was out of the office. I'll be gone tomorrow, but I just had to say something before the weekend. And I wanted to tell *you* myself."

"Thank you. Let me know once you've shared the news on Monday." He waved as she left the office.

Travis turned and nearly bumped into Mari.

"Careful." She reached out but stopped short of touching him.

He wished she hadn't stopped short. "Sorry. I didn't realize—I thought you were—well, that was quite the announcement."

"I'm happy for her, though."

"I am too. Filling her spot will take some work."

"Would you like me to take that on? Like Anne did when I was hired?"

"Please. I'd appreciate it, and I know Roger would, too." He glanced back toward his office. "It's late. You should head on home."

"Dinner?" She opened her desk drawer and picked up a stack of menus.

If it had been an invitation to join her, he'd have said yes, but it wasn't, and nothing from a restaurant sounded good anymore. "I'm so tired of restaurant food. I'll figure something else out."

"You sure?" She hooked her purse on her shoulder and walked to the elevator.

He nodded. "See you tomorrow."

Settled at his desk, he set aside the idea of food and responded to emails. An hour passed before his stomach reminded him that dinner was required. He jotted a list of tasks he had to take care of the next day. As soon as he finished, he'd go find dinner somewhere.

When the elevator opened, he jumped up and walked out to the front lobby. As late as it was, someone showing up unannounced was unusual.

Mari stepped into the lobby holding a foil-covered plate. "I couldn't let you starve."

Stunned, he reached out to grab the food but ended up sandwiching her hand between his and the bottom of the plate. She only smiled at his touch. The woman made it difficult to hide in his interest.

"This is a surprise." Travis let his hand linger a second more before taking the plate. "What about you? Have you eaten?"

She glanced at the elevator then focused on him. "I should go."

"Mari—"

"Yes?" The anticipation dancing in her eyes excited him.

"Thank you." He wanted to say so much more, but the timing wasn't right.

She waved and left, leaving him alone again.

He lifted the foil off the plate and smiled. A home-cooked meal was such a treat. He inhaled the aroma before wandering into the kitchen. Utensils were required. He couldn't remember the last time he'd had meatloaf and mashed potatoes. She'd even included bacon-wrapped green beans.

After devouring the food, he washed the plate and set it on Mari's desk with a note.

Best dinner I've had in a while. Thanks!

The next day, Mari said nothing about the delivered dinner or his note, but she did slip out of the office earlier than usual for a Friday. Travis was looking forward to dinner that night.

As soon as Fran and Erika left, he shut off his computer and headed home. After a shower and a quick change of clothes, he climbed into the car to head over to Mari's. He pulled up her address and plugged it into his map app before backing out of the driveway. She lived only five minutes away.

When he pulled up to the curb, he sucked in a deep breath before walking to the door. Nervous was a feeling he hadn't dealt with in a while. He knocked and waited a full minute until she opened the door.

Mari wore a vivid blue dress that was a perfect match to his shirt.

He grinned. "Great minds."

Shaking her head, Mari grabbed her purse. "Maybe Kate and Alex will be wearing blue too, then we'll look like a club." She flashed a silly smile. "How many times do you think we'll hear the word 'Twinkies' tonight? Any bets?"

"Twinkies, huh?" Travis opened her car door.

She shot him a confused look. "The snack that comes two in a package. They look alike."

"I know what Twinkies are, Mari." He winked when her cheeks colored.

"Of course you do." She turned and stared out the window.

Travis sensed her embarrassment and guessed that the matching outfits bothered her, even though she'd only joked about it. He brushed his hand against her arm, which did little to make him want to take things slow. "My place is close. I can stop and change my shirt."

"No. Don't. That color is good on you." She patted his hand. "That's my favorite shirt of yours."

He fought the urge to grab her hand after shifting gears. "I'll have to remember that." That tidbit would be filed away for the future.

When they arrived at the restaurant, he opened her door and offered his hand to help her out. She ignored his hand and his gaze and climbed out of the car herself.

Just when he thought she might be interested, he got mixed signals.

Kate and Alex weren't wearing blue, and they didn't match each other. Wanting to save Mari any more embarrassment, Travis hoped that no one would point out the color coordination. Touching his hand to her back as she walked through the door, he noticed her hesitate and look back over her shoulder.

He pulled his hand away.

"You look amazing." Kate wrapped Mari in a hug. "I love that color on you."

Agreement was likely etched in Travis's expression.

"Thank you." Mari smoothed the front of her dress. "I brought the checklist with me—what we discussed on the phone."

"Oh good." Kate caught Alex's hand as the hostess stepped up holding menus.

"Right this way. Your table is ready." She led them to the room off the main dining area.

Travis fell in line behind Mari. Focused on the way her curls bounced as she walked, her short hair brushing against her neck, he nearly bumped into her when they arrived at the table.

Chapter Six

Mari sat in the chair that Travis pulled out, taking in the details of the room, which she assumed was used for events such as the rehearsal dinner. Steering her thoughts away from the man beside her proved difficult. *Stop. He's your boss. This isn't a date.* That became Mari's silent mantra throughout the evening.

The most disturbing moment was when they'd walked into the restaurant, and she realized that she wished it was a date. She blamed the lady from the wedding venue for sparking the idea. Fueling the idea might be a more accurate way to word it. Hearing him discussed in the break room at work had caused Mari to stop and take a bit more notice of Travis.

"Mari, Dad mentioned that your son was headed to college. I bet he's excited." Kate smiled, which brought out her resemblance to Travis.

"Carlos is very excited. I'm taking it a bit harder." Mari laughed, trying to keep it light-hearted. "He won't be too far away, but it's a big change for me."

"Change can be hard, but it can bring new opportunities." Travis eyed her as he spoke.

"You're right." Mari scanned the menu. "Different isn't always bad. So, Kate, has Vivian been a help?"

"Yes. I'm glad you suggested it. I'd still love it if you came with me to tastings and such, if you don't mind."

"I'm happy to." Mari wondered how many of those Travis would be attending also.

The waiter approached, and they ordered drinks.

Because her head was spinning, she couldn't decide what to order. She read the menu options over and over, hoping for focus.

Travis leaned in close. "If you like seafood, the salmon is very good."

Could he read her that well? Did he know she couldn't decide?

"Sounds good. I'll try that." Mari made the mistake of meeting his gaze.

Blue eyes the color of a Texas summer sky made her want to kiss the man. That was all kinds of a bad idea. She reverted to her mantra.

Travis pulled a piece of paper out of his shirt pocket. "I worked up a list for invitations. If that's too many, let me know, and I can trim it." He handed it to Kate.

"I'm sure it will be fine." She scanned the sheet. "Oh, bless you. You marked people with how they are connected."

"Thought it might help when figuring seating and such. And I emailed you that in a file."

Alex laughed. "We might need to practice with flashcards beforehand, so we can recognize people the day of."

"That might not be a bad idea." Kate chuckled and tucked the paper in her purse.

When the food arrived, conversation shifted to honeymoon destinations—sort of.

"He won't tell me where. Says it's a surprise." Kate poked Alex in the side.

He grinned, clearly enjoying her reaction. "I promise that you'll like it."

"You're right. She'll like it." Travis didn't look up from his plate.

She gaped. "He told you?" She focused on Mari. "Do you know, too?"

Mari shook her head. "Haven't heard a word about it." Watching Kate's anticipation made her wistful. Mari needed a way to shove the emotions back into whatever bottle they'd spilled out of. And she needed a way to recork it.

"So, Dad, I had lunch with Gram the other day. She was telling me about some of the pranks you pulled as a kid."

Mari wanted to hear those stories.

Travis slowly shook his head. "I can't believe Gram ratted me out to my own daughter."

"It's better if she hears your stories and not mine," Alex said.

Kate whispered in his ear, and his expression made Mari chuckle.

Mari turned to Travis. "Pranks?"

His lopsided grin preceded his response. Arm draped on the back of her chair, he cleared his throat. "I will only divulge my stories if you promise not to hold them against me."

His last words bounced around in Mari's head, creating an image she desperately wanted to dismiss.

"I promise." She crossed her heart.

"I need to see your other hand." He winked. "I can't risk you having your fingers crossed."

She held up her hands and wiggled her fingers. "Satisfied?"

"Growing up in a tiny town required that my brother and I find ways to entertain ourselves."

Mari hadn't heard him mention his brother in years and took

it as a sign that with Kate back, some of Travis's wounds were healing. "And was your entertainment destructive?"

"We—I never meant any harm. I honestly can't say the same for Scott. Anyway, back to the stories." He shifted, including Kate and Alex in the conversation again. "We managed to catch a raccoon."

"Seriously?" Mari couldn't even begin to imagine how to catch one.

"With a trap?" Kate looked almost concerned.

Travis bit his bottom lip. "With a pillowcase. It just so happened that Hubert Crenshaw had just gotten his truck. Months before that, he'd pummeled Scott for some reason or another, and that night seemed the perfect time for repayment."

Alex started laughing, which only fueled Travis.

"We filled a small trashcan with scraps—because of course we didn't want the raccoon to starve—then waited until late at night and closed the raccoon and the trashcan into the cab of that pickup."

"Oh no." Mari dropped her fork and cringed as it clinked against the plate. "How long did you leave it in there?"

"We put the window down a little and figured they'd find it in the morning."

"Did they?" Kate pushed her plate away from her and leaned closer.

Travis wrinkled his nose. "Turns out they'd gone away for a long weekend. That poor creature was in there three days."

Mari covered her mouth to keep from laughing out loud. "Did they ever figure out who did it?"

He shook his head. "Thankfully, no. Please don't say anything about it if—when you're in Schatzenburg. There are a few Crenshaws still in the area."

She gently swatted his arm. "That's horrible, Travis."

"But you haven't heard the best part, yet." He glanced down at her hand. "One of the Miller boys had been feuding with Hubert and promised loudly that he'd get even. Anyway, that Miller boy went to Hubert's truck—no telling what he was planning. The family had just gotten back and were in the house when they heard a loud commotion. Miller was fighting off the angry raccoon."

"No way!" Kate's jaw hung open.

Mari wasn't sure there was a bottle big enough to hold what she felt. "Travis Bentley, I had no idea you were so—so—"

"Entertaining?"

"That's one way to put it." She'd only ever known Travis as a gentleman and a businessman. Picturing him hauling around a raccoon in a pillowcase made her laugh.

After dinner, when they were back in his car, Mari reminded herself yet again that it wasn't a date. Just because Travis was good-looking, charming, and engaging did not mean that he was flirting or had any interest in her beyond their work relationship.

But even after reciting her mantra many times, she resigned herself to the fact that those twinkling blue eyes were going to be in her dreams that night. She was quite sure of it.

Mari couldn't wait to chat with her friends. When Travis stopped in front of her house, she grabbed his hand. "I had the best time tonight."

"I don't share my stories with just anyone. For good reason." He hopped out and ran around to open her car door. "What are your big plans for tomorrow? Besides dinner."

"This flower bed needs attention. I'll be pulling weeds, putting in some low-maintenance plants, and laying mulch."

"Need help?"

About to say 'no,' Mari stopped herself. There was no harm in accepting his help. "I don't have an extra set of garden gloves."

"What time should I be here?"

"Whatever works for you. I plan to start around eight-thirty. It'll be cooler then."

"Sounds like a plan."

Mari walked toward the house. "I'll see you in the morning."

"Maybe I'll tell you about the time we helped Gram with her garden."

She laughed. "I look forward it. Night."

Inside, she forced herself not to peek out the window and watch until he drove away. She ran up the stairs, opened her laptop, and shot off a message while she changed out of her dress: *The four of us had dinner tonight. Travis is so much funnier than I ever realized. He told stories about when he was a kid, and I almost embarrassed myself laughing in the restaurant.*

Uh oh. Charlie's reply popped up first.

Remi startled Mari with a question. *Was it a date?*

Not at all. I thought I told you that we are trying two places this weekend. Kate is trying to choose where to have the rehearsal dinner. Mari regretted saying anything, but she'd have exploded otherwise.

So it was a double date. Remi twisted everything into romance.

No, Remi. Just because we work together doesn't mean we can't be friends, right? Mari hoped they'd see things her way.

Of course not. Charlie came to the rescue. *Did Carlos find an apartment? How are you doing with that?*

Tears slipped down Mari's cheeks before she could reach for a tissue. *He found a place. Pictures look nice. I'm not ready, y'all.*

Aww. Remi followed her message with a crying emoji.

And don't think it's because I don't want to be alone. That's not the reason. He's my only kid, and he won't need me anymore. Typing the words made Mari cry all over again.

Charlie understood. *You'll always be his mom, but it doesn't make this transition any less difficult.*

I'll be okay. I'll just have to buy extra tissues. Mari yawned.

After a long day, crying had drained her even more. She needed sleep if she was going to be awake and sociable at eight thirty. *I'm headed to bed.*

You'll keep us posted about your … friend. Remi thought she was funny.

Goodnight! Mari snapped her laptop closed and crawled under the covers. When she heard Carlos come home, she pulled on a robe and ran downstairs.

"Hey." He stood in the kitchen, digging leftovers out of the fridge. "Sorry I woke you."

"I was still awake." She snatched a few cherries from the bowl. "Good day?"

"Not bad. Need me for anything tomorrow? I thought I might spend the day with Tori—take her to the zoo or something. That okay?"

"Sure. That's fine." Mari stifled a yawn. "Goodnight. Holler if you need anything."

⌒

Mari woke up before her alarm, a tad too excited about Travis coming to help her with the flower bed. She downed a quick breakfast and two cups of coffee before he showed up at the door.

"Morning." In jeans and a faded blue t-shirt, he looked way more relaxed than he ever did in a suit and tie.

"I appreciate your help."

"With all the help you're giving Kate, I figured this was a way I could return the favor." He held up a pair of gloves. "I brought my own."

"I'll meet you out front. Let me open the garage." She left him standing on the porch and shut the door before running through the kitchen. As she hit the button to raise the garage door, she fanned herself. It wasn't even hot out yet.

He was already kneeling in the grass, his gloves on, pulling weeds.

She dropped down next to him. "There are drinks in the garage fridge if you need anything. Just let me know."

"Thanks."

They worked quietly for a little while, and Mari tried to keep her focus on the weeds. Humming, he tugged weed after weed out of the ground, making a job she'd put off look easy.

"Have you lived here a long time?" Travis yanked out a tall, prickly weed.

"Eight years. And once upon a time, I had these beds looking pretty all the time."

"You like to garden?"

"I like having pretty flowers in front." She rested back on her heels. "Wow. This usually takes me hours and hours. It's going much faster with help."

He looked around. "I don't see flowers or mulch."

When she'd told him how she was spending her morning, she hadn't expected him to offer his help. "I haven't bought them yet."

"Well, when we're finished with the weeds, we'll make a run to get stuff."

Mari couldn't imagine loading mulch in his Porsche. "We can take my car, so we don't get dirt in yours."

"I'm not worried about a little dirt."

It had been a long time since she'd had someone work alongside her in the flower beds. Carlos had pitched in a few times, but he'd done the job alone or with his buddies.

She shifted, stretching her back. "Every Spring, George would show up with a plant. A few days later, we'd shop for more flowers together, then pull weeds and plant everything. He'd surprise me with something different every year." She blinked away the mist brought on by happy memories. "I haven't been great about keeping them up since he died."

Sharing memories came easy because Mari knew Travis understood.

"What kinds of plants do you like?"

"Anything with color that attracts butterflies."

He shifted to the far edge of the bed, working the last section. "I can't say I know much about which plants attract butterflies."

"The nursery usually has them labeled. Are you going to tell me about when you helped Gram with the flower bed?" She only caught a glimpse of his grin before he leaned forward, reaching for the weeds close to the house.

"I was young when I did it, and it was a garden. Your promise from last night still applies."

"You're stalling."

"Mom sent us down to help Gram. She had all these little plants that she'd grown from seed that she wanted us to put in the ground. Over and over, she emphasized that we needed to put them deep into the dirt."

"What did you do?"

"We buried the entire plant. Thought it'd be funny. Not even a leaf poked through."

Mari shook her head, imagining mischief sparkling in those blue eyes. "What did she do?"

"Besides giving me a tongue-lashing? She made us dig them all back up and replant them correctly. It made for a very long day."

"You must have been such a handful." She yanked off her gloves and wiped her hands. "Something to drink?"

"Anything cold would be great."

"Coke, water, Dr Pepper, sweet tea, or Big Red?"

"Water." He pulled the last few stragglers while she ran to the fridge. "I think the beds are ready for weed paper, plants, and mulch."

"Thank you." She handed him a cold bottle and sat down in

the grass next to him. "If I made it sound like Carlos doesn't help me, that isn't the case at all."

"You didn't make it sound that way." He stood and held out his hand. "I can drink this on the way."

Mari grabbed his hand and let him pull her up. "I'll get my purse and lock up the house."

Chapter Seven

After dusting the mulch off his shirt, Travis closed the trunk. They'd spent more than an hour shopping for flowers and supplies, and it was nearing lunchtime.

"Should we stop and grab a bite?"

Mari looked at her clothes. "I'm such a mess. Maybe just something from a drive-thru."

"Works for me." Enjoying the companionship, he was happy with whatever she wanted.

At her house, he unloaded her purchases, and she carried in the food.

He reasoned that spending most of the day with her made it easier to keep his interest in check. They were building a friendship, and that would help his interest stabilize. Whether that was true or not remained to be seen.

He knocked before stepping inside. "Hello?"

"Come on in. I'm in the kitchen." She'd kicked her shoes off and was setting drinks and utensils on the table.

While washing his hands, he surveyed the large kitchen. Short, colorful curtains hung above the window. Red walls contrasted with the white cabinets. It fit Mari well.

"I'm not sure I want to go back out and work after lunch. It's getting hot, and we have the dinner tonight." Mari sat down at the table.

"I can come help tomorrow."

"You really don't have to do that."

"I don't mind at all." He dug into his food. "Just to avoid the Twinkie issue, I'll let you decide what color I should wear tonight. Pink or grey?"

Her brown eyes widened, and her lips twitched into a smile. "Grey."

His phone rang, and Kate's picture popped up on the screen. "Hi, sweetheart. What's up?"

"I'm glad Mari's coming tonight."

He hadn't expected Kate to discuss Mari and was glad he hadn't answered on speaker phone. Not ready to let others know how he felt and very conscious of the woman next to him, he gave a cautious answer. "It's great that she's helping you."

Mari perked up at what was clearly a reference to her.

Kate persisted. "I'm glad for lots of reasons. I need to call her to make sure she has the name of the restaurant."

Travis wondered how much of Kate's end of the conversation Mari could hear. "I told her I'd swing by and pick her up. She doesn't live far from me."

"She won't need directions then. It's good that she doesn't have to drive over alone." The longer the conversation, the more Kate would not-so-subtly press for his reaction.

"I'll see you tonight."

"Dad?"

"Yes?" If people could read him so easily, he needed to consider retiring from the business world.

"Where are you?"

"Bye, sweetheart."

"Love you." She giggled before the call ended.

He laid the phone on the table. "Sorry about that. Not sure how much you heard."

Mari wrinkled her nose, a hint of tease in her dark eyes. "You were talking about me?"

"Kate wanted to make sure you knew where we were dining this evening."

"You didn't mention that you were here." She avoided his gaze, making it hard to read her expression.

"I hope that doesn't bother you." He relaxed a little when he saw her smile.

"It could have easily been misconstrued, so I appreciate you not saying anything."

"The last thing I want is for *anything* to be misconstrued."

A bump against his foot caught him off-guard. It lasted only a second. His quick glance at Mari met with a smile. He shifted his foot a bit, expecting to meet hers again.

"Wentworth. What are you doing under there?" Mari jumped up and pulled a bag of cat treats from the cabinet.

A grey cat brushed Travis's leg again as he ran toward Mari. She bent down, and Wentworth stood on his hind legs, bumping his head against hers.

"Pretty cat. What kind is he?"

"Russian Blue. Softest cat I've ever owned." She returned to the table after washing her hands. "After eating, I definitely don't feel like going back out there."

"Instead of hogging your afternoon, I'll run back to the house until dinner. Five thirty still okay for me to pick you up?"

"Perfectly." She walked him to the door. "I really appreciate all your help."

"Anytime." He made a quick exit before he slipped up and said something he shouldn't.

Before he went to dinner, he needed to clear his head. His attraction was growing faster than circumstances were changing.

At home in his office, he pulled out the folder where he'd laid out his road map of change. Monday, he'd know if his timeline was on track. After staring at the page, resigning himself to the fact that there was nothing he could do to hurry the process, he yanked off his shirt and ran upstairs to change into a swimsuit.

A few minutes later, he dove into the pool, the cool, clear water stilling his brain as he swam back and forth. After several laps, he pushed up out of the pool and stretched out on a lounge chair.

Though delighted that Kate liked the idea of him spending time with Mari, he had more to consider than just Kate's opinion, or even Mari's. But the more time he spent with Mari, the more hints he saw that maybe—just maybe—romance was a possibility.

Three hours later, Travis was back at Mari's. When she opened the door, he had to bite his tongue. Her tanned skin glowed against the bright coral blouse. Her smile lit up her whole face.

"Hello again." She slipped on a pair of sandals.

The cat strolled up, flicking his tail.

She stroked his fur. "Wentworth, behave, sir."

Wentworth sauntered off, and Travis guessed the fuzzy feline had no intention of behaving in her absence.

Travis stuffed his hands in his pockets as they made their way to the car, only pulling them out when he needed to open her door. Restraint was his word for the evening.

Chapter Eight

Outside the restaurant, Mari stayed in her seat, waiting until Travis opened her door. She enjoyed the warmth of his hand, his amazing cologne, and that deep blue gaze. Not ready to admit those things to anyone, she savored each moment, convincing herself there was no harm in her one-sided attraction.

Forever the gentleman, Travis made it difficult to remember it wasn't a date. Helping her out of the car, pulling out her chair, resting his hand on the small of her back as she stepped through a doorway—those things sped up her heart rate and required her to start her silent mantra. *He's the boss. This isn't a date.*

Dating the boss wasn't just a bad idea; there were probably rules against it, corporate regulations that would jeopardize her job.

Mari blinked away the thoughts of corporate policies and dating to focus on the reason she'd come. The private dining room had more atmosphere than the restaurant they'd been to the night before.

Seated across from Kate, Mari remembered the earlier phone

call and determined not to behave in a way that could be misconstrued.

"Have you been to a Brazilian steakhouse before?" Travis pointed to the card next to his plate.

"This is my first time. But this place smells incredible." Mari let her finger bump his as she pointed at the same card. "So, what's this for?"

"Green side means to keep offering you food. Red side up lets them know that you don't want any more at the moment. Sides are served family style on the table, along with cheese rolls, which are delicious."

Kate and Alex walked away from the table.

"Before we start on the main course, let's visit the salad bar." Travis motioned to the middle of the dining room.

"Okay." Mari tried to remember her mantra as she crossed the room.

After savoring a salad, they all flipped their cards to green and the servers appeared with skewers of various cuts of meat: filet mignon, sirloin, ribeye, lamb, ribs, chicken wrapped in bacon. The deep aroma of seasoned, roasted meat promised deliciousness.

Her mouth watered. Once her plate was full of food, Mari flipped her card to red.

"So, what did y'all do today?" Kate asked the question ever so casually.

Mari choked on her filet mignon. Travis hadn't mentioned he was at the house. How did Kate know?

Travis shot Mari a concerned look. "You okay?"

"Yes. Wrong pipe."

He played with the card, flipping it from green to red, then back to green. "I swam laps this afternoon. It was the perfect day for the pool."

"I worked in the yard. Got weeds out of the flower bed and bought plants and mulch to make it look nice." She grabbed another cheese roll, feeling guilty even though she'd told the truth, at least part of it..

"Alex and I—mostly Alex—spent hours clearing brush from along the fence line." Kate patted the table. "Talking about brush reminded me of flowers. Mari, would you have time next week to visit the florist with me? When I ask Alex his opinion on flowers, he tells me I can have whatever I want."

Travis laughed. "I see nothing wrong with that answer."

The look exchanged between Alex and Travis gave Mari all the feels. Both men clearly loved Kate. Alex turned his gaze to Kate, and the feels exploded.

Mari wished Travis would look at her that way. "I would be happy to look at flowers with you. Have you chosen colors yet?"

"Bridesmaids dresses are red, sort of a cherry color." Kate scanned through photos on her phone. "This is what the dresses look like." She held up a picture of Alex's sister modeling the dress.

"That'll be beautiful." Mari hoped time would slow down a little and let her enjoy these months of spending time with Alex, Kate, and Travis. Once the wedding was over, she'd see much less of them, and she'd see less of Travis outside the office.

Travis pushed his plate toward the middle and leaned back in his chair. "What do y'all think? Should we have the rehearsal dinner here?"

Kate glanced at Alex, her eyebrows raised. "What do you think?"

"Food's excellent; room's nice. It gets my vote." Alex draped his arm over the back of her chair. "So, if you like it, then I think we found the place."

"I'm willing to try a few more places if need be." Travis turned his focus to Mari. "Do you like it?"

"I like it a lot." She hadn't had a better meal in ages.

"That settles it then." Kate smiled.

Mari could've been disappointed that choosing a place meant they wouldn't be going out to dinner, trying places out, but instead, she focused on the possibility that Travis would be next to her again tomorrow as she prettied up her flower beds. She wouldn't say anything, just wait and see if he brought it up.

"Could I interest you in dessert?" The waiter's Portuguese accent added a certain charm to the evening.

Travis glanced around the table. "Cheesecake?"

"Sounds delicious." Alex glanced at Kate. "Want to share a slice?"

"Yes, please."

Travis focused on Mari, eyebrows raised.

She loved cheesecake, and even beyond full, she couldn't resist a taste. "Yes, but only a little."

He ordered two slices, and the waiter hurried away.

When he brought the cheesecake to the table, Mari hesitated.

"Ladies first." Travis pushed the plate toward her.

Alex and Kate clearly had no trouble sharing.

Mari took a bite. The creamy cheesecake almost melted on her tongue, the strawberry topping adding a delicate sweetness. "Mmm."

Travis popped a bite into his mouth. "Yum. It's been too long since I've had cheesecake."

Back and forth, they took bites until only one remained on the plate.

"Go ahead." Mari had no room left, even for the last bite of her favorite dessert.

"You sure?"

She nodded and watched him savor the last morsel. "You, uh … there's a little bit of strawberry …" Mari pointed to the corner of his mouth.

He wiped every spot near his mouth except where the red glaze was. "Gone?"

"No." She picked up the napkin.

He leaned closer. "Help me?"

"Of course." Mari had never been so keenly aware of an audience as in that moment.

Kate's eyes sparkled when Mari dared look that direction.

Mari would need a better mantra after sharing cheesecake with Travis.

She held her tongue all the way home, resisting the urge to mention plants or mulch. Disappointment thudded in her chest when she unlocked her front door, and he still hadn't brought it up.

"Night, Mari. Thanks for going tonight—for everything." He stuffed his hands in his pockets, something he didn't do often.

"Goodnight. Drive safe." She stood at the door until he climbed into his car, then waved.

She checked her phone for the first time all evening and found messages waiting.

Tell me about dinner! Remi had little to no patience.

Charlie seemed just as eager for information. *We want to know how it went with Travis.*

Mari laughed as she typed out a message: *I should have messaged this afternoon. Today was a good day. Travis helped me weed the front beds, then we shopped for plants. Dinner went smoothly. Kate found the perfect spot for the rehearsal dinner. Did I cover everything?* She knew her message would only spur more questions.

If the man showed up to pull weeds, he's interested, Mari—really interested. Remi considered herself an expert on men.

Who was Mari to argue?

Charlie didn't respond, which made Mari nervous.

If he were interested, I think I'd see it. I don't. Sadly. Outside the office, the man oozes charm. Now that I've seen that side of him, that's all I see no matter where we are. It's going to make for a rough work week! Mari felt silly for even typing out the message but hit send before she deleted it. *But he's my boss and is just being nice because I'm helping his daughter. That's all.*

Don't sell yourself short, Mari. You're attractive. Working closely together, maybe he's developed feelings, BUT workplace relationships are complicated. And you are his direct-report. Be careful. Charlie's message reminded Mari of the many reasons dating the boss was a bad idea.

I'm sure it's not like that. She thought about having to choose between keeping her job and dating Travis. *And I love my job. Enough about me. Remi?*

I'm good. I started a new book. It's about a cowboy. When I head that way in September, I'll need to see some—for research purposes. LOL. Not quite forty with a house just off the beach, Remi lived, breathed, and wrote romance.

Mari giggled as she typed out a suggestion, trying to brush aside the image that popped into her head of Travis in a pair of cowboy boots. *I think we can arrange a night of two-stepping while y'all are here. Might meet a cowboy or two that way.*

Charlie chimed in first. *I love that idea!*

Remi sent a string of hearts.

Charlie, what's up with you? Mari tucked into bed, her brain still racing from the excitement of the day.

Bubbles danced on the screen a full minute before Charlie's answered appeared. *My daughter closed on the house in Ohio. My son-in-law has been out there for a couple months already, but the family is moving this weekend. It'll be so different with the grandkids gone. My other daughter decided to extend her lease in England. She's loving it over there. My son is the only one left here in town.*

Mari wiped at tears. *Aww. You okay?*

Oh yeah. I'll be fine. Charlie wasn't one for wallowing.

She woke up to a knock at the door. Carlos must've have forgotten his house key, but she was surprised he was up and out so early. Glancing at the clock, she discovered it wasn't as early as she thought. She yanked on her robe as she ran down the stairs and opened the front door.

"Oh! Good morning. I guess I should've called first." Travis held out a coffee cup. "But I brought coffee."

Mari didn't even want to think about how disheveled she looked. "Come on in. I thought you were Carlos. I never would've answered like this if—" There was no need to finish her sentence. She accepted the coffee and pointed to the kitchen. "Make yourself at home. I'll be back down in a few."

He didn't move. "Mari, I didn't mean to intrude. I can come back later."

She didn't want him to leave, and if she hadn't been half-asleep, she might've squealed when she saw him at the door. "Don't leave. Please."

"I won't, but I'll be outside laying weed paper." His gaze did away with any hint of sleepiness. "I am sorry I woke you."

"I'll open the garage." She closed the door and pushed the button on the garage door before heading upstairs to change.

Ten minutes later, she joined him outside.

"Will you hold that end down while I cut it?" Travis already had beads of sweat forming on his forehead.

She grabbed the end, and he sliced through the black paper. As he put it in place, she gathered the large staples and the mallet. While she secured the weed mat, he cut the next piece.

All the years spent working together translated well to their efforts in the yard.

With the air like soup, the heat stuck to them. But after an hour, half the plants were already in the ground.

"Take a break." Mari handed him a bottle of water. "After we're done, please let me buy—or rather, please let me make you lunch." She remembered that he'd exhausted his taste for most restaurant food.

"How can I say no to that? I accept." He downed the entire contents of the bottle in a few gulps.

"Mom? Hey. Mr. Bentley, I didn't expect to see you working in our yard." Carlos rubbed his eyes and smoothed his hair. "I could've done that for you, Mom."

"I know, but with school ending, I know you're busy. I didn't want to bother you."

"Let me wake up, then I'll take care of the mulch. If Mr. Bentley likes digging holes for the plants, I'll let him. I hate that part."

Travis laughed but didn't quit digging.

Mari guessed Carlos might ask about Travis later and hoped she could offer an explanation that didn't tip off that she was crushing on her boss—the boss that was currently next to her, elbow-deep in dirt, planting flowers on a too-warm day. She allowed her thoughts to wander toward the possibility that Remi was right.

What if she was? How would that change things at the office? *The office.* That ended the happy thoughts.

"Just two more." Travis started digging the next hole while Mari filled in the dirt around the plumbago plant.

"I can't thank you enough." She wiped her forehead. "I'll make you anything you want for lunch."

He glanced up at her, dirt smudges on his face. "Anything?"

She silently prayed he wouldn't ask for something she'd never made before and had no idea how to make.

"Pancakes." He sat back, resting on his heels. "I haven't had homemade pancakes in ages."

Mari wanted to kiss him but was quite sure that was an inappropriate response to someone asking for pancakes. "I can do that. Plain? Chocolate chip?"

His grin widened as she continued listing options.

"Banana Nut? Blueberry?" She wiped the smudge off his face. "Whatever you want."

He leaned closer, and Mari held her breath, her heart doing flip flops.

The front door opened, and Travis jerked away.

"Mom, just letting you know we're out of milk. Will you grab some if you go to the store later?" Carlos didn't seem to notice he'd interrupted something.

Travis focused on the dirt.

Mari smiled in spite of wanting to scream. "I'll get some. Thanks for letting me know."

Interrupted, the moment passed, leaving her to wonder if Travis would have kissed her and if he even wanted to.

Chapter Nine

Travis arrived at the office early Monday morning, anticipating a response to his offer. Before even making coffee, he checked his email.

His heart sank. He read the email a second time, disappointment stabbing at his chest. The deal had fallen through; his timeline for change had been completely derailed.

After the weekend, the news tasted even more bitter. When he checked the calendar and discovered that he had no meetings until late afternoon, he shut off his machine and scrawled out a note for Mari.

Will be back in the office after lunch.

He hopped on the elevator and hurried to his car. Hours and hours of work had gone into creating a pitch, and the response initially had been good. Normally, he didn't take business matters personally, but in this case, he made the exception.

In his car, he headed west, not even sure where he wanted to go, just knowing he wanted to be out of the office for a while.

When he passed the mall on the edge of town, he decided to go see Gram. Without bothering to call, he drove to Schatzenburg.

Sitting on her porch, she waved as he parked in front of the house. Easily ninety, she'd been a fixture in his life since before he could remember.

She smoothed the stray silver strands that had dared escape her bun. "This is a happy surprise. It's rare that you show up here during a workday." She wrapped him in a hug as soon as he hit the top stair. "Have a seat. I'll pour you a cup of coffee."

"Thanks." He needed more than coffee, but it was a start.

She returned a minute later and handed him a mug. "Talk to me, Travis. You clearly have something on your mind."

As much as he wanted to talk about all of it, company secrets needed to remain so, and he wasn't ready to discuss Mari with anyone. He wasn't even sure what to say.

"Kate's been telling me all about a Mari that's helping with the wedding. She works with you?" Gram had a way of yanking thoughts out of his head.

He nodded. "She does."

"You want to tell me more about her?"

He sipped his coffee and watched a squirrel bound across the yard, a large pecan in its mouth. The critter flicked its tail then started digging, which pulled Travis's thoughts to the hours with Mari working in the flower beds.

"She likes colorful flowers, the kind that attract butterflies." He remembered the feel of her fingers on his face, wiping off the dirt.

Gram let his words dance in the breeze a minute before responding. "Sounds like someone I might like."

"I think you would." He wished Carlos hadn't walked out when he did, but at the same time Travis was glad for the interruption. Kissing Mari would have made his interest abundantly clear.

The squirrel scampered up a tree and pulled off another pecan.

"She makes great pancakes." Travis thought twice about the implication. "She made them for lunch."

Soft chuckles said that Gram understood.

"Her husband died years ago. Her son is heading to college." He listed facts to avoid broadcasting his feelings.

Gram stayed silent, rocking in her chair. A soft creak filled the quiet, marking the passage of time.

After a few minutes, he ran his fingers through his hair. "When Kate came back, my perspective shifted, so I'm making changes."

"Any you care to share?"

Travis sighed. "It can't leave this porch."

She continued rocking.

"I'll be selling the house. That's not the only change, but I can't talk about all of them yet."

Gram patted his hand. "Mari part of these changes?"

"That remains to be seen." He said more than he'd intended, but withholding info from Gram was nearly impossible.

She stood up, signaling the end of the pow wow. "When can I meet her?"

"Wait. Please."

The sparkle in her brown eyes acknowledged his request. "Thanks for the visit. I've gotta get ready for my bridge club."

"Thanks, Gram." In his sixties, he felt young again sitting on her porch. "I'll let you know when."

She winked and disappeared inside, leaving Travis alone on the wrap-around porch.

Driving back toward San Antonio, he made a few decisions. Until he'd put a new plan in place, he'd avoid spending time with Mari outside the office. Shaking his head, he shifted gears, thinking about pancakes and near-kisses.

Hopefully he could get the plan back on track before the wedding.

⌒

Fran and Erika were away at lunch when he returned, making it easy to slip into his office. But almost as soon as he sat down, there was a knock at the door that led to Mari's office.

"Come in." He slipped a rubber band on his wrist, ready to snap it as a reminder to remain professional.

Mari grinned as she walked in, as happy as she was when they were in her kitchen eating pancakes. "Hi." She hesitated and stopped a few steps from the desk, crossing her arms. "I wondered if you'd be back in time for your meeting."

"I'm here." He forced himself to stay in his chair, praying he didn't come off as a jerk. "I ran out to Schatzenburg. Went to check in on Gram."

Continuing to behave like he had all weekend risked putting Mari in an awkward predicament, and he wouldn't do it. But behaving in a completely professional manner risked hurting her and having her think he'd been toying with her. He was wedged between the proverbial rock and hard place.

"Is she okay?" Perceptive, Mari had read his body language, and her tone cooled.

"Oh, yes. I think she may outlive all of us." Travis shuffled papers, hoping the strained conversation would end.

"I'll leave you to your work." Mari left the office, taking a chunk of Travis's heart with her.

Chapter Ten

Two weeks and three days before the wedding, Mari made herself comfortable on the sofa, a steaming cup of tea on the end table, the laptop balanced on her crossed legs. Music sounded from upstairs, and she closed her eyes, making a memory.

Carlos would move out in a month, and she wasn't ready for it. For five years, it had been just the two of them, and an empty house would feel lonely.

A few clicks of the mouse, and new message to her friend opened on the screen: *You busy?* Desperate times called for desperate measures.

Remi was never far from her phone or computer, and the quick reply confirmed that hadn't changed: *Nope. Just out walking on the beach.*

Mari could almost picture her friend, her blonde, unruly curls dancing in the evening breeze. *Remember how I told you I was helping my boss's daughter with wedding preparations? I think maybe that was a bad idea.*

Dots appeared as Remi typed. Messages popped up one at a

time. Mari could almost hear Remi yelling: *Is he taking advantage of you? Working you too much? I'll come down there and set him straight! How dare he!*

Mari shook her head and tapped out a reply: *Nothing like that. We spent so much time together outside of work and ... I think ... I should NOT feel this way about my boss.*

Happy faces with hearts for eyes chased each other up the screen. After way too many, Remi stopped sending the faces and sent actual words: *Send me a Vjnkonkjlp.*

The message made no sense.

???

Remi answered: *LOL sorry. Had to wipe chocolate off my screen. I need a picture.*

Mari scrolled up to make sure she hadn't misread the first message. *Chocolate? I thought you were out walking.*

I am. And eating chocolate. I can do both at same time.

I miss you, Remi! Mari loved her friend's take on life.

Mari had intentionally chosen to message Remi about the crush. It sounded silly to call it that, but that is what it was. Instead of her feelings cooling when he'd pulled away and kept the relationship strictly business, they'd ramped up, which made absolutely no sense. The last month had been near torture.

Remi wouldn't tell Mari that she was trying to fill the void of Carlos leaving by focusing her attentions elsewhere or that work relationships always end badly.

Mari sent a link to the boss's profile on the company website. The photo was recent, a good likeness. *That's him.*

Staring at the photo, she smiled. Even with more salt than pepper in his hair than when she'd first started working for him, he still looked good. His age had improved his looks, made him more distinguished, but one thing that hadn't changed—his eyes. Deep blue, they held the vibrancy of a perpetual summer.

The same happy faces appeared again, only fewer this time.

Remi messaged: *And I don't see a problem. AT ALL. Have you told Charlie all this?*

Mari wasn't ready for that conversation. *I've told y'all about him.*

Charlotte spent all day at a desk crunching numbers, and crocheting took up much of her free time. She would point out all the reasons dating someone at the office was a bad idea. She would say Mari was trying to mask the pain of Carlos leaving by feeling infatuated. Mari had told herself all those things. She'd also been through the list of why work relationships don't work, over and over.

When it all boiled down to facts, dating Travis Bentley wasn't even a possibility. All month, there hadn't been a hint of the man that leaned close when talking about pancakes.

But Remi could always be counted on to suggest the crazy, adventurous path, the outcome Mari wanted to entertain while she sipped her tea.

A group message popped up: *Charlie, Mari wants to date her boss. Here's his pic. What say you?*

Mari couldn't type fast enough: *I said nothing about dating the boss!*

Charlie's answer came swiftly and as expected: *Bad idea. Really bad idea. Relationships at the office should stay professional.* Charlie sounded more adamant than before.

Remi offered her usual banter: *Whatever! Love doesn't follow your rules. Happens all the time in my books.*

The reply from Charlie made Mari giggle, and she couldn't remember the last time she'd done that. *They call it fiction for a reason. He is a hottie, though.*

Are you suggesting she quit? Remi followed her message with a wink.

No! Charlie left no room for confusion.

Mari sighed as she responded: *Not quitting. Not dating. He's been strictly business all month. I think maybe I—whatever I did, he's pulled back, which makes it sound like there was something going on, and there wasn't. But after being so carefree and charming outside the office, he's different. I should never have made him pancakes.*

Identical messages from Charlie and Remi appeared on the screen: *You okay?* Kindly, her friends didn't ask about the pancakes.

I am. Just needed to say it. Mari typed one last message. *And this has nothing to do with Carlos leaving. Thanks for listening.*

Mari stared at the words on the screen. Was she being honest with herself? And even if it did have something to do with Carlos moving out, was that bad?

Widowed after sixteen years in a happy marriage, Mari never pictured herself in another long-term relationship. Love once was a blessing; love twice seemed too much to ask.

Her heart had other ideas.

Mari still noticed every twinkle—because some things hadn't changed—and tried to stand at least eighteen inches away, so she wouldn't be tempted to sniff his shirt. A grown woman shouldn't have to battle such impulses. But her mantra came in handy and got used a lot. *He's the boss.* She even added to it. *And he's not interested.*

With great effort, she managed to corral her feelings. When she was around Travis, no one watching would be any the wiser, but she worried she'd slip and say or do something that would make her feelings obvious to him.

Falling for the boss hadn't figured into Mari's summer plans, but if she was honest with herself, she'd come dangerously close. The professional wall she'd worked so hard to maintain lay in crumbles, but only on her side. His side stood solid, not even a chink out of the mortar, at least that's how it seemed to Mari.

Embarrassment awaited if he discovered her feelings.

She couldn't pinpoint when her feelings had changed, but all that time together outside the office had—well, it had wormed him into her heart in a dangerous way. She didn't have any expectation that the feelings would be reciprocated, and at the end of next month, the wedding would be over, and Carlos would be gone.

If Mari didn't clear her head, heartache waited at the end of the summer.

After admitting her crush to her friends, Mari made peace with the situation, ready to face another day. She walked into her office and found a cup of coffee from the local coffee house down the road sitting on her desk. A note stuck out from underneath it.

Hope you have a great day! -T

It was the most unprofessional he'd been in a month.

She glanced at his door and then at the phone. His line was lit up. She wouldn't bother him while he was on a call. Running out to the lobby, she checked the front desk. There were no coffee cups or notes for Fran or Erika.

All the progress Mari had made last night crumbled into a heap, and little green sprigs of hope sprouted from the pile of rubble.

He'd singled her out.

She dropped into the chair at her desk, waiting, wanting to talk to him. She didn't have to wait long.

Travis knocked as he walked into her office. "What time are you meeting Kate?"

She smiled as she typed the last few details in a report. "Dress fitting is at two. She's picking me up at one thirty. You sure it's not a problem if I leave?"

"Not at all." He leaned on her desk. "Will you send me a pic?"

Mari stood up, then dropped back into her chair. Being

eye-level with his chest—since he was leaning on the desk she might have been eye-level with his chin—was dangerous. Sitting was safer. "If I get a chance, I will."

"Thanks, Mari. From the bottom of my heart."

She picked up her cup, giving her hands something to do other than touch him. "Thanks for the coffee."

"Sure. How are the flowers doing? Everything thriving?"

Mari hadn't expected him to bring up that weekend. "I was afraid they were dying, but just this morning all of them were covered in blooms."

"Great. Glad to hear you have your pretty flowers in front." He strolled back toward his office. "I'll check back in before you leave."

She couldn't wait.

⌇

As promised, he walked back into her office as she opened the bottom drawer. "Headed out?"

She pulled her purse out. "If I don't make it back to the office, then I'll just see you tomorrow." Lollygagging would only ignite her already troublesome thoughts.

"Mari."

She stopped, and the troublesome thoughts stomped and waved. "Yes?"

"When you and Kate are finished, go home. No matter what time it is."

"Thanks." She didn't know what to make of his change in behavior. "I'll see you in the morning, then."

The elevator dinged, and she hurried to catch it. One more minute alone with Travis, and she would've said something she regretted—probably something about pancakes.

Kate pulled up just as Mari stepped through the double doors.

She slipped into the passenger seat when the car stopped by the curb.

"Excited?" Mari tucked her cheaters in her purse and fished her sunglasses out.

Kate grinned. "Like you would not believe. I'm just not sure how I'm going to make it two more weeks."

"I'm so happy for you."

"How long have you worked with Dad?" Her question came out of nowhere.

Mari hoped shock wasn't written all over her face; she didn't want to talk about Travis. "Seven years." Seven years, three months, and two days, but adding the months and days made it seem like she'd been counting, and she hadn't. Until recently.

"Tell me, honestly. I—well, I mean. You know my story, right?"

"I do."

"Then you know I only returned in January and have known him only a short time. I learned so much about him from my mom's letters, and he seems wonderful. Everyone in Schatzenburg talks about him like he's—I don't know—amazing. I want your opinion."

Mari hadn't been to the small town a few miles outside San Antonio that Travis spoke of so fondly, but she wanted to visit. "My opinion? Well, he's honest, almost to a fault; he treats his employees very well. And from everything I saw, he treated your mom like gold. The people in Schatzenburg who talk about him like he's amazing—they're right." Mari tried not to lay it on too thick, but Travis had earned every bit of that praise. After she answered, the thought occurred to her that maybe Kate had asked only to gauge Mari's opinion of Travis.

Kate sniffed. "Thank you. I didn't doubt he was a good guy, but—" She shook her head. "I'm a little worried about him."

Talking about Travis would only make it hard to keep feelings hidden. Mari needed the conversation to change, but she couldn't ignore a statement like that. "Why?"

"Gram says—Have you met Gram?"

"No, but Travis has mentioned her. She's your grandmother?"

"She's not related, but she's almost like a mother to Dad. Anyway, she said something that I can't shake. You think Dad is happy?"

Mari didn't know where the question was leading. "He's very excited about the wedding."

"I don't mean about that. Just seems like he works a lot. Never mind. I shouldn't have said anything."

"I'll keep my eyes open." Mari thought about the late-night timestamps on emails and saved documents, the shift in his behavior, and it all made her wonder if there was something bothering him.

"I appreciate that." Kate turned into the parking lot. "You spend more time with him than anyone."

The words bounced around in Mari's head. She did spend more time with him than anyone else, even when they weren't spending time together outside the office.

Staring out the window, she tried to replay every interaction during the last month. He'd worked late most nights but didn't talk about it much. Was he happy? He seemed much more relaxed when they were outside the office—driving in his convertible, out to dinner, eating pancakes.

Mari promised herself she'd pay more attention.

Chapter Eleven

Leaning back in his chair, his desk cluttered with papers, Travis texted Mari: *Thanks again for going with Kate to the fitting. And thank you for the picture. Looks like everything is ready for the big day.*

He stared at the picture of Kate in her dress. She was beautiful, and in just over two weeks, he'd be giving her away.

He wanted Mari by his side that day.

She responded to his text: *I'm thrilled she invited me to go along. She's going to be a stunning bride.*

He glanced at the file open on the computer. His plan was back on track, which meant he could relax his guard a little—but only a little.

Another message popped up.

Helping with the wedding has been a privilege I'll treasure. It's been more rewarding than I ever dreamed.

Travis stared at his phone. Fingers hovering over the screen, he debated about what to send in reply. He wanted to tell her that he'd relished every minute they'd spent together inside and outside the office, but it wasn't quite the right time for statements like that.

I'm very glad. It's great when something benefits everyone involved. See you in the morning. He sent the message before shutting off his machine and heading home.

～

Earlier than normal, Travis stepped off the elevator. Mari's car was in her spot, which meant they'd have a few minutes to chat before anyone else was around. After dropping his briefcase beside his desk, he strolled into her office.

Her bottom drawer wasn't quite closed all the way, and her shoes lay on the floor next to her desk. Water ran the kitchen, and the pot clinked. She was making coffee.

He dropped into her chair and waited.

Mari froze in the doorway when she spotted him.

"Morning. I wondered about these shoes' missing owner. You're in early." He stood but didn't move closer to her.

"I haven't been here long. Coffee's brewing." She avoided his gaze, and her cheeks flushed.

Travis didn't miss the signs that her interest was still a strong possibility. "I was wondering if you knew of a good realtor. I'm going to be selling my house."

Her jaw dropped open, and she met his gaze. "Really?"

"Please don't say anything. I haven't mentioned it to anyone except Gram."

In a second, she was right in front of him, tears brimming in her eyes, a hand pressed to her mouth. After a deep breath, she blinked, sending a droplet sliding down her cheek. "Are you leaving?"

"Leaving?" He shoved his hands in his pockets to avoid reaching for her. "No, nothing like that."

"Sorry. That's none of my business." She wiped her eyes and

crossed her arms. "You could call Alex's sister, but I'd suggest waiting until after the wedding."

"Good idea. I forgot she was a realtor." Travis leaned on the desk. "I'm not leaving, Mari. Just making some changes. My house is too big for one person, and Kate hasn't set foot in it since the incident, not that I can blame her." Travis nodded toward the kitchen. "Coffee should be ready."

"I'll call her—Marisa is her name, I think—and set up an appointment."

"You don't have to do that; just send me the number."

"I'll do that"—she followed him into the kitchen area—"after the wedding."

He filled two mugs with liquid ambition and added cream to hers. "Thanks."

She accepted the cup he held out to her. "Will you be attending that gala in August? The info for that arrived yesterday."

He wrinkled his nose, unsure about the timing. "I don't know. Depends on if I'm taking a date. I'd rather not attend one of those alone ever again."

A hint of a smile flashed on Mari's face. "Chum in the water?"

He raised his eyebrows. "Chum?"

Had she really just referred to him as chum?

"Handsome, unattached man in a tuxedo. I wonder how many ladies Googled you during the event. Have you read your Wikipedia page? Owning your own company probably only made you more of a target." Her eyes widened, the color left her face, and she stared into her coffee cup. "I'm sorry. That was rude of me."

"That pretty much described my evening. Handsome, huh? Get me two tickets. Anything else?"

"The foundation's charity fundraiser was moved to September?" She glanced up, her cheeks still flushed.

"Because of the wedding. Yes."

"I'm happy to help with whatever you need."

He hoped that life would be different by September. "Thank you. I could use the help."

The back and forth, always working down an invisible check-list, that routine had developed over the years they'd worked together, and Travis enjoyed it.

"Two weeks." Travis imagined dancing with Mari and thought his heart might gallop right out of his chest.

"I'm so happy for Kate."

"Mari." He leaned on the counter, choosing his words carefully. "You've been spending quite a bit of time on this wedding. It's meant the world to Kate, and"—he glanced up, mesmerized by her brown eyes—"I appreciate more than I know how to express. If there's anything I can ever do to help you, please ask."

She rested a hand on his arm. "Spending time with Kate—with you—has been its own reward."

That was his cue to exit before he said more than he wanted to. "I'll stop bothering you. I'm sure you came in early to get stuff done, not talk to me."

"I checked the calendar. Your schedule is pretty clear today. Only an afternoon meeting." She hurried back to her office.

Why did it have to be so complicated? If they'd met at a party or a café, he'd have asked her out already, but they'd met at work. If that wasn't complicated enough, she was his direct-report. Asking her out would make the legal team twitchy.

Chapter Twelve

Instead of leaving for the day, Mari lingered at her desk, waiting for Travis to poke his head into her office as he did every day at half past five. In the seven years she'd worked as his personal assistant, they'd developed a routine, a way of doing things. It was rare that he was late.

She shuffled through the menus in her drawer. Should she order him dinner? He didn't stay as late every night like before, but he spent more time at the office than he should, not that it was her place to tell him that.

When she'd lost her husband five years before, work gave her focus, making it easier to get out of bed in the morning, easier to breathe, so she understood. Even parenting was hard back then. Travis had given her all the leeway she needed to grieve. He'd shown her generosity and kindness.

More recently, in the last year, following Mrs. Bentley's death, he was the one that found focus in the job. Mari hadn't missed the signs. As a result, her feelings for him deepened, not so much in a romantic way, not at first.

She kept tabs on him to make sure he ate, ran interference when he needed time alone in the office, helped with his charity foundation, and made sure nothing fell through the cracks. Mari did her best to protect him while he grieved.

His daughter's return—that was a story all its own, an incredible one at that—had marked a change, and Mari loved to hear him talk about Kate and her fiancé, Alex.

When Kate came home, Mari met a new Travis, and she liked him. A lot.

That marked the beginning. Her professional wall started to crumble, only small chunks fell at first, but in the last few months, there were days when nothing of Mari's wall was left.

During the holidays, she'd shopped with him for toys for the charity—something he'd always done with his wife. Mari stepped in, so he wouldn't have to shop alone. That time together didn't stir notions in her head, but the time together since May had been different.

Thirty minutes past when she normally left, Mari riffled through the menus, settled on one, and picked up the phone. She ordered his favorite, grabbed the pressed tuxedo from the hook on the back of the door, and knocked.

"Come in." His smooth voice held no hint of irritation.

She pushed open the door. "Here's your tux, all ready for the wedding, and I ordered you dinner. As soon as it arrives, I'll head out, unless you need me for something." She hung the suit in the closet and held her breath, hoping maybe there was a last-minute project that required her help.

He glanced at his watch. "I'm not sure where the time went." He walked around the desk. "Now I just have to keep that clean for two weeks."

"Hopefully you don't plan to wear it. Leave it covered in the closet. It should be fine."

"Did you order something for yourself?"

"I didn't."

Travis motioned toward the phone. "Call them back. Get yourself something. It's not fair that you stay late to take care of me, then have to go home and cook."

"It's not a bother." Mari could lose herself in those eyes, but that would not be professional.

"Kate wanted me to make sure you knew you were invited to the rehearsal dinner." He leaned his tall frame back against the desk.

Mari stayed glue to the floor, even though her brain screamed "run."

Good-looking didn't begin to describe the man. Thinking himself old, he failed to notice the stares he received from many of the young women at the office. His name rippled through conversations in the break room, more often of late since he was single again.

Mari stifled a shudder prompted by the deep blue gaze. Protective didn't accurately describe her feelings, and at forty-eight, no one would mistake her for one of the young ones, but she couldn't disagree with their whispered comments.

The man was irresistible.

She hoped he didn't notice her surveying glance.

Nodding, she hoped attending the dinner wouldn't be awkward. "I'd love to be there."

"Great. Go order something, and if you have a few minutes, you can listen to my toast and help me iron out the wrinkles." He handed her cash. "If it's not a bother."

"Absolutely. I'm happy to." She hurried back to her desk and redialed the restaurant, adding her favorite to the order. While she waited at the reception desk for the delivery to arrive, she texted her son: *Working late. Everything okay?*

Friday night meant he likely had plans with friends. With a license and a car, he came and went as he pleased. With him gone so much of the time, maybe it wouldn't seem all that different in a matter of weeks.

He responded quickly, which she appreciated: *All good. Going to the movies later.*

Mari followed up as she always did: *Be safe. Love you.*

She scanned Facebook while she waited and jumped when the elevator opened.

The delivery guy stepped into the office. "Another late night, eh?"

"Seems so." She handed him cash. "Keep the change."

"Thank you, ma'am." He stepped back onto the elevator and waved as the doors closed.

She balanced the containers in one hand and reached out to open Travis's office door, but it opened as soon as her hand touched the handle.

Travis stepped back. "Oh, I was just coming to find you. Instead of the conference room, let's eat in the little room."

"The sunny spot." She loved the quaint little room off his office.

Filled with the warm rays of the late afternoon sun, the room seemed an escape from the rest of the world. He stood until she took a seat, then sat on the same small sofa even though there were two. She caught herself, trying not to add meaning to the commonplace.

"I'm not keeping you from Carlos, am I?" He slipped off his tie and rolled up his sleeves before digging into his food.

"Oh, no. He's going out with friends. He has a car. I hardly see him."

"I imagine having a teenager is rough." A sparkle filled the space that once held sadness. "I'm trying to navigate the stage after that."

"I think you are doing splendidly. She's a sweetheart."

"I can't take credit for that."

Talking about the years his daughter was missing always brought the sadness back, so Mari changed the topic. "Let's hear that toast."

Travis set his food on the table and fished a folded page out of his pocket. "You'll tell me if it sounds cheesy, right?"

"I'm sure whatever you've written is wonderful."

"I'm depending on you to be honest with me, Mari."

She picked up a napkin and wiped at a spot of sauce on his shirt. "Always."

He grinned and stared at her hands.

When Mari realized, she stopped, horrified. "Sorry. I'll stop. I just didn't want it to stain. Read the toast."

When he finished reading his toast, she needed another napkin to dab at her tears. "It's perfect. There won't be a dry eye in the place."

"The part about Emma is okay?"

"It is. Mrs. Bentley will be smiling down that day for sure." She set her food down. Thinking about the conversation with Kate, Mari wondered how Travis was really doing. "How are you doing with all this? Kate hasn't been back long, and now you'll be giving her away."

His eyes misted, and he set his food on the table. Reaching for her hand, he took a deep breath. "I could ask you how you're doing?"

Mari hoped he couldn't feel her shaking. "We are both facing big life changes, aren't we? But I have to say, I think you are handling it well."

"Kate's not mine to hold onto, and I couldn't have hand-picked someone more suited to love her."

Mari squeezed his hand. "That makes you sound like such a romantic."

"Do you like working for me?" His question surprised her.

"Yes. I do. It's easily one of the best jobs I've ever had."

He let go of her hand and picked up his food. "I'm glad to hear that."

Mari got the sense that her answer wasn't what he wanted to hear. "Travis, are you happy?"

Eyes wide, mouth full of food, he stared at her. After swallowing, he wiped his mouth. "What?" His brow wrinkled.

She stood and walked to the windows. "I worry about you sometimes. Now that you're alone, with the stress of running a company—I know you are thrilled to have Kate home." She shook her head. "I'm rambling. I don't know why I asked."

Embarrassed that she'd said way too much, she closed her eyes, wishing she could click her heels together and disappear.

"Mari."

She started, realizing he stood right behind her. "You don't have to tell me anything."

He rested his hands on her shoulders and turned her to face him. "Your question caught me off guard. Completely." He chewed his lower lip and stared out the window, his hands still on her shoulders. "I am happy. There are things that I wish were different, and I'm working on that." He focused on her again. "But right now, right here, I'm happy."

Before her brain registered what she was doing, Mari hugged him, and arms much stronger than she'd anticipated hugged her back. "I'm glad."

"Our food is getting cold." He stuck his hands in his pockets, a new habit of his.

They moved on to more casual conversation.

"I couldn't have pulled off this whole wedding thing without you, Mari. I'm not sure how to—" His phone squawked a familiar tone, and he smiled at the picture of Kate holding a stuffed bunny. "Hey, Kate. ... Just sitting here getting Mari's help with something."

Mari guessed that the interrupted comment would never be

finished, but she didn't need to hear him express the gratitude in words. The smile on his face did that often.

"Dad, it's Friday. You shouldn't keep her so late." Kate's chastisement rang through the line clearly.

An apology etched on Travis's face. "She said she didn't mind."

Mari gathered the empty containers and carried them to the trashcan in the kitchen, giving Travis privacy while he chatted with his daughter. Mari kicked off her heels and used the minutes to clean out the refrigerator, a task she'd neglected to do earlier.

Her head buried between shelves, she bumped it when Travis cleared his throat. Oh, what a sight she must've been when he walked in. She stood and tugged at the bottom of her dress, hoping it hadn't ridden up. "Sorry. I forgot to clean this, and it'll be nasty by Monday."

"There are others who can clean the fridge, you know." His blue eyes twinkled with a new spark.

"Those people never know what to throw away." She forced herself not to look away and hoped her cheeks weren't as red as they felt.

His rumble of a laugh echoed in the room. "Kate invited us to her place."

Mari replayed the words in her head. The "us" got the most attention. "Go ahead." She tied off the trash bag. "I'm almost done here. I can let myself out."

He stepped up next to her. "Please come. She specifically asked me to invite you." He ran his fingers through his salt-and-pepper hair. "And I'd like for you to come."

Her heart threatened to stampede out of her chest. She braved a glance at him, and the earnestness in his gaze made not going impossible. "Okay. What do we need to, I mean, what should I take?"

"Nothing." He smoothed out his sleeves and buttoned the

cuffs. "Thought maybe you could leave your car here and ride out with me, if that works."

She glanced around for her heels. "Yeah."

"Shoes are optional." He winked before turning around and walking back to his office.

The look that accompanied his tease was not commonplace.

⌇

Mari gazed out the window, fighting the urge to message Remi and Charlie. One would squeal; the other would lecture. There'd be time to fill them in later. Sitting next to Travis was not the appropriate place.

"Is Kate nervous? I think—except for a few items—everything is ready." In spite of all the time spent together and the help with planning, Mari hadn't been to Kate's, and the closer they got to the house, the more her nerves coiled into a knot.

"She doesn't sound it. I am, though. I want every detail to be perfect."

"It will be. In the end, they'll be married. That's what they both want most."

"You're right." He shifted gears, then rested his hand on hers. "I was hoping that maybe—"

Mari's phone rang, but she didn't reach for it. Whatever he wanted to say, she wanted to hear.

"Go ahead and answer it." He moved his hand back to the gear shift and exited the highway.

She fished her phone out of her purse, hurrying to catch it before it stopped ringing. "Hello."

"This is Officer Steve Duncan. I'm looking for Marianna Gonzales."

The call, all too reminiscent of the one she'd received five years before ripped the air from her chest. She managed to choke out one word. "Speaking." Instinctively, she grabbed Travis's hand and squeezed.

Travis pulled off to the side of the road.

Officer Duncan cut straight to the point. "There's been an accident, but …"

The words after that dissolved into a jumble of syllables, and her brain refused to make sense of them.

She handed the phone to Travis. "I can't. Please talk to him."

Without letting go of her hand, he took over the call. "This is Travis Bentley. What's going on?" He nodded as he listened. "Is Carlos okay?"

Mari rested her head on his arm, terrified to hear the answer.

"Which hospital?" He flashed her a weak smile, an encouragement.

Breath returned to her lungs.

"We're headed that way. Thank you, Officer Duncan." Travis ended the call. "Carlos is alive. He's been injured, but he asked them to call you, even gave them your number. The officer didn't know the extent of the injuries."

She wiped her eyes. "He's alive."

Travis let go of her hand and whipped his red Porsche back onto the road, heading back the way they came. "He is, and I need to get you to the hospital."

Mari stared out the window, imagining the worst. Losing Carlos would crush her. She couldn't bury him, too.

As if reading her thoughts, Travis clasped her hand. "He's alive. Focus on that."

"I'm trying." The Hill Country passed in a blur, and she held tight to a man who understood what she faced. Thinking of Remi and Charlie, Mari let go of his hand. Fingers flying across her phone, she messaged them as Travis raced toward the hospital: *Police called. Carlos was in an accident.*

She hit send too soon, probably panicking her friends.

Is he … Remi didn't finish the question.

Charlie's response popped up a half-second later: *Is he okay?*

Mari sucked in a deep breath. *He's alive but injured. He asked the officer to call me.*

What do you need? Charlie was probably booking a flight.

Prayers. Mari needed those more than anything else her friends could do.

Impulsive Remi messaged: *I can hop a plane and be there in a few hours.*

Not yet. Let me get to the hospital and find out more. I'm not alone. Travis is driving me to the hospital.

Charlie's reply surprised Mari: *Good. Please keep us posted.*

I will. Mari wanted the car to go faster.

Remi chimed in in true Remi fashion: *Give the hottie a hug for me and tell him thanks for being there since we are so far away.*

Mari wasn't even sure how to respond. Normally, she might've laughed, but worry had cut off her ability to appreciate the humor.

"Everything okay?" Travis glanced down at the phone.

"I was letting my friends know, asking them to pray." It sounded too simple for what it was. She needed to explain the importance. "After George died, I met a few ladies online through a Facebook group. Two of those ladies had recently been widowed also. I know it's weird when people talk about their internet friends, but these ladies were there for me. Together, we waded through the worst of the grief."

"They sound like amazing friends. And friendship doesn't depend on proximity." The man said all the right things.

"We get together once a year, at least. In September, they're coming to San Antonio." She wiped her eyes. "I want it to be a happy get-together. I can't lose Carlos. Not like this."

"He was alert enough to talk."

"I keep telling myself that."

Travis shifted gears, then rested his hand on hers. "We'll be there soon." He didn't offer imagined promises of health or wishful thoughts. He was there, making sure she wasn't alone and driving her to Carlos.

"I'm glad I wasn't alone."

"Me too." He released her hand as he exited the highway. "Oh, Mari. Me too."

Chapter Thirteen

Travis pulled up to the emergency room and grabbed Mari's hand. "I'll be in as soon as I find a parking spot."

Brown eyes, rimmed in tears, begged him to hurry. "Thank you."

He watched as she walked through the double doors, tempted to leave his car and run after her. The parking lot was full, and it took a couple minutes before he spied an empty space. Texting Kate, he ran across the parking lot. *Mari's son was in an accident. Don't know any details. At the hospital with her.*

He shoved the phone in his pocket and scanned the waiting room as he cleared the double doors. Mari stood near the glass-in reception area, her arms wrapped around herself.

Wanting her not to feel alone, he pressed a hand to the small of her back, and she leaned into him.

"What did they say?" He prayed for good news.

Turning to look at him, she opened her mouth, but no words escaped, only tears.

Travis wrapped her in an embrace. "Have you spoken with anyone?"

She nodded into his shoulder. "She's checking. Said to wait, but what if—"

A doctor pushed through the double doors and walked toward her. "Mrs. Meyer?"

Mari shook her head.

The doctor surveyed the room and hurried away to another woman. "Mrs. Meyer?" When she nodded, he said, "I'm very sorry …"

The woman's wails drowned out the rest of what the doctor said.

Mari glanced up at Travis before burying her face in his chest.

"The officer said he was conscious." He offered what encouragement he could.

Holding her, his chin resting on her head, he waited. Aware of how it would look to anyone they knew, he didn't care. He'd have to deal with that if it came up.

A woman stepped up to the desk and leaned out. "Mrs. Gonzales, your son is being prepped for surgery."

"Can I see him?" Mari turned around but didn't leave his arms.

"Not until after. If you'll have a seat, I'll find out what floor."

Mari stepped closer to the window. "Surgery for what? What happened?"

The woman shook her head. "I don't know. Let me find out where you need to go." She made her escape before Mari could ask any more questions.

Mari turned around and stepped back into Travis's arms. "Why won't anyone tell me what's wrong with him?"

Without any clue how to answer, he held her a minute, then led Mari to a chair and sat down next to her.

She wrung her hands. "Kate's expecting you. You can go."

The idea of leaving her was laughable. "I texted her. Once we know more, I'll call her." Travis reached for Mari's hand and tucked it between his. "I'm staying."

She laid her other hand on top of his and stared at the reception desk.

Minutes crawled by, and Travis could feel her muscles tightening with every tick of the clock hanging on the wall. He brushed his thumb along the side of her hand, hoping it would soothe her at least a little.

The woman at the desk reappeared and motioned them over. "Fourth floor."

After she gave them directions to the surgical waiting room, Mari and Travis headed that way. Navigating hallways that all looked the same, they made their way to the elevator, then to the waiting room.

Mari and Travis were the only people in the room.

Almost as soon as they sat down, a man in a white coat pushed open a door at the other side of the room. "Mrs. Gonzales?"

She jumped up but didn't let go of Travis's hand. "Yes?"

"Your son has a compound fracture of the humerus, but I'm going to fix that. Surgery will take two hours at least, but it depends on what we find when we get in there." He stepped away, then turned around. "We're hoping for no surprises."

"Which arm?" Her hand tightened around Travis's.

"Left. If it goes long, I'll send someone out to update you." He nodded as he left the room.

Mari continued standing even after the doctor left and pulled her hand away. Pacing, she circled a group of chairs over and over. A message popped up on her phone from someone named Remi: *Any news? How does he look?*

Phone in hand, he crossed the room. "Mari, your friend is asking about Carlos."

Mari barely acknowledged him but took the phone and started typing.

Travis stayed beside her. When her eyes went wide and panic registered in them, he glanced at the screen.

Is the hottie at the hospital with you?

He hadn't meant to see it but wasn't sorry that he did. It eliminated any hesitation he had about holding her, comforting her. His ego appreciated it, too.

She turned the phone away from him, her cheeks a beautiful shade of pink.

He slipped an arm around her waist. "Please sit. When Carlos is out of surgery and awake, he'll need you. At least get off your feet for a bit." He wanted to be close to her but knew there was little he could say to ease her worry.

Glancing around, he spotted a small loveseat, which was essentially two chairs shoved together without an armrest in between. When he steered her that direction, she didn't resist.

Mari sat down and shook her head. "Compound fracture. That means—it was bad, wasn't it?"

"He was alert and old enough to give consent, so they didn't have to wait. Let's see what the doctor says after surgery before we worry."

"But the bone came through the skin. That's what it means, right?"

He nodded. That was what he understood that to mean, but he was no doctor. "I'm going to find us something to drink. Soda or coffee?" He didn't want to leave her, but with a long wait, they both needed a drink. A Coke or coffee would have to do.

"Either works. Thank you." She glanced down at her phone but caught his hand before he stepped away. "You don't really have to stay. It'll be a long wait."

Why she thought there was any possibility he'd walk out of that hospital before he knew Carlos was okay, Travis didn't understand. Instead of making declarations about what wild horses couldn't do, he squeezed her hand. "Be back shortly."

In the hall, he called Kate. "Hey, sweetheart. Just wanted to update you. Carlos is being prepped for surgery. Bad break on his left arm."

"Alex said he'll come get me. We can be up there in an hour or so."

"No need for that right now. Surgery will take a couple hours. I'll text when I know more."

"Dad …"

He sensed where the conversation was headed. "I'm not leaving here until Carlos is out of surgery and I know Mari's okay. I'll call you later."

"I don't care how late it is, please keep me posted."

"I will. Love you." Travis ended the call and walked into the cafeteria, heading for the coffee.

A worker with the hospital's logo on his t-shirt shook his head. "All the pots are empty. We'll be making more in a bit."

"That's all right. I'll grab something from the machine." Travis glanced around, wondering which direction would take him to the snack area.

"Through those doors, turn left, take the fourth right. You'll see them. Or there are some in the sub-basement."

"Thanks." Travis hurried out before more directions got tossed at him.

He found the soda machine just where expected and dropped in coins.

Out of habit, he checked his work email. The most recent message caught his attention. From a Charlotte Potter, the subject line read *I'm a friend of Mari's.*

He opened the message.

> *Hi, I'm a friend of Mari's, and explaining how I got your email would take too long. I'm not sure*

when you'll get this message, but Mari mentioned you were at the hospital with her. Thank you.

I'm worried about her. Is Carlos okay? Is she okay?

Charlotte

Travis stared at the message. Her number was included at the bottom.

He dialed, wondering how she'd gotten the email address. Based on the other message calling him a hottie, Mari had discussed him with her friends.

"Hello."

"Charlotte, this is Travis Bentley."

"You got my message? Is she okay? Are you with her?"

"I'm at the hospital. Stepped away from her to get us something to drink."

"I cannot thank you enough for being there for her. If she gets bad news, please let me know as soon as possible so I can grab a flight out."

"Sounds like he'll be okay, but I'll let you know. Is it okay if I text you at this number?"

"Absolutely. She'll be horrified that I emailed you, but I was really worried."

Travis hurried back to the waiting room. "You weren't the only one worried. I'll keep you posted."

He tucked his phone away and pushed open the door, a can of Coke in one hand and a Dr Pepper in the other. "They were out of coffee."

Mari reached for the Dr Pepper. "This is good."

He glanced down at the spot next to her, wanting to sit with her but not wanting to crowd her.

She shifted. "There's room." It was so like her to read his mind. What else had she picked up on?

He sat down. "Charlotte emailed me. She was worried about you, so I called her and told her what we knew."

Mari paled. "I'm so sorry. I can't imagine why she'd do that. I messaged her."

"Don't be sorry. Your friends care."

Minutes dragged by. The clock on the wall continued its constant ticking. The more time passed, the more Mari tensed.

He draped an arm around her. "Waiting is a beast. It'll eat you alive if you let it." After thirty years of waiting, he considered himself well-informed on the topic.

"I keep imagining the worst." She rested her head on his shoulder.

"I know."

Dealing with the unknown was hard; watching someone else deal with the unknown was torture.

A young woman slipped in and sat in the corner, her eyes red and swollen. Shortly after, a couple wandered in, engrossed in conversation. The small room began to fill. One hour felt like ten.

All the while, Travis kept his arm around Mari, rubbing her shoulder from time to time. Nothing he could say would change the situation, so in near silence, they waited.

He closed his eyes and rested his head against the wall. When she shifted, he opened one eye. "You okay?"

"It's been more than an hour. Almost two."

"I expect someone will be out soon with an update."

She leaned her head against him again, and they continued to wait.

As the two-hour mark came and went, Mari fidgeted more and glanced at the door more often. "It's taking too long."

"He said at least two hours."

"Have you updated Kate?"

"I have. She said to let her know if we needed anything."

She looked up at him. "Travis, thank you for staying."

He met her gaze, ready to explain that nothing would have made him leave her alone, but the door swung open. Every person in the room turned to see who had entered.

Recognizing the surgeon, Mari jumped up. "Is Carlos okay?" Travis stood behind her.

The surgeon nodded, smiling. "We're done. He's being moved to recovery. You'll be able to see him soon." He showed her x-rays and explained what they'd done. "I expect a full recovery. Radial nerve is fine; no palsy."

"Thank you so much." She leaned back against Travis, relaxing for the first time in hours.

"Have a good evening." The doctor slipped out the door.

She turned and hugged Travis. "Carlos is okay."

He held her close. When she stepped back, after a longer-than-typical hug, he kept an arm around her. "Once you can go see him, I'll run and get whatever you need to stay the night. I mean, I assume you're staying."

"I am, but I'm fine. You've done so much already."

"Mari, you're in a dress and heels. Surely something else would be more comfortable. I can go to whatever store is open."

She dug around in her purse and pulled out her keys. "If you don't mind the weirdness of digging through my things, you can get stuff from my house."

"I'll manage." He stuck them in his pocket and tugged her into the seat next to him. "Let's sit. What do you need me to get?"

Phone in hand, she started typing out a text. "I'll send you a list."

His phone beeped a minute later, and he glanced at what she'd sent.

She gripped his hand. "I sent my friends a link to your page on the company website. That's where she found your email address."

"They running a background check on me?" He glanced down, anticipating her reaction.

"Because of the picture." She shook her head. "And I feel like I'm in high school all over again."

He tightened his grip on her hand. Saying anything risked saying too much. He flashed her a smile.

"I never intended to tell you, yet here I am, prattling on. Please say something."

"Something." He winked.

Before he could say more, a woman pushed open the door. "Marianna Gonzales?"

Mari popped up out of her chair. "That's me."

"Right this way."

She glanced back over her shoulder and smiled.

Travis waved and headed out to the parking lot. He called Kate as he walked to his car.

She didn't even wait for him to speak. "Dad, is he okay? He came through the surgery okay?"

"He did. Mari just went back to see him." He slid into the driver's seat and started the engine.

"You aren't with her?"

"I'm headed to her place to get stuff, so she can spend the night. And to get a few items for Carlos."

"Oh, Dad. I'm so glad y'all have each other." Kate summed up his feelings quite well.

"Me too. Listen, I'll talk to you in the morning. I need to get going."

"Love you, Dad."

When he arrived at Mari's, Wentworth waited in the front window.

Travis unlocked the door and stepped in, careful not to let the cat out. "Hey, fella. Let's make sure you have food. Mari and Carlos aren't going to be back tonight."

Wentworth followed as Travis wandered into the kitchen.

Only a few morsels remained in the bottom of the bowl.

Thankfully, he didn't have to hunt for the food. As soon as he stepped into the pantry, Wentworth ran toward the shelf where the cat food was stored.

"I won't let you starve." Travis dropped a large scoop into the bowl, then refilled the water.

While Wentworth munched his kibble, Travis worked his way down the list, gathering what Mari requested. As he stuffed the last few items in the bag, Wentworth jumped up on the bed.

Travis zipped the bag closed. "I only have time for a quick scratch. Then I have to get back to the hospital."

Wentworth purred.

"Night, sir. Behave." Travis didn't expect that his admonition would make the slightest difference to Wentworth, who only flicked his tail in response.

Chapter Fourteen

Mari sat beside the bed, clutching her son's hand. Nurses and doctors all seemed happy with how Carlos's recovery was going, but Mari would believe it when he opened his eyes and spoke to her.

A soft knock sounded at the door.

"Come in." She almost hoped her answer would wake Carlos.

Travis stepped in, a small overnight bag in his hand. "I had to convince the nurse to let me in after visiting hours." He set the bag in an empty chair. "How is he?"

"Still asleep." Mari tried not to think about Travis rummaging through her drawers.

Carlos moaned as he opened his eyes. "Mom? Hey. How long have you been here?"

"A while. How are you? Need me to call a nurse?" She sprang out of her chair, reaching for the call button.

"Not right now." He shifted and winced. "Mr. Bentley, sorry I yanked her away from work."

Travis shook his head. "You gave your mom quite a scare. I hope your car fared better than you."

Carlos's smile fell away, and he tried to sit up. "I wasn't driving. Is Liam okay? Have you heard?"

Mari wracked her brain trying to remember Liam's last name. "I don't know. What's his last name? I'll find out for you."

"Jones."

She breathed a sigh of relief that it wasn't Meyer. "Let me go see what I can find out."

Travis laid his hand on her shoulder. "Stay here. I'll ask on my way out." He swung the door closed behind him as he left.

"Didn't expect to see him here, Mom. Oh, that's right. You were *working late*." Carlos apparently felt well enough to make insinuations.

"I stayed to help him with wedding stuff. He's my boss. There isn't anything like that going on." She'd left out the part about being on the way to Kate's when she'd gotten the call or the hand-holding or the near-kiss. "He ran to the house for me. I had him grab some of your clothes for later."

"Don't try and change the subject." His teasing eased her fears and made it easier to believe he would be back to himself in short order.

Her phone beeped, and she yanked it out of her purse.

Travis texted: *Liam is down the hall. I talked to his parents. He's banged up with a few broken bones but will be okay.*

Mari turned so that her back was to Carlos as she typed: *What a relief. I cannot thank you enough, Travis.*

His reply made even the memory of a wall disappear: *Anything you need, call me. No matter what time. See you in the morning.*

If ever a heart would have been the answer most representative of the way she felt, that was the time, but she only answered: *Okay.*

She glanced up as the door opened, hoping maybe Travis had returned.

"Mrs. Gonzales, here's a pillow and blanket. That chair pulls out." The nurse set the items in the chair next to the bed before heading back out of the room.

Carlos sobered. "Did he say how Liam was?"

"He's down the hall. Sounds like he'll be okay. What happened?" Mari fiddled with the chair, trying to get it ready for sleeping.

"Some guy jumped the median. Liam swerved, but the guy still hit us."

She blinked away the tears that threatened. "I'm glad you're going to be okay. Why don't you get some more sleep?"

"Maybe." Instead of closing his eyes, he switched on the television and flipped through channels.

Mari unzipped the overnight bag and pulled out a change of clothes. Travis had picked up everything she requested. A small shopping bag tucked in the side caught her attention. After changing, she settled in the chair and opened the bag. Inside, she found her favorite kind of chocolates, a paperback, and a note.

> *Since I'm guessing you won't sleep much, here's something to read and a little snack for when you're awake in the middle of the night. I picked up a random book with a nice cover, so I hope you like it. Text or call if you need me.*

How did Travis know her favorite? She rarely had it at the office, and then she remembered. The first Christmas she worked for him, she'd been charged with ordering gifts for the staff. She'd intentionally left herself off the list. When she returned to work after the holiday, a gift card lay on her desk for an amount she deemed too much. The following year, she requested that he let her order her own gift. He agreed, and that year and every year after, she'd ordered that brand of chocolate.

What else had he noticed over the years?

Mari snapped a picture of the book cover and sent it to Remi along with a text. *Look what Travis surprised me with tonight. He doesn't even know you're an author.*

He's a keeper! A man with such great taste is rare. Remi responded like Mari expected.

While Carlos stared at the television, Mari read.

Eventually, Carlos drifted off to sleep, and the room got quiet. Mari slept in fits and spurts. If Carlos moved, she woke up. When the nurse came in, she woke up. He was getting the care he needed, but Mari prayed she'd be able to survive on those tiny snippets of sleep.

$$\backsim$$

"Good morning." Carlos kept his voice low.

Mari opened one eye, not ready for the sunlight. "Oh, hello." Sitting up, she rubbed her face. "You brought me coffee?"

Travis held a paper bag and two cups of coffee. "Flat White. I figured it was a Venti sort of day."

"You guessed right." She smoothed her hair. "I'm not sure what Carlos can have."

"I checked with the nurses. They approved." He pushed the rolling table up to the bed and handed over breakfast tacos.

"Thank you, Mr. Bentley." Carlos wasted no time digging into the food.

Travis sipped his coffee. "I don't want to intrude, so I'll go, but I can bring you lunch. Just let me know what you want." He flashed a half-smile before turning toward the door. "Oh, and I drove your car over. It's in the garage—third level near the northwest staircase." He handed her keys. "Forgot to give those back last night. But if you want me to check in on Wentworth, I can do that."

"Thank you. I would appreciate that." She slid the house key off the ring and pressed it into his palm, wanting to say so much more.

"Keep me updated." He stepped out of the room.

Mari followed. "Travis."

He stopped, looking surprised that she'd come after him.

"I'm not sure how to thank you for—for everything. I don't know what ..." She shook her head, erasing the visions of what could have been.

He rubbed his forehead. "Mari, I'm not sure I would've survived the last year and a half without your friendship. I'm just glad I can do something to help you."

Friendship. He'd gently explained how he felt and gave her a place to hide her emotions.

She wrapped her arms around his neck. "You're a good friend."

He patted her back. "I'll be back later."

"How are you getting back to your car?"

"I'll manage." He squeezed her hand. "Go eat before your tacos get cold."

Her feet refused to comply. She stood in the hall, staring after him as he walked away. Part of her yearned for the professional distance that made it easy to work alongside him, but another part of her yearned for something else entirely.

Chapter Fifteen

Travis crossed his arms as the elevator descended. *A good friend.* He guessed that phrase didn't exactly explain her feelings, but it worked as cover in the current situation—not that he wasn't her friend. He just wanted more than that, and he held on to the indications that maybe she did, too.

When he reached the bottom floor, instead of exiting the elevator, he pushed the button to go back up, hoping that during the short ride he'd think of a reason for showing up again.

He stepped off the elevator, still unsure of what to say.

Mari walked out of the room when he was only steps away. Surprise registered on her face. "You're back."

He pointed toward the room. "Everything okay?"

"Yeah, I was going to find something sweet."

He had the perfect opportunity to spend a few more minutes with her. "I'll walk with you down to the snack machine."

"Thanks. Did you need something?"

"I forgot to ask about Wentworth. Besides refilling water and giving him kibble, is there anything else?"

"There are little cans of wet food in the pantry. He'll love you forever if you give him that."

"I'll make sure and do that." He wondered what would spark the same response in Mari. At the snack machine, he dropped in coins. "What would you like?"

"Cookies."

He punched in the code, and the package fell.

After handing them to her, he moved toward the wall as a nurse pushed a cart down the corridor. Mari did the same, getting out of the way. When she moved closer and rested a hand on his chest, it nearly undid his restraint.

"Thank you, Travis. Did you apologize to Kate for me? I felt so bad keeping you away from her."

"No need to apologize. You didn't keep me here. I chose to stay, and Kate understood completely."

Mari stared at the floor, her hand still on his shirt. "I loved the chocolate."

"I'm glad. Has the doctor said how long Carlos will be here?"

"Said maybe tomorrow he could go home." She sighed and allowed him a glimpse of her brown eyes. "In the car, I worried that would never happen."

Travis pulled her close. Watching her cry wasn't easy.

"I'm crying about what didn't happen. How silly is that?" She let go and wiped her eyes.

"It turned out mostly okay." He didn't quite know what to say. "I'll walk you back up."

She clutched his arm as they wandered back to the room. "Will I see you tomorrow?"

"You'll see me later today. I'm bringing you lunch and dinner after that. Text me when you decide what you want."

"I will." She stopped outside Carlos's room.

"Promise me you'll call if you need anything. And if you give me a shopping list, I'll get groceries for you or whatever."

"What would I do without you?" She hugged him before walking back into the room.

⌒

That night, while Travis was at the office working when he should have been home, Mari texted: *Carlos gets to go home tomorrow.*

Great news! Any idea what time? Tired, he yawned and focused on the screen. He'd reviewed the numbers for his meeting more times than he could count, but as important as it was, he didn't want to miss any details.

Not sure. You should go home, Travis.

He stared at her message, wondering how she knew where he was. *How do you know I'm at work?*

I guessed. She sent a smiley.

He saved the file. *Shutting down now. I'll be by in the morning unless they release him really early.*

Unlikely. I'll see you then.

Although plans were back on track for his big project, closing the upcoming deal would put the company in a better situation, which is exactly what he needed.

He swung by Mari's on the way home and was greeted at the door by a very lonely Wentworth. "Hello, sir. You don't like being home all alone, do you?" Travis squatted to give the cat a scratch. "It's not fun being all alone."

Travis dropped kibble into the bowl and gave the cat fresh water.

Purring, Wentworth ran to the pantry, sat next to the shelf where the little cans waited, and stared at Travis.

"I wonder what you want." He grabbed a can, sending Wentworth into a tizzy. As soon as the bowl touched the floor, the cat buried his face in the food. "Now that we're such good friends, you'll put in a good word for me, won't you?"

Wentworth couldn't be bothered to respond.

"Enjoy. I'll be back to check on you tomorrow." Travis locked up the house, but before leaving, he stopped to check on the flower beds.

After two days without water, the leaves were looking droopy. He turned on the hose and gave the plants a much-needed drink. Keeping those flowers alive and beautiful was a priority.

Chapter Sixteen

Mari shifted in the chair, uncomfortable and ready to go home. Reliving the exchange with Travis, she cringed. How could she have said that to him? And grabbing his arm that way seemed silly in hindsight.

The emotional rollercoaster of the last few days had her saying things she never intended to say. So, when the door swung open and Travis arrived with breakfast, she sucked in a deep breath, steadying her heart rate before jumping up to greet him.

He set the food down and motioned toward the hall. "Morning. How is he? I figured out here we wouldn't wake him."

"Good. He woke up once last night, but the pain is manageable." She kept her hands to herself, shuddering at how she'd behaved yesterday.

"Listen, I'm going to cancel tomorrow's flight. I can reschedule once things have calmed down, and—" He'd worked way too hard on that account to postpone the meeting.

"No. That is a big account. You will get on that plane *first thing* in the morning." With more authority than she'd ever used with him, she met his gaze. "The meeting is first thing Tuesday morning. You need to fly out tomorrow."

He raised his eyebrows, but the corner of his mouth twitched into a slight grin. "I guess that settles that."

"Please, Travis. Carlos is being released this afternoon."

"Good to hear. You'll both sleep better at home." He slipped his hands into his pockets. "About tonight …"

Mari held her breath, unsure of where the conversation was headed.

"Do you need help getting him home?" There was more he hadn't said.

"We'll be fine." She laid a hand on his arm, worried about his pensiveness. "Everything okay?"

"Oh, yeah, it's fine. I just—Kate invited me to a surprise party tonight. It's for her detective friend that's helped them so much and for Alex's sister."

"You should go."

He stepped closer and lowered his voice. "If you need me, I'll skip it."

Tempting as that was, she wouldn't take advantage of him. There was a difference between needing and wanting. "Go to the party."

"I will go on one condition."

"What's that?"

"Give me a shopping list. You don't need to be running through the store when you are trying to get Carlos home."

How could she say no to that? "I'll text you what we need."

"My flight leaves early, but if you need anything else, call me. And I'll make sure Erika and Fran know to call me if there is any trouble on Tuesday."

"They can call me. I just don't want to leave Carlos."

"You can stay home with him as long as you need." He glanced down at her hand still on his arm. "Promise to call if there's any-thing I can do?"

"I promise." She pulled her hand back and crossed her arms. "And I'll keep you updated on the patient."

"I'd appreciate that."

They lingered awkwardly in the hall. Conversation had never been difficult, but the last sixteen hours had changed that. She hoped maybe he had to choose his words more carefully because feelings were developing, but the possibility that she'd over-stepped, making their working relationship strained, also played in her head.

"I should …" She nodded toward the door.

"Oh, yeah. I'm sorry. Your food is getting cold." He smiled and turned to go.

She'd miss not seeing him. "Travis."

"Yes?" Anticipation lit up his eyes.

Surely, she wasn't misreading the signs. Stretching up, she wrapped him in a hug. "I'll see you when you get back."

"Until Thursday, then." He smiled and turned to go.

She stood in the hall, watching as he made his way to the elevator. The doors opened as he walked up, and he gave one last wave before disappearing from view. She stepped back into the room, and Carlos raised his eyebrows.

"You're awake. Travis brought breakfast."

"You gonna fill me in on what's going on with your *boss?*"

Mari sat down with her food, hoping the questioning would be brief. "Nothing. He's being kind."

"If you say so." He unwrapped his tacos.

While she ate, she replayed the conversations over the last few days. Nothing said was out of the ordinary. The pauses and glanc-es in between sparked a wonder, a possibility of hope. As soon as the thought took shape, she swatted it away. Dating the boss was a horrible idea.

Just when she'd convinced herself that the relationship must remain professional, Travis texted: *I'll be back by in a bit to drop off your keys. You'll need those.*

Seeing him again would only weaken her convictions.

Once Mari had Carlos home and settled on the couch, remotes and snacks within reach, she texted Travis and let him know they'd made it. She had promised to update him.

He replied a minute later: *Good to hear. I think you'll both get more rest at home.*

Mari couldn't disagree with that. *We will. Have a safe flight and good luck with the account. And have fun tonight.*

A smiley popped up followed by: *I'll message when I land in Boston.*

Something had definitely changed. He'd never sent a smiley before. Ever.

Snacking on chocolate, she responded with a smiley. Finding chocolate on her counter and cheesecake in her freezer—items she hadn't put on the list—made reining in her emotions a harder task. Thankfully, when Travis dropped off the keys, it hadn't been too awkward. There was perhaps a little more finger contact than necessary, but she wasn't about to complain.

At the end of the day when Carlos was settled in for the night, Mari went upstairs. Inviting and comfortable, her bed swallowed her as soon as she laid down. She woke up twice during the night to check on Carlos but managed good sleep in between.

When her phone buzzed early, she grabbed it, still half-asleep. "Hello?"

"Mari, I'm so sorry to bother you, but I need a favor." Travis sounded flustered, which wasn't like him at all.

She sat up. "What's wrong?"

"My departure was delayed, and I'm afraid I'll miss the connecting flight. I can't find the email with the itinerary to sort it all out. I should have it. I'm sorry."

Mari jumped out of bed and opened her laptop. "Give me a second. I'll resend it. Or would you rather—just let me handle it."

"I don't want you to go to any trouble." Flight announcements over the airport loud speaker made him hard to hear.

"I'll take care of it. Stay by the phone."

He thanked her again and again. "What would I do without you, Mari?"

"Let's just hope you never have to find out." Had she really said that out loud? She focused on getting his travel plans untangled.

After sorting it out, she called him back. "Sent you an email with the details. Also sending a text."

"Thank you, Mari."

"Text me when you land in Boston. I don't care if it's late."

"I will."

When she wandered out to the living room, Carlos was awake, eating cereal.

"I would've gotten you breakfast." She brewed a pot of coffee.

Carlos shook his head. "I have one good arm. Breakfast was easy."

"Need anything?"

"Nope. You going to the office?" He slurped the milk out of the bottom of the bowl.

"I have off today. It's the Fourth of July, but I'd stay here to help you anyway."

"Oh yeah. Guess no backyard barbeque for me." He winced when he shifted. "I appreciate everything, Mom. Makes me feel like a slug, though."

She shook her head and gathered his dishes.

Mari snuggled into her spot at the end of the sofa, book in hand. Carlos gave up trying to play Xbox and turned on a movie. The afternoon passed quietly.

When her phone beeped, she launched toward it, and Carlos chuckled. Her eagerness wasn't going to help convince him there was nothing going on with her boss.

Travis texted only two words: *Made it.*

She tapped out a quick reply: *I let the hotel know the flight was delayed.*

Another smiley.

"The *boss?*" Carlos raised an eyebrow.

Mari worried Carlos would read the truth in her expression. "What?"

"Everything okay with *Mr. Bentley?*" His emphasis on the name hinted at the deeper question, which Mari chose to ignore.

"Yes. He had some trouble with his flight, so I had to help him. It's all good now."

"Mom." He shifted to look her in the eye. "You don't have to keep things from me. If you are dating, I'm okay with that."

Shocked that Carlos had said anything like that, Mari wasn't about to tell him about her one-sided feelings. "There isn't anything like that going on." She wasn't sure if she was trying to convince herself or daring the universe to make a liar out of her.

By Tuesday afternoon, Mari had a severe case of cabin fever.

Carlos crashed on the sofa, controller in hand, attempting to fill time by playing on the Xbox—not an easy task with only one good hand.

She settled at the kitchen table within earshot and tried to get a few work items out of the way. Glancing at her phone between tasks, she forced herself not to text Travis. She'd only end up interrupting his meeting. When her phone chimed, she smiled at the text on the screen: *Landed the account. Thanks for all your help.*

She tapped out a reply: *So glad. Enjoy your evening in Boston. See you when you get back.*

Dots bounced on the screen, and she waited.

How's Carlos?

She texted: *Good. Not in much pain.*

Good to hear. Travis knew how to play the knight in shining armor.

She wished it was more than just a role. *Be safe.*

Too antsy to continue working, she got up. Chopping vegetables and sausage, she kept busy in the kitchen while the oven preheated. She'd let the oven do most of the work. After sliding it onto the rack, she went back to her laptop and checked the schedule for the next day. Perhaps tomorrow, she'd work a half-day. With Travis out of the office, it would be quiet, and she could get a ton accomplished. Besides, Carlos seemed well enough to leave alone.

She had more trepidation about leaving him than he did about staying alone. What would she do when he moved out in a few weeks?

〜

After washing the last few dishes, Mari picked up her phone.

Charlie had messaged: *I've been waiting for an update. Are you going to make me ask Travis for one?*

I'm so sorry. Even alone, Mari felt the flush of embarrassment, remembering what she'd admitted to Travis. Including Remi in the answer, Mari updated her friends. *Carlos is home and is healing. After being at the hospital and now at home for so many days, I'm going stir crazy.*

Should we talk about Carlos or Travis first?

Mari didn't have to look to know that question came from Charlie. Remi would've started with Travis.

Mari answered honestly. *I already told you that Carlos was doing well. And I'm not sure I want to talk about Travis at all.*

When is the wedding? Remi finally joined the conversation.

Mari hadn't thought much about the wedding since the accident. *Less than two weeks away.*

Are you going with Travis? The question had come from Charlie.

I'm going; he's going. We aren't going together. Mari typed as fact what she hoped wasn't true. She wanted nothing more than to be by his side at the wedding.

When does Carlos move out? Charlie kept lobbing questions.

Mari had tried not to think about that. *Two weeks after the wedding.*

Remi chimed in: *Please don't make us beg for information. When you messaged last week, Travis was strictly professional. Has anything changed?*

Uh, yeah. Charlie answered before Mari could even think what to type. *When I talked to him, there was a definite hint of unprofessionalism—don't think that's a word but whatever.*

Charlie was morphing into someone Mari didn't recognize.

You talked to him?????? Remi clearly hadn't expected that.

Emailed him because I was worried about Mari. He called me right away. Has an amazingly smooth voice. Charlie was just having fun at Mari's expense. That was the only explanation.

Like a pillow talk sort of voice? Or a late-night radio host? Remi was probably creating a new character. *With those blue eyes? Totally swoon-worthy.*

Stop! Mari couldn't let herself get caught up in that sort of chatter. It wasn't true—well, the part about his smooth voice and swoon-worthy blue eyes was totally true—but because she and Travis worked together, they couldn't be more than friends. Talk like that would launch her out of the friend mindset. *We're friends. That's all.*

I'll stop teasing. My best advice is to appreciate the friend-ship for what it is and enjoy every minute of it. Charlie's message prompted tears.

Are you sad that Carlos is moving out or sad that you'll be alone? Remi couldn't just let the conversation end on a happy note.

Mari stepped away from the keyboard, hunting a box of tissues. She'd need it. *Here goes. When George died, I was terrified of being alone. Having Carlos around kept me sane, I think. He needed me, so I couldn't sink too deep or shut myself off. But now, being alone doesn't—it bothers me a little, but not like before.*

She waited for a response.

When none appeared, she continued. *I'm not unhappy that he's leaving. I'm not sad that he'll be on his own and won't need me—maybe a little sad about that part, but mostly the unknown has me nervous.*

I wish I could hug you right now. Remi gave the best hugs.

Charlie sent a message: *I completely understand. And I get that your friendship with Travis has an element of the unknown also.*

Mari stared at the screen. That explained how she felt. As much as she liked Travis, dating him would mean giving up her job. In her heart she knew that, and it scared her. She didn't want to start over somewhere else or learn someone else's routine.

Those thoughts always wrapped back around to the fact that Travis hadn't said a word about dating. They were friends, and she could live with that.

Chapter Seventeen

Mari woke up early, wanting to be sure Carlos had everything he needed—pain pills, breakfast. The smell of food and coffee wafted from the kitchen. She hurried down.

Carlos stood at the stove, whistling and stirring eggs with one hand. "Morning. I made enough for two."

"I was planning to make you breakfast." She poured herself coffee and leaned on the counter.

"I can manage. Go ahead and go to work." He dropped eggs onto a plate. "But eat first."

"Sure you'll be okay?"

"Mom, I'll be fine." He'd grown up the last few months, and only a hint of the kid he used to be was left. "Really."

"But you'll call if you need anything?"

"Yes. I promise."

"Maybe I'll work a half-day then." She hurriedly ate before running upstairs to change.

Travis in Boston meant she wouldn't be dealing with clients, so she opted for more casual attire. She traded her dress and heels for jeans and flats. A simple fitted blouse made her look at least somewhat put-together. It didn't much matter because she'd hide in her office most of the day, getting things done.

⤳

She slipped into the office before anyone else arrived. Her productivity was at its best when no one else was around to distract her. She hadn't even sat down at her desk when the door leading to Travis's office opened. Thinking she was alone in the office, she jumped, and a squeal escaped before she realized who it was.

"Didn't mean to startle you. I'm sorry." Travis rubbed at his five o'clock shadow, an unusual look for him first thing in the morning. "I didn't expect you in today." He leaned against the doorframe, his hair tousled, his shirt wrinkled and untucked.

"I thought you were in Boston." She glanced down at her jeans.

"I flew in late last night. Just came in to get the details about tomorrow's meeting. I figured they'd be on your desk. They called late yesterday about moving it to today."

"Give me a minute to find it." She shuffled through the stack of papers she'd pushed to the edge of her desk. "I didn't hear about that. No one called me."

"You didn't have to come in. I'd have survived. *Maybe.*"

"I'm not sure about that." She looked him over. "I'll call the caterers and see what we can do about moving it to today."

"I hadn't even thought of food. That could be a mess."

"I'll figure it out. And Carlos is okay. He doesn't need me as much as I want to think he does." Handing Travis the meeting agenda, she eyed him. "Is everything okay?"

"That lunch is my only meeting today. Good."

"I didn't schedule anything because you weren't *supposed* to be here."

He raked his fingers through his hair.

"Travis Bentley, what's wrong?" She stood up and positioned herself between him and the door. "You look like you slept in your clothes."

"I didn't." His blue eyes lacked their normal sparkle. "I haven't slept."

"Why not?"

"You know the new account—they wanted a contract in hand today. I flew back last night and came straight to the office after I landed. Worked on that most of the night."

"What in the world?" In all the years she'd worked for him, she'd never seen him so uptight about a new contract and wondered if something else was bothering him.

He yawned and stretched. An image of snuggling with him on the couch with his head in her lap, her fingers trailing through his hair flashed in her head. Sheer will-power kept her hands off him. The flashes made her job more difficult. "I'll work on the contract. Just send me your notes. Then go sleep. I'll wake you with enough time to change before your meeting."

"It's close to done. I don't want to dump more on your plate."

She reached for his hand. "Please let me help. That's why I'm here."

"Thank you." He squeezed her hand and stared at her several seconds before saying anything more. "The notes are on my desk."

She followed him into the office. He gathered the papers into a stack, tucked a file folder under his arm, and handed the rest to her. It wasn't like him to hide papers from her. *What's in that folder that he doesn't want me to see?*

Flipping through to make sure she had what she needed, she noticed a missing page. "I think a page is missing. I'll grab it." She moved papers around, searching for the errant page. On the edge of the desk were tickets—tickets she hadn't ordered. Only the corners stuck out of an envelope. She couldn't see what they were for. He'd ordered them himself, which meant he didn't want people knowing about it. It also meant he didn't trust her not to share information about his personal life.

All the signs were there. He'd told her to get two tickets for the gala, so he could take a date. The walls started to close in, and her chest tightened.

She pulled her gaze away from the tickets, hoping he hadn't noticed her staring at them. He'd hidden the file folder; maybe he thought the tickets wouldn't be noticed.

"I appreciate this." Standing close, he startled her.

She grabbed the missing sheet and put a few steps between them. "Do you have a clean shirt here at the office?" Thinking about what he needed kept her mind off the pair of tickets and the file folder, temporarily.

"Think so." He crossed the office and opened the closet at the far end. "Yes. This should work." He held up that vibrant blue shirt, the one that made his eyes come alive.

Mari hurried toward the door and pointed at the large leather sofa. "Sleep. No one knows you're here. I'll wake you before the meeting."

He smiled as she pulled the door closed behind her.

She spread out his notes and opened the contract file. It was close to completion. She scanned it for mistakes and typed up the rest. While her fingers stayed busy, her mind drifted to the tickets. *Am I jumping to conclusions?* Maybe he'd planned something with Kate. Mari shook her head. That didn't explain why he didn't ask her to order the tickets like he did all the time.

She wasn't sure what bothered her more—that his attentions were focused on someone else—which left Mari feeling stupid and somewhat betrayed, but mostly sad in ways she couldn't explain—or that she had no idea who the mystery someone was.

Mari slipped into his office, letting her eyes adjust to the darkness before making her way to the couch. Sprawled on the couch, arm hanging off the edge, he snored. She hated to disturb him.

The file folder lay on the table. It'd be so easy to take a quick peek before waking him.

But she didn't. "Travis, your meeting starts in forty-five minutes."

His eyelids fluttered open, and alarm registered on his face as he inhaled sharply. "Mari, I, uh …" His tone cautious, he glanced around the room as if trying to figure out his surroundings.

A sleepy dazed smile cut across his face once he shook off the haze. His tousled hair, untucked shirt, and wrinkled clothes took irresistible to a new level. There went the wall.

He pushed up to a sitting position and scrubbed his face. "Wasn't sure where I was for a second. I thought—never mind about that. Hopefully there's a clean pair of slacks in that closet."

Flipping on the light, she opened the closet. "There is." She gathered the shirt and pants and carried them across the room.

"Good. These look like they've been slept in." He stood and began unbuttoning his shirt. "Lunch get worked out?"

Still clutching his clothes, she swallowed the growing lump in her throat. "Maybe. Yes. No. I should go check on that." She rushed out of his office. It wasn't like she'd never seen him without a shirt. To clarify, she'd seen him without a dress shirt—once—but he'd been wearing an undershirt. But she hadn't given a second thought to what was under the t-shirt. Until just that moment.

Before her brain could derail the train of thought, she mulled the possibility that someone else was seeing him without a shirt—someone who would be using that second ticket.

"Mari." His shirt buttoned up, he stood in the doorway. "I'm sorry I made you uncomfortable."

"Oh no. Why would you think that?"

"You left in a hurry … with my clothes."

She pushed them to him. "I'll go check on lunch."

∽

When lunch was over and the conference room empty, Mari packed up the leftover food and returned the room to order. The cleaning crew would take care of wiping everything down and vacuuming.

She glanced at the time. *2:48* So much for only working a half-day. She hadn't checked on Carlos in hours. It rang several times before he answered.

"Just checking on you." She figured he must be on speaker based on the way he sounded.

"No! No way." He groaned, and a loud thud echoed near the phone. He must've slapped the couch. 'Sorry. I died."

She'd miss so many things when he left, but the outbursts when he lost a round weren't on the list. "Need anything?"

"Yeah. Milk, chips, and we're out of sliced cheese."

She scrawled the short list on a notepad. "Anything else?"

"And maybe some Thai food for dinner."

"Thai food? Sure. I think I can manage that. Text me if you think of anything else." If she left soon, she could be at the grocery store before the rest of San Antonio showed up, which always seemed to happen in the late afternoon.

She'd finish up a couple tasks and then leave. That was her plan, anyway, but she needed to check with Travis. Spinning around to head into his office, she bumped into him.

"Couldn't help but overhear when I stepped in. Let me grab y'all dinner. I know a fabulous Thai place."

"You don't have to do that." Turning away, she stacked papers, getting her desk in order for the next day, avoiding a face to face discussion.

He leaned closer. "Please."

"As long as you order for yourself and stay and eat with us." Her tongue had a mind of its own.

Having dinner with him wasn't going to change anything—wouldn't change who'd be by his side when he handed over those tickets.

He rested a hand on her back. "What do you want, Mari?"

She whipped around and blinked. She hadn't expected him to ask about her intentions or her feelings. Did he know she'd seen the tickets? Could he read the disappointment on her face?

"Um, what do you mean?"

"To eat. What do you and Carlos want to eat?" His half grin and puzzled look made it hard to remember what Thai food she liked.

She flipped to a clean sheet in the notepad and scrawled the name of Carlos's favorite dish, then added her choice. "Thanks."

"I'll see you at the house about five. You should take off."

"I think I will." She grabbed her purse and started for the elevator. Pushing the down button, she said a quick goodbye to Fran and Erika. "Oh, the list. And my phone."

The doors opened, but she hurried back to her office. She should've been watching where she was going. If not for his hands catching her by the shoulders, she'd have plowed right into him. Again.

"Your phone."

"I'm so sorry. I was just running back to get it."

Loosening his grip but not pulling his hands away, he gazed down at her and cocked his head. "Everything okay with Carlos? You seem a bit—not quite yourself."

She forced a smile. "You can say it. I'm jumpy. I'm a bit of a mess." A deep breath helped keep the tears buried. "Carlos is fine. Not sure I can say the same for me."

The emotional blur of the last few days had pushed her to the limit. Worrying about her son, then discovering he didn't really need her was both bitter and sweet. At least she knew he'd be fine when he moved out in a matter of weeks.

Heaped on top of everything else, the discovery that Travis had a special someone he wasn't disclosing to the world knocked her off-kilter. Then she'd done a freefall into crazy and invited her boss to dinner.

She focused on the carpet, wishing Travis would pull her close like he had at the hospital. She wanted the comfort of his arms around her, wanted to hold off the loneliness that waited to fill her soon-to-be-empty nest, wanted to imagine that the ticket was for her.

He tugged her back into the office and swung the door closed. Arms wrapped around her, he asked, "Are you okay?" His words sounded soft, like the fur of her Russian Blue cat.

Nodding, she looked up at him. "I will be."

Holding her close, he rubbed her back. "I wish I knew what to say."

She wiped her eyes. "I'm okay."

The concern in his eyes betrayed the tight smile on his face. "See you at the house." His hand grazed her arm as it dropped to his side.

Thankfully, the last sentence was delivered in hushed tones. If the receptionists heard him, Mari could only imagine how that would stir the rumor mill. People would assume she was breaking office rules, corporate policy that Travis had no intention of violating.

Somewhere in her head she had a mantra. She needed to remember it, especially if Travis was dating. The one thing that didn't line up—it seemed odd that he'd be so attentive to Mari if he was seeing someone else. As much as she wanted to entertain the idea of being that someone, they worked together. Those two ideas didn't seem compatible.

☙

At five minutes to five, Carlos answered the knock at the door. "Mr. Bentley, thanks for bringing dinner."

Mari listened as the guys chitchatted about the weather and Carlos's sling.

Footsteps approached the kitchen, and she sucked in a deep breath before they cleared the corner.

Wentworth sprung out of wherever he'd been napping and dashed up to Travis.

"Hello, Wentworth. You miss me?" He grinned as the cat wove between his feet.

"Seems so." Mari laughed. "He's usually not so friendly with strangers."

Travis still wore the blue shirt he'd changed into earlier. Had he even gone home? "Where should I sit these?" He held up the bags.

"Right here." She patted the counter. "I'll grab plates and silverware."

Travis leaned down and scratched the cat. "Wentworth and I aren't strangers, and you were right about the wet food, by the way."

Carlos picked up his container. "I'll just eat out of this."

Seeing Travis loving on her cat melted Mari's heart even more. She laughed. "He's begging."

"He is. May I give him a can?" Travis pointed toward the pantry.

"Yes. And, help yourself to some of this Pad Thai if you'd like. I only want part of it." She scooped a portion onto her plate.

"You're welcome to some of mine, too" He served Wentworth his dinner before serving himself food.

At the table, as they ate and talked, she relaxed. Perhaps it was the friendship and companionship she appreciated. It didn't have to be a romantic attachment. Friendship was easier anyway. It didn't violate any corporate policy.

Chapter Eighteen

Travis lingered at the table, enjoying both the conversation and the company. Watching Mari in her own space, interacting with her son, only affirmed Travis's feelings.

When Carlos disappeared upstairs, Travis sat with Mari in the den, waiting for the perfect opportunity to begin a difficult conversation.

"I ordered tickets for the gala. I couldn't remember if I mentioned that." She ran a finger along a seam in the cushion.

With Wentworth in his lap, he sucked in a deep breath. "I hope you know I appreciate you—not just because you're a great personal assistant but because—"

"You're a great friend, too." She used the word he wasn't going to use and didn't even glance at him as she said it.

The timing wasn't right.

Driving home, Travis tried to think of some way to show Mari how much he cared. Saying it to her was a given, but a surprise would add weight to his words.

On a quest to come up with the grand surprise, he sat down

at his computer, and searched for ways to surprise a girlfriend, not that Mari was his … yet. He clicked the list of ideas. He didn't hold out high hopes that he'd find the right idea when the first item on the list suggested showing up at her workplace. He did that every day.

As he stared at the list, an idea sparked. He replied to the email Mari's friend sent him.

> *Charlotte-*
>
> *I'm sure Mari has updated you, but Carlos is home and doing well.*
>
> *His move date is approaching, and I know it will be a difficult transition for Mari, especially after the surgery.*
>
> *I'd like to do something special for her, surprise her somehow. Any ideas you could suggest would be greatly appreciated.*
>
> *Travis*

Travis sent off the email, hoping he wouldn't have to wait long for an answer.

Thursday morning, the elevators opened earlier than Erika and Fran arrived. Travis guessed that Mari had come in early. He wouldn't complain about having a few minutes alone with her before the workday started, but he wondered if maybe he should have talked to her last night.

He stood when she poked her head around the door, her smile lighting up her eyes. "Hi. You're in early."

"Good morning." She glanced behind her. "I'm going to drop my stuff in my office and then make coffee."

"I'll come with you." He sauntered next to her as they walked through her office to the kitchen. "Thanks for having me last night. I really enjoyed it."

"We did too." Busy with the coffee, she didn't look at him. "We'll have to do it again sometime."

His heart fluttered at the thought, and he waited to respond until she glanced up. "I'd like that."

The coffee trickled into the pot, and Mari sighed. "Carlos is till planning to move out. I know he can't pause school for a broken arm, but he acts like everything will just be fine. With his arm like that, I think he needs help with the move, but he insists that he doesn't."

"He can't carry much with that sling."

"Exactly. I get that he doesn't need me anymore, but why won't he accept help?" The coffee finished brewing, and she filled two mugs, adding cream to hers but leaving his black. "Thank you for letting me rant and ramble."

He sipped his coffee, trying to hide his grin. "Always happy to listen. And my guess is that he's trying not to load on you what he feels he should handle himself."

"You might be right." Her shoulders sagged.

Travis leaned in closer. "I can talk to him if you'd like." He wasn't sure what she'd think of the idea.

She patted his arm. "He'll think I put you up to it, but thank you."

Travis laid his hand on hers. "Thanks for making coffee." He wanted to tell her that she made his day brighter by just walking through the door and that he wasn't sure how he could do his job without her organization and help, but he didn't. In the office was not the place to have that conversation.

The rest of the day didn't allow for stolen moments or casual chat. In late afternoon, he buzzed Mari's phone.

"I'll be on a call for a while. Hold everything. And don't wait for me. I'll see you in the morning."

"All right." She hesitated. "Is there something I forgot to put in the calendar?"

With nothing scheduled, she probably wondered about the call, but he wasn't ready to bring her in on his secret … not yet.

"No, this is something I planned. See you in the morning."

"Bye."

Sitting in the little room, he dialed. "Hi. This is Travis. Have you had a chance to look over the information I sent?"

The man on the other end of the line didn't hesitate before answering. "Yes. And I very much like what I see. I have a few questions, but I'm still very interested."

Travis relaxed. What was only a remote possibility days ago morphed into a big change, hopefully one of many changes.

"I'm really glad to hear that."

Chapter Nineteen

Mari went home, made dinner, and fussed over Carlos. She tried not to think about the call that Travis hadn't added to the calendar. It was so unlike him to do that. Before Mari tucked in for the night, she messaged Remi and Charlie. *Spent the whole day at work. Carlos is doing well.*

Remi sent a happy face followed by a question: *How's the hottie?*

I was going to ask the same thing, just in a different way. Charlie's message surprised Mari.

She didn't know how to answer them. *Travis is fine.*

We know that! Remi was probably laughing at her own joke.

Mari pounded out a response. *Nothing has changed. He came over for dinner last night, but it's nothing. Just friends. Wedding plans are on track. After next weekend, things will go back to normal.*

In the moments she believed that, and it made her sad. Weddings were supposed to make people cry for an entirely different reason.

⌒

At work the next morning, she didn't ask about the phone call, and Travis didn't mention it. After making coffee and some casual chitchat, Mari settled at her desk.

Minutes later, Kate texted: *Could I get some ideas from you?*

Of course! Mari closed her office door. *What do you need?*

I'm trying to decide what to get my bridesmaids. I want to find something they'll love. Any ideas? Kate's excitement was unmistakable, even over text.

Hmmm. Mari tried to think of something unique and fun. Her lack of ideas made her feel old. *Do you want a thing or an experience?*

Oooh! An experience. That's a great idea. I may do a combination. Now I just have to think of what.

What about all of you spending a day at the spa together? Mari would love a day at the spa, hopefully Kate's bridesmaids would like that, too.

Perfect! And I can get them plush robes, monogrammed. But I need to order ASAP. Thank you, Mari. Kate followed her text with a heart.

Mari loved the relationship that had developed with Kate in the last couple of months. Pushing aside thoughts of the wedding, Mari focused on work. .

⌒

At the end of the day, when Travis poked his head in to say goodbye, his grin was as wide as the doorway. "One week!"

"You going to make it that long without exploding?"

"Not sure." He sat on the edge of her desk. "Have a busy night planned?" He almost sounded as if he was fishing for an invitation.

"Nothing exciting. Just dinner. Carlos isn't cleared to drive yet, so I assume he'll be home." She rubbed at an ink smudge on the desk. "You're welcome to come over."

"I don't want to intrude."

She didn't dare look up. "You aren't. Not at all."

"Going home to a quiet house is—it's not fun, especially with all the excitement."

Kate had been right. Why hadn't it occurred to Mari that he might be lonely?

She stood, and with him resting on her desk, she wasn't eye-level with his chest, which helped. She wanted to say something meaningful about friendship and being there for each other, but everything she thought of sounded sappy or cheesy. "Maybe we can figure out a theme for the charity event. You coming straight to the house or stopping to change first?"

"I'll swing by my house on the way over. Anything I can bring?"

"Just you." That was what Mari wanted.

⌒

Mari hadn't even pulled out of her parking place when Carlos texted: *Tori and I are headed to Liam's. I'll be home late.*

Have fun. She resisted messaging Remi and Charlie right away, telling them what she'd done and asking for their advice. Instead, she drove home. Hopefully, Mari would have a few minutes to tell them about her predicament before Travis arrived.

When she got to the house, after sliding the already-assembled casserole into the oven and dropping kibble into Wentworth's bowl, she ran up to change. While she stripped out of her work clothes, she messaged her friends: *Invited the boss over for dinner because he seemed lonely, AND he asked if I had a busy evening planned almost like a hint. But I found out after I invited him that Carlos isn't going to be home. He's spending the evening at a friend's house. What have I done?*

You invited him AGAIN?

Mari didn't need to see the round little picture to know Charlie had sent that message.

With everything that happened, he was so kind. I'm trying to be a friend. Mari's motives were somewhat divided, but she did want to be Travis's friend.

Remi could always be counted on to offer the romantic perspective. *Maybe he needs a girlfriend. Then he wouldn't be lonely.*

Neither of y'all are any help! Mari tapped out the truth and read it over before hitting send. *I like him. A lot. But I'm not sure it will ever be more than friendship. Right now, I'm okay with that. I just want to be around him, and that makes me sound pitiful.*

He's your boss. That could get complicated. Charlie cared, but her pragmatism didn't always feel warm and fuzzy.

Remi sent a heart. *Just have fun.*

A knock sounded, and Mari yanked on her jeans and t-shirt. *He's here!* Her friends would have to wait to hear more.

Barefoot, she ran to the door. "Hey. Carlos ditched us for friends. He went over to Liam's."

"How is his friend?" Travis wore shorts and a t-shirt. It was the most casual she'd ever seen him. His legs weren't too shabby.

Friends don't check out not-shabby legs. Mari needed to update her mantra.

"Healing. He's been home a couple days." She headed into the kitchen. "What can I get you to drink? I'm out of Cokes, but I have juice and milk. I also have a bottle of premixed margarita."

"That last option sounds pretty good."

"With or without salt?"

"Without."

She poured the margarita over ice and added a small straw. "Your drink. Shaken, not stirred."

The grin that spread across his face made her want to say it again, but it wouldn't have been funny a second time.

"Too many of these, and I'll have to take Uber home. Good, though." He took another sip.

"I figured you'd be out with the guys tonight. Aren't they all doing their bachelor party stuff tonight?"

"They are. Alex invited me, but they don't need an old guy hanging around."

"What exactly do you think they'll be doing that you'd be cramping their style?"

"Nothing like that. The other two guys are happily married, and Alex—that guy wouldn't cheat on a pop quiz he graded himself."

"Sounds like Kate found someone a lot like you." A little honesty couldn't hurt anything. Mari meant every word.

Travis snapped his head up, his eyes wide. He opened his mouth, then closed it again, still staring at her. After a sip of his drink, he turned toward the counter. "On nights when Carlos isn't home, what do you usually do?"

"Depends on how the day went. Good day, I might throw together a salad or warm leftovers. Then I watch tv or make cards or something."

"What about the bad days?"

"I stop and grab ice cream or cheesecake and have that for dinner, usually in front of the television."

"So, you only cooked because I was coming?"

She'd be lying if she said anything other than yes. "It wasn't a bother. I had the casserole ready to slide into the oven." She poured herself a margarita. "And like you said, spending the evening alone can sometimes be tiresome."

He lifted his glass. "To friends. And not being alone."

She clinked her glass against his. "To friends."

Either his relaxed manner or the margarita had taken the edge off her nervousness, and her romantic notions faded away as she took Charlie's advice and simply enjoyed the company.

Chapter Twenty

Travis finished his second serving of the casserole. "That was delicious. Thank you." He picked up both empty plates.

"Don't worry about the dishes. I'll get them later." She pointed to the den. "Let's go where it's more comfortable."

"Whatever you say." He sipped the last of his drink. "You mentioned working on the theme. I'm open to suggestions. Christmas in July won't work now that we've moved it to September."

"It's the first event since Kate came home. What if we used that somehow?" She curled up on the end of the sofa, her bare feet tucked underneath her.

Travis dropped down next to her, leaving a polite gap. "I hadn't even thought of that. But the foundation is named for Claire Bentley. How would we work that in without everyone calling Kate the wrong name?"

Mari jumped up and ran into the kitchen. She returned holding a notepad. "What if we wrote it like this?" Dropping down next to him, without leaving the gap, she wrote out *Meet Claire*, then crossed out the name and scribbled *Kate* above it.

"That's a great idea. I'll mention it to Kate to be sure she's okay with it, but I really like the idea."

Mari pointed at his empty glass. "Refill?"

"Sure. But I'll get it. Want me to top yours off?" He reached for her glass.

"Please." She smiled up at him. "Thanks."

In the kitchen, he added ice to each glass, then refilled them, all the while, berating himself. *Why had he toasted to friends?* Using that word would leave her with the wrong impression, but maybe for the time being, friendship was the best option. Surely lawyers wouldn't mind that.

It was a fine line that demanded attention. Although he cared much more about Mari's opinion, there could be ramifications of blatantly ignoring legal advice, not that he'd asked, but he knew what they'd say.

"We could watch tv or play a game." She'd padded into the kitchen with nary a sound.

Travis nearly spilled the drinks in his hand.

"Sorry." Her lips apologized, but her eyes laughed.

He grinned when he noticed the games in her arms. "What are my options?"

"We could save the world from a virus, work on our pattern matching, or try to avoid exploding kittens." She laid out games on the table, an inviting smile shaping her mouth.

"I think I'm up for saving the world." He'd be up for kissing her too, but she hadn't offered that option, and that was somewhere on the far side of that fine line.

Settled at the table, they laid out the board and stacked cards. After quickly reading the directions, they began playing.

Laughing and talking, they strategized, thinking through moves, trying to eliminate the virus.

When Travis draped his arm on the back of her chair and leaned in close, reading the card in her hand, Mari sat perfectly still. *Is she holding her breath?* That was the moment he sensed her attraction. She said nice words about friendship, but her body language sang a different tune, and it was music to Travis's ears.

Working together, they eventually saved the world from a pandemic.

After another refill and a few rounds of Exploding Kittens, Travis couldn't stifle his yawn. "I should head home. Mind if I leave my car here and get it in the morning?"

"Not at all." She glanced at her phone. Notifications filled the screen.

"Someone really wants to talk to you, it looks like."

"Charlie wants an update before heading to bed. Thus, the spam of messages." She tucked the phone in her back pocket. "With all that's happened this week and all."

Since her husband died, Travis had never heard her mention any guy other than Carlos. Perhaps the assumptions about attraction had been way off the mark. "Go give Charlie his update. My ride should be here any minute."

Mari touched his arm but didn't speak until he turned to look at her. "*She* is one of the friends I mentioned the other day. Charlie is short for Charlotte."

Why hadn't he put that together? "Oh. I didn't realize. I thought—you should go chat with them. Tell them I said 'hi.'"

"Charlotte Potter and Remi Carrington. Remi is a romance author. She lives out west. She's spamming messages because she wants to know how dinner went. Suffice it to say, I don't get out much." Mari shrugged.

"Sounds like they don't either." He stepped out the door as a car pulled up to the curb. "Thanks for tonight. I had fun."

"Me too. Would it be weird if I asked you to text when you got home?"

He winked but didn't give an answer. Of course he'd call her.

After sliding into the backseat and greeting the driver, Travis turned to look out the back window and waved.

Mari stayed on the porch until the car turned the corner.

❧

At home, he shot off a quick text: *Made it home.* It had been one of the most enjoyable evenings in a long time. He tossed his phone on the bed and turned on the television. The low hum helped lull him to sleep when his brain wouldn't be quiet, which lately was almost every night.

His phone beeped, and he grabbed for it.

Mari's response kicked his brain into overdrive. *I had a fantastic time. Thank you for coming over.*

Travis climbed out of bed and wandered down the stairs and into his office. He wanted to ask her out before revealing the secrets he'd been keeping, but that meant asking her to sneak around or change jobs. He wasn't sure about either option. Contemplating how and when he might broach the topic, he scrawled out ideas, feelings, and thoughts.

He checked his email before going back up to bed and found a message from Charlotte, or Charlie as she was known to her friends.

> *Let me be clear. I care about Mari and do not want to see her hurt. Especially now.*
>
> *Charlotte*
>
> *P.S. What sort of surprise?*

Travis typed out a response as fast as his fingers could move.

> *Mari is important to me. I wanted to plan something for the day Carlos left.*
>
> *Travis*

He expected that he wouldn't hear from her right away, but he was wrong.

Let me think about it. Budget?

-C

Travis tapped out a quick reply. That question was easy to answer.

Not an issue. Will consider ALL ideas.

-T

He hoped he wouldn't have to wait long. Moving day was fast approaching.

Chapter Twenty-one

After cleaning up, Mari went upstairs. Snuggled in bed, she messaged her friends: *I had such a good time. We laughed, played games, and drank margaritas.*

Romance? Remi had a one-track mind.

Friendship. That's what I need more than romance right now. Mari's answer felt truer seeing it on the screen.

I like this guy. Charlie's message almost sounded like someone else had sent it.

Mari typed *Me too* but deleted it before hitting send. *I'm falling asleep. Night.*

Remi sent hearts, and Charlie sent a sticker of a sleeping kitten. Mari couldn't wait to see them in September.

Before turning out the light, she texted Carlos: *I'm going to bed. There is leftover casserole in the fridge.*

He answered: *Won't be too much longer. See ya in the morning.*

Deliriously happy but exhausted from a full day, she laid her head on her pillow and closed her eyes.

⁓

Saturday morning, Mari made herself coffee and sat at the table, wondering what time Travis would be by to get his car. The flutters that had accompanied thoughts of him had been replaced with a deep contentment. Truthfully, the flutters hadn't been replaced, but they'd been joined by the contentment. Whatever the case, she liked the new direction.

The front door opened and closed. "Carlos? I'm in the kitchen."

He walked into the room, stone-faced. "When did he leave? I'm not mad or anything, but you could've been honest with me. I'm not a kid anymore."

She replayed his words in her head, trying to make sense of them. "What are you talking about?"

"Mr. Bentley spent the night. What happened to 'nothing like that is going on' and 'he's my boss'?"

Mari wasn't sure whether to laugh or be angry. His accusation was preposterous, but his tone made her want to lash out.

After a deep breath, she calmed her anger. "His car is gone?" She cradled the pang of disappointment.

"Uh, *yeah*. Why do you sound so surprised?"

"Travis left last night. We drank margaritas while we played games, and he took a ride share home." She emptied the last of her coffee into the sink and rinsed her mug. "Anything else you need to say?"

"I thought ..."

"Clearly." She rested her hand on his cheek. "Travis is my friend. Why would I lie to you?"

Carlos looked as uncomfortable as a cat after a bath. "I'm sorry."

"Forgiven. What's on your agenda for today?"

"Tori is coming to help me pack." He shifted his sling.

"Need more boxes?"

"I could use a few more probably."

Mari loaded her plate and silverware into the dishwasher. "You eat. I'll go get some."

He needed space after their conversation, and she wanted to get out of the house. In the car, she picked up her phone then dropped it. She wasn't sure she'd tell anyone—not even Remi and Charlie—about Carlos's assumption.

The tiny part of Mari that didn't laugh at the idea of Travis spending the night held her back. She'd dated a few times over the years and was always upfront with Carlos. His reaction to Travis struck her as odd.

Could Carlos sense what she hadn't said? Or did he not like Travis? She hoped that neither was true. The notion that maybe she wasn't as content with the idea of only a friendship poked at her. That he'd come by and hadn't even knocked or texted disappointed Mari.

⌒

Monday morning kicked off a week that Mari knew would be a blur. She could not have been happier that Kate hired a wedding coordinator because without her the week might have been a nightmare.

Anytime Mari was around Travis, she recited her friendship mantra. Silently, of course.

At the end of the day, when he leaned on her desk asking how the day had gone, she remained in her seat. "I've been going over resumes for the admin position. I'm grateful that Anne stayed an extra month. I need to find someone soon."

"Any good candidates?"

"None of them are bad. After reviewing the job with Anne, I'm trying to find a good fit." Trying to be diplomatic, she didn't go on about how Roger Talbot wasn't the easiest person to work with.

Travis rubbed the back of his neck. "When is her last day?"

"End of the month."

"We can chat about having Fran or Erika cover for Anne until we fill the position. Anything else?"

"I marked you out of the office Thursday and Friday."

"I'll be here Thursday, but leave the calendar that way. I might be able to get some stuff done."

Against her better judgment, she stood. "You going to sneak around and expect me to cover for you?"

His fingers brushed her hand. "Would you?"

Mari couldn't remember her mantra. "In a heartbeat."

His smile was the reward for honesty. "I'll see you tomorrow."

Tuesday went by in a blink. When Carlos called Tuesday afternoon, Mari was just finishing work.

"Hey, mom. Just letting you know that I'm headed out. I'll be home late."

"Have fun. Call if you need anything."

An idea grabbed her, and before she lost her nerve, she popped into Travis's office. "Carlos is out with friends again. Want to grab dinner?"

Attributing time spent together to friendship made it easy to extend an invitation. She liked being with Travis but refused to unpack all the reasons why. It didn't have to be complicated, and there was no corporate policy against friendship. That was her new mantra.

That warm smile lit up his eyes. "Is it a cheesecake or leftovers kind of day?" Travis shut off his computer.

"Busy, but not bad, so maybe real food with a cheesecake chaser."

"Dinner sounds good, but it's my turn to cook."

Mari couldn't even imagine him standing at a stove. Her expression must've shown that because he laughed.

"Don't look so surprised. It won't be fancy, though."

With a promise to meet him at his house, she ran home to change. She called Charlie on speaker while driving home.

When she answered, Mari started with what was on her mind. "I'm having dinner with Travis again. At his house."

"Hi. So glad you called. How is your week going?"

"Charlie, I need your advice."

"I gave you my advice already." Charlie didn't approve of any hint of office romance.

Mari regretted calling. "I know you did. I was just hoping that maybe—"

"But I might've been wrong."

Mari replayed her words, wondering if she'd heard correctly. "I don't need Remi talking me into things."

"You know me better than that. Having a friend that isn't a two-hour flight away is a good thing. So, my advice is to proceed with caution, but I can't help but like him—or what I've heard about him."

"Consider me cautious. Thanks, Charlie. I miss you. September seems so far away."

"Agreed."

⌒

Mari had been to Travis's house a time or two over the years, but not since—not for almost two years. She knocked and tried not to wonder what the neighbors were thinking. *The neighbors don't care about who he has over.*

"Come in." Travis held a spatula in his hand. "I hope grilled cheese and bacon sandwiches are okay. I even have pickle spears as a side."

"Sounds good."

"I told you it wouldn't be fancy. I don't keep a lot of groceries around."

"This a family recipe?" Mari couldn't resist a tease.

Travis winked. "We call it a grilled Bentley. Please don't share the recipe."

She laughed.

"So, tell me something about the Mari I don't know."

"There's really just the Mari you know. Too hard to keep secrets."

"Okay then, no secrets. I can work with that." He flipped the sandwiches. "Where do you want to visit?"

She didn't need to ponder that question. "I've always wanted to see Ireland."

He set the food on the table. "Ireland?"

"The pictures make it look so beautiful and lush. Then you add castles and what's not to love?"

"It is beautiful." He'd been there, apparently.

"What about you?" She took a bite of the sandwich. "Tell me about the Travis I don't know."

He opened his mouth and closed it again, shaking his head. "What?"

He draped his arm over the back of her chair, a tease dancing in his eyes. "You already know about my gardening and raccoon-catching skills. What more do you want to know?"

There was plenty she wanted to know. "How long ago did you go to Ireland?"

"It's been eight years—maybe longer. I took Emma for her birthday."

The questions bounced back and forth as they ate.

"So what else is on your bucket list?" Mari finished the last of her pickle.

He wiped his hands on a napkin. "Cheesecake."

"Why is cheesecake on your bucket list?"

"It's not." He pushed back from the table, laughing. "It's time for cheesecake. I don't have any, so we'll have to go get some."

"I don't *need* cheesecake."

"I think I might." He jingled his keys. "Tell me what else is on your bucket list."

"Am I going to get to hear more of yours?"

"Sure." He opened the car door for her. "I've always wanted to drive a road course."

"Like racing? I had no idea." She buckled into her seat. "Sounds exhilarating."

That night, she learned more about the man she'd worked with for seven years. He'd been interesting before, but his interesting factor tripled.

Chapter Twenty-two

Thursday afternoon, Travis poked his head into Mari's office. He couldn't wipe the smile off his face if he tried. "Thanks for helping me hide out today. I won't be in tomorrow, but I'll pick you up at five for the rehearsal dinner."

"Don't forget your tux. Is it still in your closet here? And I'm happy to meet you at the restaurant if that's easier."

"I like the company." Travis pulled an envelope out of his pocket and hoped his hands didn't shake when he handed it over. "You don't need to come in tomorrow. In fact, you might not have time. Open it."

She peeled up the flap.

"I asked Kate for ideas on how to thank you. She suggested this." He couldn't wait to see her reaction.

Mari slipped the paper out and unfolded it. She jumped out of her chair and met him at the door. "A day at the spa? Travis, this is too much."

"Not nearly."

"If I'd known that Kate was fishing for ideas for me when

she called, I would've suggested something more affordable." She stretched up and hugged him. "Thank you."

He drew blood biting his tongue. "See you tomorrow evening."

"Yes. I can't wait." She blocked out Friday on her calendar and gathered her things. "I'll walk down with you."

"Great. Did you talk to Fran and Erika about covering for Anne until we find a replacement?"

"I did." She shouldered her purse, and they walked to the elevator.

"And?"

"They agreed, but neither was happy about the idea. They are hoping I find the perfect candidate before the end of the month. Poor Roger."

"He's great at his job." Travis resisted the solution that popped into his head. "But it is hard to find people that work well with him."

In the parking lot, he stopped near her car. "Say 'hi' to Carlos and Wentworth for me."

"I will." She climbed into the car and started the engine but didn't back out of the spot.

He guessed she was messaging her friends about the spa day, at least he hoped the gift would make it into their conversation. In his car he checked his email, hoping to hear back from Charlie.

A message awaited him.

T-

I have an idea, but I need to check with Remi.
Mari will love it.

-C

Travis answered from his phone.

C-

Can't wait to hear the idea.

-T

He drove home, wishing Charlie would have shared the idea and not just dangled a tease.

⌇

When he pulled up to the curb Friday night, he took a deep breath before running up to the door. Why was he nervous about seeing her? He was too old for flutters.

She pulled open the door only seconds after he knocked. "Come in. I just need to grab my purse."

Travis smiled, at a complete loss for words. She'd never looked as stunning.

When he spotted Carlos near the kitchen, Travis waved. "Hi, how's the arm?"

Mari spun around, her eyes wide. "Hey, sweetheart. I'm headed to the rehearsal dinner." Her brow wrinkled, and she tensed.

"My arm is good." Carlos sounded nothing like he did before. His tone was flat. "Mom, you going to be *late?*"

"Probably, yes. I'll text you." She hugged him. "Tori coming over?"

"Maybe, not sure." He glanced from his mom to Travis. "I hope you have a good night. See you in the *morning.*"

Travis had no idea what bothered Carlos, but something did, and it included Travis. Watching Mari's reaction bothered him. The tension caused her stress, and that irritated him.

He nodded to Carlos as Mari stepped out the door and followed her out to the car. After opening her door and helping her in, he slid in behind the wheel. "What's going on with Carlos? He seemed unhappy to see me."

Throwing the question out probably wasn't the best way to handle it, but it needed to be asked.

Mari sighed. "He thinks I'm lying to him. He thinks …" She let the sentence trail off and stared out the window.

"Mari, what's wrong?"

She shook her head. "He thinks we're sleeping together, and that I'm keeping it from him. Not that it's any of his business if we were."

Thoughts bounced around in his head faster than he could process them. "The night I took Uber home?"

"He saw your car and assumed you stayed over. I told him it wasn't true."

"I'm so sorry. I never meant—"

"You haven't done anything to apologize for."

But he had. He'd been careless with how he'd behaved. "Mari—"

"Please, can we just not talk about it?"

Deflated, Travis continued the drive to the dinner. He hated to see her upset, and although she brushed it off, the way she shut down the conversation made it clear she was bothered by the whole thing.

He cared for her, and if she wanted nothing more than friendship, he'd accept that, as hard as it would be. His heart wanted so much more.

Until she wanted to discuss it or at least until she gave an indication of what she wanted, he'd be more cautious. Staying at arm's length seemed a good starting place. Every time he touched her, he wanted to pull her close and whisper how beautiful she looked and how happy he was to have her with him.

He pulled up to the valet stand, and as he handed over his keys, a young man helped her out of the car.

Chapter Twenty-three

Mari wished she'd kept her mouth shut. The evening was enjoyable, and Travis was the same as he always was, except with an additional eighteen inches between them at all times. There was no hand on her back, no pats on the shoulder. He made sure no one else jumped to the same conclusion Carlos had. Mari shouldn't have cared, but it made her mad—mad at Carlos for the way he acted, mad at herself for saying anything and even more so for wishing the relationship was more than friendship. She missed the feel of his hand on her back.

At the end of dinner, while Kate, Alex, and a handful of others mingled, Mari eased up next to Travis and rested a hand on his back. "Tonight was wonderful. Don't you think?"

"You look beautiful." He slipped an arm around her waist and leaned in close. "And yes, tonight has been perfect. I hope tomorrow goes as smoothly."

With that one touch, the eighteen inches disappeared.

When Travis pulled up to the curb in front of her house, she hoped he'd walk her to the door. The shift at the end of the evening gave her hope.

He jumped out and opened her door. "Mind if I come in for a few minutes?"

Caught off-guard, she blinked before nodding. "Yes, of course. I mean, I don't mind."

"Hard to believe tomorrow is the big day."

"I'm not sure who was more excited, Kate or Alex." She unlocked the front door and stepped in as he held the door open. "Can I get you something to drink?"

"Coffee sounds good." He glanced around, and she guessed he wondered if Carlos was around.

The dark and quiet house indicated he wasn't.

She kicked off her heels and headed to the kitchen. "Oh, I loved my spa day."

Travis followed her. "That's a pretty color on your nails."

"It was a real treat. Thank you."

"If someone—other than Carlos—assumed there was something going on, would that bother you?" He stood at the counter pushing a stray crumb in circles.

"You know what assuming does." She pulled two mugs out of the cabinet, keeping her back to him as she poured the coffee. "I can't control what people think. Why should I let it bother me?"

"Then we're on the same page. I didn't want you to be upset or feel trapped in a … a bad situation." He moved closer.

Mari shook her head and slid his cup toward him. "I haven't felt pressured to have you over or help with the wedding. I've enjoyed it. Every minute." She sipped her coffee, choosing her words. "There is no rule or policy forbidding being *friends* with the boss, right?"

"Right. No rule against friends."

Using the word friend felt almost dishonest. She wanted so much more.

Mari peeked out the window. Wedding guests occupied all but a handful of chairs. Music would start any moment. Travis paced, inhaling and exhaling with intention.

She stepped up behind him and rubbed his back. "Everything is perfect. You can relax."

He flashed a nervous smile. "I'm trying."

She turned him to face her, then adjusted his tie, making sure it was straight. "I'm going to go sit down before the music starts."

He clasped her hand before she stepped away. "Thank you for everything, but especially for being here today."

Mari couldn't imagine not being at the wedding—with him. He'd never looked more attractive. She could tell herself that happiness looked good on him, and it did. But in truth, she cared about him in a way she hadn't cared about anyone in a very long time, and friend didn't describe those feelings well.

She squeezed his hand and kissed his cheek. "I wouldn't want to be with anyone else. I mean, I wouldn't want to be anywhere else."

Before Mari could set right her Freudian slip, the click of heels signaled the approach of the wedding coordinator.

"I think we're all ready." She pointed outside. "Everyone's in place."

Mari tried not to think about what assumptions were being made. "See you out there, Travis."

The twinkle in his eyes warmed her cheeks.

An usher escorted her up the aisle, and she took a seat in the second row. In front of her, an older woman sat next to Travis's empty chair. When the music started, she eyed Mari as all the guests looked down the aisle.

That must be Gram. Mari smiled before turning around. The woman nodded, a smile in her eyes but not on her lips.

The bridesmaids and groomsmen made their way toward the front. When the music changed, Mari stood. Double doors at the back of the mansion opened, and Travis and Kate stepped out onto the porch and down the steps. He patted her hand before continuing to the front.

Kate made a beautiful bride, but it was the man escorting her down the aisle that gave Mari hot flashes. Friendship wasn't enough.

∼

While guests mingled inside, enjoying hors d'oeuvres, Mari stood off to the side as the photographer snapped pictures of the wedding party. When Kate and Alex headed toward the reception to make their grand entrance, Mari slipped in a side door and checked the table assignments.

She smiled when a hand pressed into the small of her back.

"We're sitting over here." He pointed to a table near the front.

We? It started to feel as if she were his date, but as soon as the thought formed, she tried to rein in her runaway imagination. Just because she wanted something to be true didn't make it so.

Seats at the table filled with Kate's family and friends, many of which Mari hadn't met. The few people she had met sat at the tables reserved for bridesmaids and groomsmen.

Travis introduced Mari as others joined them at the table, and she filed names away, trying to memorize the connections. His sister-in-law sat to her right with her husband and daughter, who appeared to be about Carlos's age. To Travis's right was the older woman, who had been next to him at the wedding. He introduced her as Gram, and Mari wished she knew what Gram was thinking.

Conversation flowed easily, and Mari made it through dinner without any awkward looks or questions.

Travis brushed his hand along her arm. "Would you care to dance?"

"Yes." She answered too quickly, and her heart fluttered with anticipation. Willing herself to relax, she followed him onto the dance floor and slipped her hand in his.

His dancing skills didn't disappoint.

When the song ended, she smiled up at him. His intense gaze stirred a deep desire to be kissed. The music started again, and he raised his eyebrows in request.

"I'd love to." Whether his question was about dancing or kissing didn't change her answer.

Song after song, they glided across the floor.

When the deejay called for all the single ladies to gather on the dance floor, Mari hung back.

"You should be out there." Amusement danced in Travis's blue eyes.

"Will you be out there for the garter toss?"

"Touché."

⌒

Late in the afternoon, as Kate and Alex prepared to leave, the guests gathered near the exit. Mari choked back tears as Travis hugged Kate, then Alex. The entire day had been fabulous, a picture-perfect wedding worthy of a magazine spread. With bubbles dancing in the air around them, the happy couple ran to Alex's truck. Kate waved as Alex tucked the layers of her dress inside the cab.

Travis stepped up beside Mari. "And they're off."

"They look so happy."

"Yeah." The smile on his face was tempered by a penetrating wistfulness in his eyes.

"What are you doing this evening?"

He shrugged. "I'm open to suggestions. We could dance some more."

She followed him back inside and slipped her heels off. "But not in these heels. Why don't you come over to the house? I was going to order pizza and watch a movie with Carlos."

In the middle of the dance floor, he stopped. "If it's really okay, then yes. I'd like that."

"It's really okay."

"After all the excitement today, going home alone would seem rather anti-climactic. It's not like Kate moved out of the house and now things will be lonely. It's just ..." He shook his head then started moving around the dance floor again. "You know what I mean."

"I'll know much better in a couple weeks."

⁓

When Travis stopped in front of the house, Mari grabbed his hand before he turned off the engine. "Hurry back."

"I will. Just gonna get out of this monkey suit."

"What do you like on your pizza?"

"Anything but anchovies and pineapple."

"See you in a few." She climbed out of the car and waved after unlocking the door. "Carlos, I'm back. Pizza sound good?"

"Hey, Mom. Don't worry about ordering me anything. I'm headed out. Tori and I are going to grab dinner. Maybe see a movie."

"Oh. Okay."

"I hope you don't mind. I figured you'd be really late."

"No, of course I don't mind. Go have fun." She hadn't even mentioned that Travis was coming, so that wasn't the reason Carlos was leaving.

He left, promising to call if he was going to be late, and Mari ordered a large supreme pizza before running upstairs to change.

She slipped off her dress and changed into jeans and a t-shirt. Excitement kept a smile on her face. She hoped it wouldn't be awkward without Carlos around. It wasn't as if she and Travis hadn't done things together before. But after the wedding, after dancing, it all felt different. *Maybe only to you. Corporate policy, remember?*

A knock sounded at the door, and she hurried down the stairs. Expecting the pizza guy, she pulled open the door and froze. "Travis."

In jeans and an untucked button-down, he looked just as amazing as he had in his tux. "You look surprised to see me."

She glanced past him to the pizza guy getting into his car. "I have money for him."

"I took care of it; although, I was surprised it was just one pizza. I expected Carlos could eat a large by himself."

"He can, but he opted to see a movie with his girlfriend this evening."

"So, it's just the *two of us?*" Travis almost sounded like he was flirting.

"Yeah. Hope that's not a problem." She flipped the bolt on the door.

He followed her into the den. "Not a bit."

She pointed to the sofa. "Make yourself at home. We can eat around the coffee table. Choose whatever you want to watch. I'm going to grab plates and such."

In the pantry, she gathered plates and napkins. Then from the fridge, she pulled two Cokes.

By the time she returned to the sofa, he had his shoes kicked off and a show cued up and paused. "A movie about Winston Churchill okay? Maybe we'll even have time for the second movie too."

"Sounds good to me." She'd be happy with whatever kept him by her side for the next few hours.

The movie played, and they ate. Interested in the storyline, she enjoyed learning about Churchill much more than she'd expected. Side by side, but not touching, they watched history retold.

When the credits rolled, she sighed. "That was really good."

She pushed off the sofa. "I'll put away the rest of the pizza, then we can start the next one."

"Let me help." He jumped up and gathered the plates and napkins.

She slid the leftover slices into a Ziploc bag. "Another Coke?"

"Nah, I'm good." He leaned back against the counter, looking as sexy as ever.

Possessed by an unknown force, fueled by the enjoyment of the day, Mari started talking. "I want to tell you something, but you have to promise—A—that you won't fire me, and—B—that you won't act like you know."

"Now I'm intrigued, and I promise not to fire you." He crossed his heart.

Teasing about what she wanted to say was easy. Saying it wasn't. Too late for a "never mind," she wandered back to the sofa and waited for him to sit before continuing. "You are often the topic of conversation in the break room. Ladies talk about how sexy you are. It's not just the ladies at the gala who think of you as a great catch."

That lopsided smile lit up his face. "I guess I need to spend more time in the break room."

"And there's lots of speculation about whether you'll venture back into the dating world again."

He sobered, his gaze riveted to her face. "I don't intend to date—"

"I wasn't trying to imply anything." Maybe she'd wanted to test the waters, but it was mostly the truth.

"I don't intend to date *just to date.* I'm not looking to fill time. Only someone amazing could have me entertaining the idea of dating again."

Entertaining the idea of dating again? He made it sound as if he was thinking about it. While there were a couple moments when she wondered if his attention was motivated by anything other than friendship, she understood that her desires skewed her perception, adding intentions that didn't exist. The reality that there was much she didn't know about his life tempered her wishful thinking.

The tickets. Somewhere, outside the office, maybe even out of town, he had someone special who occupied his thoughts—whether that woman knew or not—and Mari had no clue who it was. But chances were, that person would be using the other ticket.

Mari sat quietly, hoping he'd say more. And he might've, but keys jingled. The door opened, and Carlos walked in. Tori walked in behind him.

"Tori, you've met my mom, and this is her … *friend*, Mr. Bentley." Carlos tried to hide a smirk but failed.

"I should go." Travis slipped on his shoes.

Mari ignored the look from Carlos. "I'll walk you out."

On the porch, Travis stopped, and she tried to figure out what to say, how to apologize for Carlos, how to apologize for talking about how the ladies at work discuss the boss's dating life.

"I'm sorry." She didn't offer an explanation.

Travis glanced at the door. "I appreciate you inviting me. I enjoyed it."

"You're welcome anytime, Travis." On impulse, she stretched up and wrapped her arms around his neck. "I mean it. Okay?"

Arms still around her, he pulled her close again. "I'll remember that."

"Goodnight."

He held her a couple seconds longer than she expected. "Night, Mari."

Lingering on the porch until he pulled away from the curb, she sighed. Monday seemed far away. She inhaled before stepping inside, not ready for the questions she expected from Carlos.

"Carlos ran upstairs." Tori sat at the kitchen island alone, sipping a Coke. "Your boyfriend is kind of a hottie, Mrs. Gonzales. You know, for an old guy."

Mari choked, trying not to spew the water she'd just sipped. "He's not my boyfriend, but, yeah, he is a hottie, definitely a silver fox." She laughed, imagining Travis's reaction to what she'd said. "He's my boss. We're friends."

"Oh? He always hang out here on Saturday nights?"

"Not always." She had no desire to explain the circumstances which had landed Travis at her place that night. Dishrag in hand, she returned to the den and wiped down the coffee table.

After cleaning up and straightening the throw pillows, her phone rang. She didn't recognize the local number. "Hello?"

"Mari, I think maybe I left my phone there."

"How are you—oh, never mind."

Travis laughed. "You too young to remember landlines?"

"Very funny. Let me look for it." She moved the pillows she'd just put in place and scanned the tabletops. When she came up empty, she stuck her hand between the couch cushions. "Found it."

"Good. At least I know where it is. Mind if I come by in the morning to get it?"

"That's fine. Do you need it tonight? I can take it, or you can come back over."

"I can live without my phone until morning. You've had a long day. We both have. Besides, it gives me a reason to see you in the morning. Night."

The call ended, and Mari stared at the phone. Had she heard him correctly?

"Everything okay, Mom?" Carlos walked toward the kitchen.

"Travis forgot his phone."

"You gonna spy?" He chuckled and looked to Tori for her reaction.

Mari shook her head and headed to the stairs. "No. I'm not. I'm tucking in for the night. Nice to see you, Tori."

"Night," Carlos and Tori said in unison.

Mari snagged an extra charger cable from her desk and plugged in Travis's phone next to hers. After a quick shower, she donned her jammies and crawled under the covers. Travis's last sentence played over and over in her head. She had no idea how she'd be able to sleep.

When a text popped on his screen, she couldn't help but read it. *Looking forward to it. I'll be in town late next week; we can meet …*

Unable to read the rest of the message, her mind filled in the blanks.

Chapter Twenty-four

Travis dove into his backyard pool, hoping that swimming laps would help relax him. After giving Mari a hint of his intentions, excitement fueled his thoughts. The email from Charlie only ramped them up further.

They had a plan, and Mari would be more than surprised. After tomorrow morning, she wouldn't question why he'd chosen to surprise her.

Back and forth across the pool, he swam. For good or for bad, tomorrow would change their relationship.

As he swam, he ordered his thoughts, planning what he would say.

⌢

Up at the crack of dawn, Travis drove to the grocery store as soon as it opened. He wanted to buy flowers for Mari. He took his time, not wanting to show up at her house too early, but finally settled on a colorful bouquet.

Sipping coffee at a fast food restaurant near Mari's house, he waited until 8 am before driving to see her.

Flowers tucked behind his back, he knocked. His heart rate matched the footsteps hurrying toward the door.

The door opened, and the smell of pancakes and bacon greeted him.

"Good morn—" She froze when he pulled the flowers from behind his back. Her furrowed brow gave way to surprise. She stared up at him, questions dancing in her eyes.

After a deep breath, he launched into his rehearsed monologue. "Maybe I am way off base, and if so, please just say so. But I'm going to go out on a limb and possibly make a fool of myself. I don't want anything to jeopardize our friendship or our working relationship, but I …" Pausing, he held out his hand. "Would you go out with me? Not just as friends. Not as co-workers. On a date. Would you?"

She stared at his hand, her smile giving him hope. "I made breakfast—pancakes and bacon—and what about corporate policy? And the message … I thought …"

"Is that a yes?"

"I'd love to go out with you, Travis." She slipped her hand in his. "I hope you're hungry."

"I love your pancakes. About corporate policy, that is a conversation we need to have, but it can wait until after breakfast. I'm not sure what you mean about the message, though."

She buried her nose in the flowers. "I thought I heard you wrong last night."

"What about dinner tonight? I know it's very late notice."

"Tonight's good. You can even stay after breakfast, and we can watch that other movie, if you don't have other plans."

He pulled her close. "Sounds like a perfect Sunday."

Mari leaned against him. "This will be complicated, won't it?"

Carlos peeked out of the kitchen and grinned. Maybe being right was all he needed.

Travis lifted her chin so that she looked up at him. "It might be a little complicated, so I'll understand if—"

"Let's eat." She clutched his hand and led him into the kitchen. When she saw Carlos, she stopped. "Carlos, I know I said that—"

"I heard." He stayed stone-faced for nearly a minute before winking at his mom. "Mr. Bentley, I saved you some bacon. Mom said you were coming to get your phone." He glanced at the flowers. "She's a great cook."

"Good to know." Travis took the plate Mari offered him and helped himself to bacon, omelets, and pancakes. "This all looks fabulous."

"Y'all stop." Mari laughed as she arranged the flowers in a vase.

Travis set his plate on the table and pulled out the chair next to him. "Are you going to eat?"

"In a sec." She fussed with the flowers a minute more before putting food on her plate.

"So, Carlos, when do you leave? It's coming up, isn't it?"

"Yes, sir. Friday after next." Carlos heaped more pancakes on his plate and drowned them in maple syrup. "I want to get settled in my apartment before classes start."

"Need help moving?" Travis cast a side glance at Mari when asking the question, wanting to see her reaction.

Carlos shook his head. "I'm sharing an apartment with a couple buddies of mine. We're all going up together. We're good."

"I offered." Mari snapped a slice of bacon in two and winked at her son.

"I'll only be like an hour away." He dragged his last bite of pancake through the lake of syrup. "And I already told the guys they'd have to move my stuff because of the sling."

"If it would help to have movers. Just let me know. I can arrange that." Travis didn't offer just because it would score him points.

"I'll ask my buddies about that." Carlos jumped up from the table. "I've gotta get ready. Tori's family is having a barbeque today. She'll be here to get me soon. I'll see y'all later." He disappeared up the stairs.

"Thank you." Mari patted his shoulder. "Whatever your reason for offering, I appreciate it."

Travis stood up and gathered plates from the table. "You're welcome. Let me get these dishes loaded."

She wiped down the table and counters as he rinsed and loaded dishes. "You caught me completely by surprise. How long have you felt this way?"

"I could ask you the same question."

"You could tell?"

"There were glimmers of hope."

"I couldn't pinpoint the moment, but gradually during the last six months. You?"

"Similar." He closed the dishwasher and dried his hands before opening his arms.

She stepped into his embrace. "And you were there for me when I needed you."

"This past year you've been there for me more times than I can count." He pulled back when a knock sounded. Until they sorted out the complicated parts, the relationship would have to be kept low-key, as much as he hated that idea.

She patted his chest. "It's probably Tori."

Travis dropped on to the sofa, knowing that a difficult conversation was looming. "That was interesting."

"Did you see Tori's expression when she walked in and you were here again?"

He laughed and nodded. "I noticed. I didn't miss the looks from Carlos, either. Later, I should probably talk to him."

"He didn't seem irritated, thankfully. Last night, Tori referred to you as my boyfriend, and I told her you weren't. I can't imagine what she thinks now."

He patted the cushion next to him. "Come here."

She sat beside him and slipped her hand in his. "What are we going to do?"

"I was going to suggest, instead of dinner tonight, maybe we'd get out of the house, spend the day together."

"That's not what I mean."

"I know."

"You're my boss, and office dating is frowned on."

Travis rubbed his temples. "It is. That's why I've stayed quiet."

"That's no longer an option, so what do we do?"

"You know that I'd quit in a heartbeat if I could."

She rolled her eyes. "You can't quit. It's your company. I know that."

"We have two options: keep it quiet and sneak around or"— he sucked in a deep breath—"change this so that you aren't my direct report."

She blinked, and he knew she was fighting tears. "Travis, I love my job. I'm not sure—what if we keep things quiet until ..." She didn't even have to finish her sentence. The meaning was clear.

"Mari, I'll support whatever you choose. Knowing where this is headed before you change jobs is wise." He tried to put himself in her shoes to understand, but he didn't like the idea of keeping it secret.

"I don't mean keeping it from Kate or anything. Carlos already knows. And thank you." She rested her head on his shoulder.

"What do you say we go spend the day out of town, where we won't be seen by coworkers. I know a great barbeque place about an hour and a half from here."

"That'd be fun."

Travis thought of all the places he wanted to take her, places and events where many people from work might see them. All that would have to wait until the relationship was public.

Chapter Twenty-five

On the road, Mari studied him, thinking of all the times she'd stayed late at work to help him, wanting to be near him a bit longer. Whatever the text from last night meant, she felt safe in assuming it wasn't another woman. But what did it mean? What secret was Travis keeping?

As if reading her thoughts, he reached for her hand. "Until yesterday, I didn't dare hope that it might be more than friendship that you felt, not for someone twenty years older."

She squeezed his hand. "Now you're just trying to score points by making me younger. It's only a fifteen-year difference."

"Did it work?" He released her hand and downshifted. "With the keeping it quiet, I feel a bit like I'm getting away with something."

"Like two renegade teenagers sneaking around behind people's backs?"

"Exactly."

"With you being my boss—when it was just friendship, I—I'm just not sure what people will say about it."

"I get it." He clasped her hand. "I would never want people to think you were coerced in any way."

"What will Kate say?"

"She likes you, Mari. That's easy to see. She sat you next to me at the reception, didn't she?"

"That wasn't your doing?"

"Kate and Alex made all the table assignments. Didn't ask me about it at all. I may or may not have peeked at the table chart, just to check."

"All right. I'll stop fretting over what she thinks. Maybe."

Travis and Mari spent hours wandering through the small town of Llano, Texas. After stuffing themselves on sirloin and some of the best potato salad Mari had ever tasted, they scrolled through shops on the square, holding hands. She didn't want the day to end, didn't want the weekend to end.

When they were on the highway headed home, Travis reached for her hand. "I was thinking that maybe tomorrow morning, I could pick you up, and we could ride to work together. It'd give us time to chat before I have to be the boss."

Mari tried not to think about what it would be like at the office. She hadn't worried when they were spending time together as friends. *Why worry now?* "I'd like that."

When they walked into the house, Carlos sat on the sofa, the leftover pizza in front of him. "Hi, Mom. Mr. Bentley, just the man I wanted to talk to."

"Hey, sweetheart, have a good time at the barbeque?"

"It was good." He dropped the slice of pizza on his plate.

"Travis, can I get you a drink?" Concerned about what Carlos might say, Mari tried not to let it show.

Travis squeezed her hand. "Water would be great." He stepped toward the sofa as she made her way to the kitchen. "What can I do for you, Carlos?"

Mari tried not to clink glasses as she pulled them out of the cabinet. Filling the glasses at a slow trickle, she listened.

"My buddies liked the idea of movers. You think that's possible?" Carlos only wanted to talk about the move.

"Absolutely. Give me your number. Better yet, text me." Travis rattled off his number.

Mari breathed a sigh of relief and started toward the den.

She wasn't even out of the kitchen when Carlos asked, "What's going on with you and my mom?"

Blue eyes watched her as she made her way to the couch. "I asked her out, and we spent the day together." Travis shifted his feet, making room for her to walk past. "I'm hoping she'll say yes to a second date."

She met his gaze and immediately wished she hadn't because she nearly spilled the water and fell in his lap. *Hoping?* As if she'd given any indication that she hadn't thoroughly enjoyed every minute. Avoiding the risk of shattered glass and spilled water, she set the drinks on the coffee table.

Carlos smiled.

Travis laced his finger with hers. "I care about your mom. A lot."

"When I told you there was nothing going on, there wasn't. Just this morning—" Mari didn't want Carlos to think she'd lied to him.

"I believe you. Now I know you didn't see it. But, it was kinda obvious he had a thing for you, Mom. But, I shouldn't have said what I said. Sorry." He pushed off the sofa. "Y'all have fun."

Mari nodded, a bit choked up by his apology. "We are keeping it kinda quiet for now until we figure a few things out."

"Mums the word." He rushed up the stairs.

She leaned her head on Travis's shoulder. "Thank you."

"For what?" Travis stared down at her, eyebrows raised.

"The movers. I worry about his arm."

"I kinda knew that."

⌒

Tucked in bed, Mari breathed in deep before sending the message to her friends: *He asked me out.*

Charlie sent a heart, which was completely unexpected.

Yay! This is so exciting. I knew he needed a girlfriend. Remi's response was less of a surprise.

Mari wished they were closer. *We are keeping it a secret for now.*

Until when? Charlie always had to ask the hard questions.

Remi replied: *Until she knows she loves him. Then it doesn't matter who knows.*

Mari didn't hide the issues from them: *Until I decide not to work for him anymore and find another job.*

No! But you like working for him. Remi thought the world should work like fictional romances.

Charlie sent another message: *That's a big decision, but you'll know when he's worth it.*

Mari was closer to that point than she wanted to admit, but the idea of working for someone else and searching for a new job overwhelmed her.

Chapter Twenty-six

Travis poured himself a cup of coffee and pulled out another mug for Mari. Behaving like they weren't dating required great effort. He'd wanted to tell her about his plans, but if they fell through again, she'd be more than disappointed, so he kept his mouth shut.

Commotion near the elevator announced the arrival of Erika and Fran.

"Go ahead. She's not here yet. Her parking spot was empty." Erika's words piqued Travis's interest.

Fran dropped her voice a bit, but not enough that he couldn't hear. "She attended the wedding."

"I'm not surprised. I'm not sure he'd know when to eat if she didn't schedule it for him and order it for him." Erika clearly thought she was funny.

"Have you seen the pictures? Lucy in accounting is friends on Facebook with"—Fran hesitated—"never mind all that. She sent them to me. Look."

"Oooh. Maybe she's angling for a raise?" Laughter drowned out Erika's next few words.

Anger ignited in his gut, and he worked to temper it before confronting the ladies.

"Poor Mari. As if she'd catch his eye. He could have his pick." Erika had no idea when to stop talking.

Tempering his anger would have to wait.

About to walk out of the kitchen, he spotted Mari standing in her office doorway across the hall. Out of sight but within earshot, she'd heard the morning gossip but hadn't been seen.

She shook her head, her brown eyes begging him not to intervene.

How could he let the ladies say that and not address it? Cooling off a bit, he nodded. After picking up her mug, he decided to poke at least a little.

"Mari, good morning." He enjoyed making his presence known.

Erika and Fran stopped talking, and silence replaced the gossip.

Travis handed Mari a mug. "When you have a few minutes, I'd like to discuss something with you." Glancing over his shoulder, he added, "In my office." He made a point of walking around through the reception area instead of cutting through Mari's office.

Erika and Fran mumbled, "Good morning" while shuffling papers.

"I have time now." Mari followed behind him, carrying her coffee.

As soon as the door closed, he took her hand and led her to the sunny spot. His coffee abandoned to the table, he forked his fingers through his hair and paced. "They—"

"Please, Travis." She clutched her mug.

"They can't talk about you like that. It's not true."

Mari set her mug next to his. Hands on his chest, she gazed

up at him. "I know it's not, but saying anything would risk our secret."

He slipped his arms around her. "I'll bite my tongue."

"Thank you." She stepped away and reached for the doorknob.

"Why are you in a hurry?"

She stopped and leaned back against the door. "Too many meetings will unravel our secret."

He stood up and closed the distance between them. "And we don't want that."

"Travis, I'm not ready to quit my job." She straightened his tie. "And I don't want people thinking you're taking advantage of your position."

"Does it bother you?"

"I in no way feel pressured to go out with you. The fact that I work for you doesn't bother me. When necessary, I'll rearrange my life so that you're no longer my boss."

"I wish there was another way." He held out hope that there would be.

"I know."

"I'll keep *us* under wraps and behave myself, but I'd much rather take you to lunch without caring who sees." He hoped his emphasis of the word us wasn't missed.

"I'll keep that in mind."

He followed her through his office and brushed his hand on hers as she opened the door to her office. "Thank you, Mari."

Travis sent Mari a text before leaving the office a little early: *Running a quick errand. Will be back to pick you up.*

Text when you are back, and I'll sneak down. Just reading her text pumped him full of guilt.

At the florist around the corner, he selected the largest bouquet they had on display. Before he pulled out of the parking lot, Mari texted: *Fran offered me a ride home since I didn't have my car at work. Do you mind?*

He tapped out a quick response: *Probably a good idea. Text me when you're home?*

I will. She followed her text with a smiley.

He drove home to wait. After changing out of his slacks and dress shirt, she texted: *Sorry we couldn't ride together. I'm home.*

Mind if I come over? He'd gone from reminding himself he was her boss to inviting himself over.

I'd like that a lot.

He hurried over with the flowers buckled into the passenger seat.

She stepped out onto the porch when he pulled up to the curb, which could only mean that she'd been waiting for him. He liked that thought.

When she spotted the flowers, her face lit up. "Again? I'm not accustomed to being spoiled like this."

"I aim to change that." For Travis, loving someone meant giving all he had. Sure of his feelings, he also knew it wasn't yet time to say it out loud, but there was no harm in showing her.

"Thank you. They're beautiful." She pushed open the door and stepped inside.

"I'm not trying to change your mind about keeping it quiet. Please know that." He swung the door closed.

She stretched up and kissed him on the cheek. "I do."

No matter the complications, asking her out was the right thing to do.

⌒)

Tuesday flew by, and only business was discussed at the office. If there was gossip, he didn't hear it.

Trying to pace the relationship, he didn't invite Mari to dinner, but when Fran and Erika went home, he wandered into Mari's office. "Thanks for beeping me when that meeting dragged on. I needed it to end."

"You're welcome, but you did have another meeting."

"Thanks all the same." He couldn't imagine another person doing that job. "You look beautiful today."

Her face colored, and she scanned the floor for her shoes. "Thanks."

"You free tomorrow for dinner?"

"Yes."

"I was thinking we could grab a steak in Waring. It's out of the way. Might see if Kate and Alex want to join us."

"Sounds great." She swung her door closed and then stood in front of him. "Are you going to find every out of the way place in the area?"

"If I have to." He slipped his arms around her. "Would I be pushing my luck if I invited you for dinner on Friday?"

"I'll double check with Carlos because it's his last weekend in town. Can I let you know tomorrow?"

"Of course." Travis felt selfish for wanting to dominate her time.

She patted his chest. "I should go."

"I'll see you in the morning."

She gathered her purse and hugged him again before getting on the elevator. Travis moved to the window and watched until she pulled out of the parking lot.

Back at the computer, he emailed Charlie.

> *C-*
>
> *I'm glad Remi likes the plan. I have no idea how
> I'm going to keep this under wraps until the big*

reveal. Thanks for all your help. I'll make all the arrangements.

-T

He leaned back in his chair, wishing he could speed up time.

Chapter Twenty-seven

Wednesday after work, Mari ran home to change before Travis picked her up. She'd had a light lunch in preparation for steak night.

Dressed in a sleeveless summer dress and sandals, she pulled opened the door and gaped.

Travis had on boots and jeans, and Mari reminded herself to breathe.

She picked up her purse. "I like your boots."

He laughed as he opened her car door. "Glad to hear that."

As he drove, she watched the landscape blur by. "Are Kate and Alex meeting us?"

"I didn't call. They've only been married a few days. Didn't want to bother them."

"Probably a wise choice." Mari shifted to face him. "I found someone I thought would be a good candidate for Roger. Anne liked her. I liked her. Roger didn't. I'm still hunting."

"I'm sorry. Do I need to step in?"

"Not yet. I'll let you know." She leaned her head back, contemplating an idea. "Not working for you—"

"Mari, I'm not asking you to quit."

She rested her hand on his. "I know, Travis. But is the problem that I work for you directly or is it that I work for your company?"

"Mainly that you report to me."

"Tell me about where we're going." Thinking about changing jobs soured her stomach. "Have you been there before?"

"I haven't. Read about it. It's steak and live music, and it's out of the way."

She wanted to relax and enjoy the evening, but finding something else to worry about seemed to be her quickly growing talent. A couple years shy of fifty, she thought she'd moved past letting others' opinions dictate her choices, but imagined whispers—and she could imagine some real doozies—made her cautious. "What happens if someone sees us together?"

Travis parked along the side of the rode. "Likely my legal team will request a meeting and tell me all the reasons that dating my direct report is a bad idea."

"You'll look bad?"

He brushed her cheek with his thumb then tucked hair behind her ear. "You don't need to worry about that."

She grabbed his hand. "I just need a little more time."

"Time for what?"

"Before I change jobs."

Clouds passed through his blue eyes as he nodded. "Let's go eat."

Inside the country store, it was easy to forget life was complicated. While her steak was grilled to order, Mari stuffed her baked potato and filled a cup with strawberry lemonade.

When the steaks were ready, they wandered outside and sat at picnic tables. A band on stage filled the evening air with songs

Mari knew almost by heart. Travis sat down next to her, and life seemed perfect, if only temporarily.

She watched as families visited around tables, and kids played corn hole. "About Friday . . . Carlos doesn't have plans. He wanted to take me to dinner since it's his last Friday in town. If you wanted—"

"Go out with Carlos. There will be plenty of weekends for us to go out after he leaves." He talked about the future as if it were a given.

"Thank you for understanding." Mari struggled to process all she was feeling.

The man next to her, her boss, stirred emotions she hadn't expected to ever feel again.

Days at work breezed by, and maintaining a professional relationship at the office wasn't as difficult as she'd expected. The stolen moments in the sunny spot, holding hands while they chatted about his schedule helped, but she knew those moments carried a risk.

Friday evening, instead of going out, Mari made Carlos's favorite—spaghetti.

Carlos added shredded parmesan to his plate, nearly covering the pile of pasta and sauce. "You could've invited Travis. I wouldn't have minded."

"Nah, tonight was for us."

"I like him, Mom. And, I'm glad you aren't going to be all alone after I leave."

Mari poked at her food. "We've only gone out a couple times."

"I've seen the way you light up when he comes around. Besides, you've known him seven years. It's not like you met on a blind date last weekend."

"I'm glad you like him. He is pretty wonderful, but enough

about all that. What else needs to be done to get you ready for this weekend?"

"Laundry." He laughed. "But seriously, I've packed everything I'm going to need."

Mari couldn't imagine life without Carlos living at home, but the idea no longer soured her stomach. "I can help you with that."

When Liam called after dinner inviting Carlos and Tori out for ice cream, Carlos shot Mari a glance, silently asking permission.

"Go. Have fun. I'm going to tuck in early. Maybe read a little."

"Thanks, Mom. Say hi to Remi and Charlie for me." He winked before running up the stairs.

Was she that predictable?

After a quick shower, she slipped into bed, but instead of messaging her friends, she did something brazen and called Travis.

He picked up before the first ring ended. "Mari, hi! This is a nice surprise. Did you and Carlos have a nice evening?"

"We did. He left to go get ice cream. I hope I'm not interrupting anything."

"No. Not at all. I was just … umm." Papers shuffled as he trailed off.

Mari shook her head. "You're at work, aren't you?"

"Maybe, but I'm leaving as soon as we hang up … in an hour."

"An hour?"

"Two then. I'm okay with that." He laughed. "How's the packing going? Carlos letting you help?"

"He's not. Tori has been over nearly every afternoon, and his buddies have come to help once or twice. But I overheard him talking to Tori, and you were right. He doesn't want me to work all day, then go home and pack up his stuff."

"You've done a great job with him, Mari." He knew exactly how to win her heart.

"He's a good kid, but I can't even call him that anymore."

"What would you do if you weren't working?" Travis's question surprised her.

"Starving." She chuckled. "It's not even an option. What about you?"

For him, it was an option. "Travel. Discover out of the way places. Hopefully chase grandkids."

"What about your charity?"

"I wouldn't give that up. I'd probably spend more time with it."

Keenly aware that their worlds were different, Mari fought the insecure voices that whispered she didn't belong in his life, in his world. Twisting the sheet around her finger, she tried to think of an answer. "I didn't mean to be flippant before, but I've never thought about it. So, hmmm, I'd probably find a place to volunteer, maybe learn to crochet. I'm not even sure."

"Maybe one day, you'll have time to figure it out." He didn't wait for her to respond, which was good because she had no idea how to follow that comment. "I was thinking. Tomorrow, if you're free, why don't you come over to the house? There's a pool. I could throw something on the grill."

Mari hadn't expected to be dating the boss, and she definitely hadn't expected that he'd be seeing her in a swimsuit. "That'd be fun." The idea of seeing him in a swimsuit swayed her decision.

"Three okay?"

"Perfect." That'd give her time to shop for a flattering suit, a coverup that didn't look like a velour bag, and maybe a cute pair of sandals. Tomorrow would be busy.

Silence filled the next few seconds, and Mari almost said she had to go, except she didn't. More than that, she didn't want to hang up.

"I have a fundraiser thing in the morning, otherwise I'd have suggested we get together earlier."

How many of those events would she be attending with him if they weren't sneaking around.

"I'm glad I don't have to wait until Monday to see you again." Mystery and coyness had been tossed out the window, and she said whatever popped into her head.

A laughed wrapped around her, as soft and warm as a fuzzy blanket. "Two days is definitely too long."

"I told Remi and Charlie about us." On the phone, spilling her guts was much too easy.

"Did you send them pictures from the wedding? Gush about the flowers?" Humor dripped from his words. "I hope you didn't tell them about the raccoon. You were sworn to secrecy."

"I'd love for them to meet you. When they come in September, maybe we could all go to dinner."

"When Kate came back into my life, all the years of hurt and worry took a backseat to the present. Days are more enjoyable, but it's because I changed."

"You have. When she showed up that day in January, I almost didn't recognize you. And then spending time with you outside the office"—Mari fanned herself—"the word irresistible comes to mind."

"I could skip the fundraiser in the morning."

"No, you shouldn't. Besides, absence does something to the heart." She yawned.

He followed suit. "Those are contagious. I should let you sleep. Until tomorrow."

"Goodnight." Mari ended the called and snuggled under the covers.

How long did she have to wait to be sure of what she felt?

Chapter Twenty-eight

Up early, Travis ran to the store before going to the fundraiser. He wanted to spend as much time with Mari as possible.

When he walked into the store, he didn't have a clue what he wanted to make, which is a horrible way to start a shopping trip. But grilling meant he needed a meat of some kind, so he beelined to the meat section. She'd liked the ribeye. Was steak twice in a week too much?

He hoped not.

After tossing steaks into his basket, he wandered into the produce section. Sides were a requirement. He wanted something he could cook on the grill and settled on asparagus.

Next course on the list was dessert. Cheesecake was an easy option, but something grilled would tie the meal together. When he spotted the local peaches, he grabbed them. Grilled and topped with vanilla ice cream, they would be a satisfying finish to dinner.

With all the ingredients he needed in his basket, he walked into an empty checkout lane. That early, he had his choice.

Excited, he didn't understand why he was nervous. It wasn't

a first date; they'd spent time together at his house and at hers. Whatever the reason, butterflies danced the conga in his stomach. Waiting would be the hardest part.

At the house, after unpacking the groceries, he slathered the steaks with butter, olive oil and spices before wrapping them in foil to marinate. He wanted to impress her.

Once the meal prep was complete, he changed clothes and rushed out the door, hoping the time would pass quickly.

When he arrived at the pancake breakfast, Roger cornered him. "What's going on with you and Mari?" The man lacked the ability to ease into a conversation.

And it was a conversation Travis didn't want to have.

He raced to think of an answer that wasn't a lie and also didn't force Mari's hand. "What prompted that question?"

"I saw the photos from the wedding." Roger glanced around but failed to lower his voice. "It wouldn't look good to be dating your secretary."

"Personal assistant."

"Whatever you want to call her—dating her is a bad idea. She's your direct report. That would reflect badly on the company." Roger scratched his chin. "But if she didn't report to you … hmm. Maybe she could—"

Travis had a good idea of what Roger was going to suggest because Travis had already thought of it, but it wasn't his decision to make. He waved at a couple across the room. "I'm going to chat with George and his wife. We can talk later."

Sitting down to a pancake breakfast, he groaned inwardly. Pictures from before he and Mari started dating were causing ripples, but he couldn't ask Mari to change jobs. That would be presuming too much, especially for a temporary fix.

When the breakfast was over, Travis slipped out and headed home, glad that the afternoon would be spent in the privacy of his own backyard. He'd have to be careful about where he and Mari went, what they posted on social media.

Falling for Mari had been so natural and easy. Dating her was beyond complicated.

Chapter Twenty-nine

Mari stood in front of the mirror. *It's not too bad.* For almost fifty, she looked pretty good, especially if she closed one eye and stood angled to the mirror. She still had curves, just a few more than she did back in the day. Considering she'd been to three stores and tried on eleven other suits, she was happy with what she saw in the mirror. She slipped the jersey knit cover on over the swimsuit. Maybe she could wear that most of the day. It bordered on cute.

Her main goal—besides spending the afternoon with Travis and seeing him in a swimsuit—was to not bring the relationship to a screeching halt when she took off the cover. She worried about how she looked in a swimsuit; there was no way she was ready to let him see her in less.

Tired of shopping, she decided to wear sandals she already owned. She had just over three hours before she had to be there.

After completing the purchase, she ran out to the car. She hadn't even backed out of the space when a text from Travis popped up on the screen: *Just leaving the fundraiser. Want to come at one thirty?*

Mari responded: *Sounds great.* The next hour would be even busier.

∽

Her heart beating on her ribcage, Mari smiled when he opened the door. At home, half her closet lay strewn across her bed, but she could worry about that later.

Wearing shorts and a top with her swimsuit underneath, she adjusted the bag hanging on her shoulder. "Hi."

Travis wore swimming trunks and an unbuttoned Hawaiian shirt. "You look great. I hope moving up the time didn't inconvenience you. You bring your suit?"

She reminded herself to keep her eyes focused on his face. "I did."

"You know where stuff is. Whatever you need, just ask. Make yourself at home." He'd never seemed so nervous.

She followed him through the house and stopped just outside the back door. "This is crazy." She set her bag on a chaise lounge.

He whipped around, eyebrows raised. "What?"

"We've known each other for years." She caught his hand. "I am trying not to be nervous. It's not like it's a blind date or even a first date."

His shoulders relaxed, and that lopsided grin appeared. "I didn't want to wait until three." He pulled off his shirt. "You gonna get into your suit, or should I throw you in like that?"

"Jump in. I'll be right behind you." She turned, giving him her back. Once she heard a splash, she stripped off her t-shirt. Resisting the urge to turn around to make sure she didn't have an audience, she unbuttoned her shorts and slid them off.

Sucking in a deep breath, she turned back toward the pool.

Chin resting on crossed arms, he leaned on the edge of the pool, grinning.

She'd definitely had an audience. "You swim laps out here?"

"I do when the weather cooperates. When it doesn't, I head up to the gym and use theirs."

"Show me."

"Laps or the gym?" He pushed off the side of the pool and glided through the water before starting his stroke.

Mari only looked away long enough to avoid falling into the pool.

As he made his way back toward her, she eased herself into the water. He surfaced and caught her around the waist. She gasped. Meeting his gaze, she parted her lips, anticipating their first kiss.

He slid his hands down her sides before pulling her closer. "This new?"

WHAT?? How would he know that? "I spent my morning shopping. How did you know?"

He fiddled with the side of her suit, and plastic poked her in the side. "This."

"Crap. I ripped off the tags before washing, but I was in a hurry. Didn't notice that only the paper came off."

He let go and pushed up out of the pool. "I'll grab scissors. That can't be comfortable."

So much for that first kiss.

After snipping off the offending piece of plastic and fishing the end out of her suit, she jumped back into the pool, not worrying about getting her hair wet or washing away her makeup.

Travis tossed two inflatable rafts into the pool.

Mari climbed onto one of them, trying not to flip it over as she did. "How was the pancake breakfast?"

Travis bit his lip. "Pretty much like they always are."

"What's wrong?" Mari knew his tells, and that was a big one.

"Roger asked me about you."

"Asked you what?"

"What was going on with us. I wasn't going to say anything. It doesn't change anything."

"I haven't said anything except to Remi and Charlie, well, and Carlos." She frantically tried to figure out how Roger knew. "Please don't keep things from me."

He shot her a glance, but she couldn't decipher the significance. "Because of the wedding."

"Oh. I should've behaved differently that day. Was Roger even there?"

He paddled until his float was right beside her then reached for her hand. "I wouldn't change anything about that day. It was perfect, and I'm glad I have the photos to remind me."

She squeezed his hand. Quitting her job would make all the issues go away, and she wanted to, but with Carlos going away to college, she could afford to go maybe a month without a paycheck while hunting for a new job. Asking for Travis's help was out of the question. The only possibility of changing jobs without a hunt made her wrinkle her nose whenever she contemplated the idea.

"What is your opinion on clowns?"

"That's an odd question." Without letting go of his hand, she rolled off her float and into the water. "Don't love them. Don't hate them."

He joined her in the water and tugged her close. "What about surprises?"

"Are we talking dark alley surprises or heart-melting boyfriend surprises?" She slipped her arms around his neck.

"Definitely the latter."

"I loved the flowers. You know how to—"

"Melt your heart?" He spun her around in the water.

"Every single day."

As the day went on, Mari stopped thinking about how she looked or even what he thought. He still hadn't kissed her, but she'd been having so much fun, it didn't seem to matter. She'd laughed harder than she had in a long time, probably since the last girls' weekend with Remi and Charlie. Mari only mentioned the private pool party to them when she'd pulled into Travis's driveway. She grinned, thinking about how many messages would be waiting for her.

She toweled off and stretched out on a lounge chair, the summer sun drying the remaining droplets. "Anything I can help with?"

"Everything is prepped. Just waiting on the grill to heat." He handed her a tall glass of iced tea and dropped into the chair next to her. "So, tell me. If you had an unlimited budget and all the time off you wanted, where would you go, besides Ireland?"

The question caught her by surprise. "I have to think about it. No one's ever asked me that before, and I can't say I've dreamed up fantasy travel plans—other than touring castles in Ireland."

He shifted closer before reclining the lounge chair. "On Grafton Street in Dublin, you can have tea on the roof of a department store."

Mari closed her eyes, trying to envision what it would be like. "It sounds so elegant, so romantic. Have you done that?"

"No, but I want to." He slid his fingers along her hand and laced them with hers. "Back to the original question."

"Okay, so second on my list is Scotland. It'd be worth the trip just to listen to people talk. Places I've heard about, and if I can still remember them, they must've made an impression, so I'd like to see them. The Salt Flats in Bolivia—the photos from that place almost don't seem real. I'd love to see the lavender fields in France, to ride a gondola through the canals of Venice, to visit the museums in Bruges and enjoy a boat tour of those canals. I'd love to see that castle, the one that inspired the Sleeping Beauty Castle. I can't remember the name of it."

"Neuschwanstein." The man was one surprise after another.

"No wonder I can't remember the name. I can't say it."

"Anywhere else?"

"Now that I've gotten started, it could be a long list: Patagonia, the limestone cliffs in England, the Sacred Valley of the Incas. The world is full of places I'd like to see, but closer to home, there are places I haven't been." She sat up without letting go of his hand. "The Marfa lights—that's something I want to see, and I haven't been to Yellowstone." Leaning back in her chair, she gazed at him. *And I want to see them all with you.* "What about you?"

"I like your list."

"Any places you'd add?"

"The Hunan Province in China, New Zealand."

"Hobbits."

"Absolutely. And Easter Island." He squeezed her hand before letting go. "The grill should be hot. I'll throw the steaks on."

After adjusting the chair, Mari rolled to her stomach and watched him as he arranged steaks and vegetables on the grill. "You'll have a hard time topping this date."

"Is that a challenge?"

"Just my way of saying I'm having a wonderful time." She could think of only one thing that would make it better.

He closed the grill and returned to his chair, facing her when he sat down. "You're beautiful, Mari."

She swallowed the lump in her throat and smiled. Complimenting him on the way he looked—and he did look so good—might come off as deflecting. "Thank you."

He jumped up and flipped the steaks before setting plates and silverware on the patio table. "Dessert will be grilled also."

"Sounds interesting." While he plated the steaks and asparagus, Mari pulled on her swimsuit cover.

"I was thinking. After Carlos leaves, maybe we could just plan on dinner together most nights. I don't want to crowd your time." He tugged on a t-shirt before sitting down.

Mari laid a hand on his cheek. "I enjoy spending time with you."

When she leaned in close, intending a quick peck, he turned his head. The man was avoiding her kisses. "Good to hear."

"And maybe if I spend enough time, I can figure out what you're hiding." Her brazenness startled her, but she couldn't retract what she's said.

He draped his napkin in his lap and winked. "When I'm ready to spill secrets, you'll be the first to hear."

Later, after a dessert of grilled peaches and vanilla ice cream, Mari folded her clothes and tucked them into her bag.

"You leaving?"

"I should go." *One week.* She'd dated the man one week and would quit her job and travel the world with him, not that he'd made her that offer.

He hugged her. "I enjoyed today."

"Me too, but you know that already."

Hand in hand, they walked to the front door, and Mari tempered her impulse to initiate a kiss. Travis was intentional, controlled in everything he did. It was who he was. So, even though her impatience was eating her alive, she chose to wait.

He slipped his arms around her and pulled her to his chest, but this time without whispered words of how much he'd enjoyed the day. Warm lips pressed to her temple. She didn't move, hoping time would stand still. *Intentional.* He wasn't working up the courage; she knew him too well to believe that.

"Mind if I call you later?" He walked to her to the car.

She hugged him again. "Please do."

Chapter Thirty

Sitting at his desk, Travis pulled out paper and pen. Spending the day with Mari had him contemplating plans for the future. Things that couldn't be said should at least be written down, so he did.

He read over the note again before sliding it into an envelope and sealing it. He scrawled her name on the front. In the drawer it would be safe, waiting for when it needed to be read.

Sleep came easy that night, and blissful dreams accompanied his rest.

On Sunday, Travis drove out to Schatzenburg. He had a hundred items on his to-do list, but lunch and conversation with Gram was what he needed.

When he got to town, he parked in front of her white Victorian. After a brisk walk down the street, he slipped into church just as the organist started to play. Gram sat in the second row where she'd sat every Sunday for as long as he could remember. He sat down next to her.

She handed him a hymnal. "Good morning. Are you alone?"

"It's just me today."

"Have time for lunch?" She pointed to the number at the top of her page.

Travis flipped to that hymn. "I was hoping you'd be free."

Familiar songs in a familiar place flooded Travis with memories. The little town held so many. He missed his parents, especially his mom. So many times throughout the years, he'd mourned the fact that he could no longer sit down across the table from her, eat her pancakes, and talk about life, but Gram reached out time and again, making sure he never felt orphaned.

After the service, he walked arm in arm with Gram back to her house.

"I have a bit of cobbler left, so you picked a good day to come." She patted his arm. "Tell me about Mari. That's why you're here, I assume."

"Can't I just show up for a visit?"

She shook her head and clicked her tongue. "Don't ever try lying. You aren't very good at it."

He laughed. "We're dating, but because she works for me, we have to keep it quiet and sneak around."

"I did my share of that as a teenage girl." She pushed open the door after unlocking it. "But you don't need to hear *those* stories." The woman clearly had secrets that she chose not to share.

"It's not ideal, but it has to be her decision to change jobs. I can't ask that of her."

"Maybe—I don't know if it's even possible—you could be the one to change jobs."

"That would be a process, and not a fast one. I don't want to wait to spend time with her, and saying we are just friends feels deceitful. I want her to know how I feel."

She pulled a plate from the microwave and set it in front of him. "I didn't plan on company today, so I hope leftovers are okay."

"I'm here for the company more than anything."

"I need to meet this woman that has captured your heart." She slid another plate of meatloaf in to heat. "Preferably, before you propose."

"We've been dating a week, and you met her at the wedding."

"Technicality. I need to have time to visit with her. And, falling in love doesn't always take a long time. Sometimes it sneaks up on people slowly; other times, it tackles you when you least expect it."

"How long did you know Sam?" Travis had fond memories of the man that was more like a grandpa than anyone else.

"A few days."

Travis never knew that tidbit but had long held up Gram and Sam as an example of happily-ever-after. Even in his last moments, he had held her hand, whispering how much he loved her.

Gram wiped her eyes. "Now for dessert."

"I'll be going out of town soon. That might be a good time for you to visit with Mari without me around. I'm guessing that's your preference."

"It is. If you're around, you'll just be a distraction." She winked and added vanilla ice cream to the top of his cobbler.

That night, Travis made it a point to be home at a reasonable hour and not stay late at the office. After a shower, he called Mari. "Hi. How was your day?"

"Good. Carlos is packed, except for laundry. I spent today tackling that for him." She laughed. "And I thought he didn't need me. How was your day?"

"I drove out to see Gram. Went to church in Schatzenburg then had lunch with her."

"Did you spill your secrets to her?"

"You'll be first, Mari. I promise."

"I hope you know I'm teasing you."

"I do." He closed his eyes, flashes of yesterday filling his head. "It's getting late. I should let you get some sleep."

"Thanks for calling. I like this nightly ritual."

He wanted to whisper three little words, but saying them too soon might scare her off. "See you in the morning."

"Goodnight."

⌒

Frustrated at how late it was, Travis glanced at the clock. Mari made booking travel arrangements look so easy. Because of her, he hadn't done it in years, and everyone he spoke with on the phone could probably tell.

Reserving a rental car shouldn't take so long. The ticket agent took even longer when he booked the plane tickets.

He needed to be in the office in time for his phone meeting, one that wasn't on his calendar. The secrets were getting harder to keep, especially from Mari.

When the itinerary arrived in his email, he forwarded it to Charlie and Remi.

Here's to a great surprise! Thanks for all your help.

-T

When he finally made it to the office, he poked his head into Mari's office and waved before answering his phone.

The call lasted for over an hour, but it brought good news.

As soon as it ended, Travis walked into her office. Her chair sat empty, and her heels lay under her desk. She hadn't gone far.

Travis stood in the doorway, waiting.

When she walked in, he grinned. "Have a few minutes?" He kept his tone professional as he leaned on the doorframe, arms crossed.

Mari marched straight through into his office. He shifted in the doorway, leaving just enough room for her to go by.

The door swung closed behind them.

"First, I need to apologize. Being late, the long phone call. I hope neither left you in a bind."

"Oh no." She studied him. "Want me to reschedule your afternoon appointments? Anything you need for me to add to the calendar? Any new meetings? Or scheduled calls?"

"No. I'll be here this afternoon."

He took a few steps, crowding her personal space.

Her lips twitched into a smile. "Not seeing you made yesterday seem long."

He trailed a finger down her arm. His phone rang, but he didn't move. "I know this is Carlos's last week here in town, so I expect your evenings will be busy. But I was hoping you'd have dinner with me on Thursday night."

"I'd like that." The way she wiggled her fingers, it seemed the ringing was making her crazy. "Should you answer that?"

"Probably, but I'm not going to." He squeezed her hand. "I need for you to make some travel plans for me, but I need them kept quiet. Please."

"Of course. Is everything okay?" Genuine concern, not just curiosity blanketed her question.

"Yes. I'll write out the details for you, and I'll make us dinner reservations."

"Which client should I put down for billing purposes?" That question was prompted by curiosity.

He continued to brush his fingers on her arm. "It's not for a client."

"As soon as I get the info, I'll make the arrangements." Mari patted his chest before slipping out of his office.

He guessed that she was pondering the hush hush travel plans and the unscheduled phone calls. He hoped her trust in him wouldn't be undone by those things. Jumping to a painful conclusion would have been easy, but she'd known him a long time. Would that outweigh the secrets?

He dropped into his chair and texted her: *Lunch?*

If you have a plan, I'm game.

He couldn't think of any place nearby where they didn't run the risk of being spotted. *Your place or mine? I'll pick up take-out and meet you.*

Your place. She followed the message with a heart.

Give me a fifteen-minute head start. I'll let you know when I'm leaving. He grinned at his phone. Sneaking around to date her was worth it.

Chapter Thirty-one

Absorbed in work, Mari jumped when Travis touched her shoulder. Cabinets opened and closed in the kitchen, and she nodded that direction before he had a chance to speak.

He winked. "I'm going to lunch now. Need anything before I go?"

"No, I can't think of anything." She needed to think of better answers for their faked conversations.

"Just text or call if anything comes up." He walked out to the hall without even looking back over his shoulder.

Mari glanced at the time. Sitting at her desk for fifteen minutes would be the hardest task of the day. She tried returning to what she was doing before he came into her office, but her mind was on him, not on the work in front of her. Risk of typos and errors skyrocketed when her head wasn't in the game.

Checking her email, she managed to kill a couple minutes. Answering a few took another few minutes. *Ten more minutes.* Counting down only made time crawl by.

She straightened her desk, carried her cold coffee into the

kitchen, and rinsed out her mug. Back in her office, she slipped on her shoes. She opened her bottom drawer to pull out her purse, and Roger walked into her office.

"Mari, have a few minutes? I need to talk to you."

"I'm about to go to lunch. What do you need?" She couldn't very well text Travis with Roger right in front of her.

"Any more applicants?"

"We've had a few. I will be meeting with three of them this week."

"I haven't gotten any meeting requests."

"I want to screen them first before having them meet with you." She slipped on her shoes and pulled out her purse. "Anything else?"

"Travis is better with people. Maybe you could hire someone for him."

Mari wasn't ready to have that discussion. "You'd have to talk to Travis about that."

"Well, I don't want to keep you. Is Travis in his office?"

"He's at lunch."

"Where did he go?"

Mari wanted to laugh. *He's at his house waiting for me to show up.* That was clearly not what she'd tell Roger.

Quickly she conjured up an honest answer. "I'm not sure what he's having for lunch."

"Okay, then. I guess I'll catch him later." He wandered out of the office.

Her screen lit up, and she opened the message from Travis. He'd sent a single heart. She headed for the elevator, determined to ignore anyone that tried to stop her.

⁓

The rest of the week continued in the same pattern. Every night, Travis called before Mari went to bed. Every day, he snuck out of the office to grab lunch, and they met at his house. The only variable was who threw a wrench in their lunch plans.

On Tuesday, Travis got a call just as he was about to leave. Mari left first and grabbed lunch, meeting him at his house again. Mari hoped she wouldn't have to eat alone in her car because Bret Coulter could stretch a two-minute conversation to twenty.

On Wednesday, Fran caught Mari, asking her how to use the copy machine, and she wondered if there was a plot against her. Fran knew how to use the copier.

On Thursday, lunch plans had to be scrapped altogether when Erika invited Mari to lunch.

She slipped into Travis's office. "Erika invited me to lunch, so … well, I think I should—I'm sorry."

He came around the desk grazed her arm with his finger, a habit she was starting to love. "That's fine. Is everything okay? That's a bit unusual."

"I'm not sure, but if I had to guess, it's about Roger. I'll let you know what she says."

"I'm taking off early today. I'm meeting Marisa about selling the house."

"Give her my best."

"Enjoy lunch. I'll see you Monday." With the door open, he made sure to say it loud enough to be overheard.

At lunch, Erika launched into concerns before Mari had even ordered food.

"I heard a rumor that Fran and I were going to cover for Anne until you could find a replacement. Is that true?"

"I met with three ladies this week, three very talented women. Roger blackballed every single one. Filling that slot is proving difficult."

"I will not work with him."

"I'll keep that in mind. I can't make promises. Having you and Fran cover for Anne wasn't even my idea, but I'll talk to Travis."

"When? He'll be gone when you get back, and he's out of the office tomorrow." Erika shifted and leaned closer. "Or will you see him *outside* the office?"

"I can talk to him on Monday." Mari stood up. "Let's order food."

Erika followed beside Mari. "You can tell me. I mean, you were dancing with him at the wedding."

"Kate invited me to the wedding because I helped her, and we became friends. If I'd known dancing with Travis would fire up the rumor mill, I might have made a different choice."

"He is good-looking."

Mari stepped up to the counter, thankful for the excuse not to respond. "I'll have the beef kabobs." Her thoughts jumped to Travis in his swimsuit, gliding through the water and pulling her close.

The girl behind the counter asked, "Ma'am? Did you want that with rice?"

Mari felt heat rush through her cheeks. How long had she been lost in her thoughts? Sneaking was pointless if her expression gave away her feelings.

After lunch, as she left the restaurant, her phone beeped. *We still on for dinner tonight?*

She grinned as she answered: *Looking forward to it.*

At the end of the day, when she pushed open her front door, she stopped, and tears started. Boxes filled the living room. In the morning, Carlos would move out. All week, she'd been preparing herself for the day he moved out, but the boxes caught her off-guard, and she nearly lost it.

Her lip quivering, she inhaled and wiped her tears. There'd be plenty of time for crying after the move. "Carlos, I'm home."

"Be right down."

In the kitchen, she dropped her purse on the counter and began unloading the dishwasher.

He tromped into the kitchen. "Got the rest packed up. Tori helped me, and Lawton carried them down the stairs."

She hadn't thought to worry about how the boxes had made it down to the front room. "What time are you meeting your friends tonight?"

He'd been talking since Sunday about how a group was getting together for a last goodbye. She didn't mind not spending the evening with her son but appreciated Travis's dinner invitation all the more. Sitting alone in the house would only invite a night of tears and cheesecake.

"Tori's picking me up at five. She's more upset than I expected."

"She's going to miss you." Mari understood. "She has one more year, right?"

"Yeah." Carlos leaned back against the counter. "You don't mind that I'm going out tonight, do you?"

"Not at all." She glanced at the time. "Travis is taking me to dinner."

"Another date, huh?" He grinned.

"Just stop. I need to go change." She reached up and wrapped him in a hug. "I'm so proud of you."

Nothing about him seemed little anymore. "Love you, Mom."

Travis knocked a few minutes before six.

"Hi. Come on in. Excuse the boxes. Tomorrow is moving day."

"I'm so sorry. When I asked about tonight, I wasn't thinking. If you want to spend the evening with him, I get it."

"Going to dinner will be a good distraction for me. He's out, saying goodbye to his friends."

"I'll do my best to keep you distracted." He held out his hand. "I'm guessing your friends have been bombarding you with messages."

Face turned toward the door as she locked it, she hoped he couldn't read her expression. Her friends had been sending messages, but she hadn't answered. Her emotions were too tied in knots to discuss the move with the two people who could see through her mask from half-way around the country. "They have."

"I can't wait to meet them."

"They want to meet you too."

"Do y'all talk about me?" He winked as he opened her car door.

"Maybe."

"I don't want to crash your September weekend, but I'd like to take the three of you out to dinner one night, if that's okay?"

"I'm pretty sure they'd love that." Mari passed along the invitation, hoping a message from her would set their minds at ease. *Travis wants to take us all to dinner when y'all are in town. Sound good?*

YES popped up on the screen twice. Remi and Charlie were in agreement.

"It's a date." Mari couldn't wait to show him off to her friends.

After your date, please message about moving day. Charlie was concerned.

As Travis drove out of town, away from people that might recognize them, Mari stared out the window, trying not to think about an empty front room, an empty house.

During the silent drive, Travis held her hand when he wasn't shifting gears.

At the restaurant, he pulled out her chair before sitting down. "So, what did Erika want to discuss with you?"

"She refused to work with Roger. I promised to talk to you about it on Monday."

He sighed. "That's problematic. I get that he's odd, but that seems a strong reaction."

"He's brusque, comes off as rude, but I don't think he intends that. Social cues mean nothing to him."

"I get it. Enough about that whole situation. We can talk about it on Monday, just like you told Erika."

"How did it go with Marisa?"

"Great. She had comps, so we decided on a price and she's listing the property. Fingers crossed that it sells quickly."

"Why are you in a hurry?"

"I'm craving change."

"Is that what I am—change?"

"The best kind." He kissed her hand.

As the waiter rushed away to get dessert, Travis laid his hand open on the table. "If I won't be in the way, maybe I could be there tomorrow, just to make sure it all goes smoothly with the movers."

"You're worried about me." Touching her fingertips to his, she absorbed the magic of the moment—the romance, the candlelight, the man.

"Worried is too strong a word."

"You won't be in the way. Please come, and I'd like to pay you for the movers."

"Like I told Carlos when he offered, consider it a graduation gift." The way he treated her son earned Travis several gold stars.

"Thank you." Mari trailed her fingers on his. "As you can probably tell, I'm a bit of a mess, so let's talk about you. Tell me something unflattering."

"Didn't expect *that*." He brushed his thumb along her fingers. "You've worked with me a long time. I imagine you've noticed a few things."

While it would have been better to ponder the question, acting as if she had to really think about it, she didn't. "You work too much. Even when Emma was around—except when she was sick, then you didn't, but after she ..." Mari left the sentence unfinished. They both knew what she meant. "You are at the office late almost every night and most weekends. I notice the timestamps on emails and saved files."

"Guilty." Back and forth he continued to stroke her fingers, which only prompted her to prattle on.

"And I see anger flare in your eyes when someone crosses you, but you swallow it all inside. In seven years, you've only ever come close to losing your temper. I've never seen you explode." Telling a man all the unflattering things she'd noticed over the years was a poor choice for a second date, but she let it all spill out. "You're controlled. Always. Not controlling that's not what I mean."

"I understand. And I've been known to hold a few grudges, but only against those who deserve to be tarred and feathered. And when I lose my temper, it's ugly."

"I'm sorry."

His thumb stopped moving.

She looked up from the table and met his gaze.

"Sorry about what?"

"What I said."

"It's all true." He stared into his coffee cup. "Bet the ladies in the break room haven't noticed those things."

"I know so much more than they do—the unflattering and the make-me-weak-in-the-knees flattering. I get that they come as a package." She squeezed his hand. "Maybe at our next dinner, you can point out my flaws."

"So just to be sure I have this right, not losing my temper is a flaw?"

"Only because you keep it all inside."

The lopsided grin appeared. "Hopefully he returns with that cheesecake soon."

"I'm thinking I should've skipped that third glass of wine."

"Good thing I'm driving." The tease in his tone made her giggle.

"A very good thing."

Chapter Thirty-two

Mari was out of bed before the sun crested the horizon. She'd taken the day off to be home on moving day and wanted to make Carlos breakfast for his last morning at home. Promising herself she wouldn't cry, she put on her makeup before going downstairs. She slid bacon into the oven, made a stack of pancakes, and waited to scramble the eggs until Carlos woke up and Travis arrived.

You okay? Travis's text showed that he cared in a hundred little ways, and each one opened her heart to him a bit more.

Not really. I made a huge breakfast. Come hungry.

I'll be there in five.

Carlos wandered into the kitchen just as Travis knocked. "Movers should be here in an hour." A yawn cut off his sentence.

"We have time for breakfast then." Mari pulled open the door.

Travis grinned in his disarming way. "Hi."

"Thanks for coming." More words risked tears, and she was determined not to dissolve into a puddle, at least not before boxes had been loaded.

Carlos filled a glass with orange juice. "Mom, you outdid yourself."

"I just need to scramble the eggs." She finished making breakfast, letting the guys talk.

The last few grains of sand fell out of the hour glass. The day marked a turning point, and life wouldn't be the same.

So much for determination. Overcome with emotion, she served up two plates, sat them in front of the guys, and then ran up the stairs, the knot in her chest threatening to burst out in sobs.

Her phone beeped before she even closed her bedroom door. *Mom?*

She answered Carlos: *I'm okay. I promise.*

The next text was from Travis: *Want company?* The wink that followed his text made her laugh.

After wiping her tears, she freshened her makeup and made her way back downstairs. "Did you guys leave me any bacon?"

"Proof of how much we care." Travis slid a plate in front of her as she sat down.

"Carlos, you sure you don't need us to help you at the apartment?" She focused on her food.

"Travis hired guys and a truck, which is awesome helpful. So, we're good. But maybe in a week or two after we get things in order, you can come see my place. Both of you."

"Sounds good to me." Travis snapped a slice of bacon in half.

Mari smiled. "I can't wait." She loved that Carlos had included Travis in the invitation.

When the loaded truck pulled away from the curb, with Carlos's car behind it, Mari waved from the porch. As the tail lights disappeared, she leaned back against Travis. "He's gone."

Emotions flooded her cheeks.

He wrapped his arms around her. "Until laundry piles up and he wants a big homemade breakfast."

"Thanks for being here." She choked out the words.

His breath tickled her ear as he whispered, "Spend the weekend with me. Pack a bag, and we'll get rooms somewhere in the Hill Country."

The weekend? Rooms?

After she was quiet for too long, he kissed her cheek, which caught her off-guard. "Two rooms, no expectations."

"That sounds wonderful." She wiped her eyes. "I could use a change of scenery."

"I'll call and make arrangements." He flashed his winning smile.

Mari ran upstairs to pack. It took twice as long because she second guessed what to wear more than once. Buried under what she normally wore to bed was a set of cute pajamas, not see-through but well-fitted. That was the safest bet. When she zipped up the over-stuffed bag, she sighed. *The weekend?* She'd packed enough for a week.

When she made it to the bottom of the stairs, Travis took her bag. "I'll throw this in the trunk. Then we're ready to go."

"What about you? We can stop at your place."

"I packed before I came. Just in case you said yes."

How long had he been dreaming up this getaway?

Nerves and excitement played out a shoving match, vying for a hold on her thoughts.

Her brave face lasted until the city limits. Her tears started anew, and she let herself sob. "I know it's silly to cry. He'll be fine."

He held her hand.

"I don't even know why I'm crying. I didn't cry when he went to camp in the summer, but that was only a week. This feels so final." She couldn't help but laugh when she caught sight of herself in the side mirror. Makeup was a bad call.

"There's nothing silly about crying. You'll miss him." He parked up in front of a boutique hotel and smiled in a way that made the light dance in his eyes. Wiping tears off her cheeks, he whispered, "Wait right there."

He ran around the car but stopped, tapping away on his phone. Wiping the black smudges off her face, she watched him in the rearview mirror, curious.

He opened her door and helped her out of the car. "Once we get our rooms, I'll come back out and get the bags."

They strolled into the hotel hand in hand, and Travis nodded to the man at the desk. "I have reservations. Bentley."

"Yes. If I can just have you fill this out, Mr. Bentley."

"Travis, I'll be back inside in just a minute. I want to snap a few pictures of that porch." Mari loved the architecture of the old building, but the porch was the gem that she'd remember long after the weekend was over.

"I'll meet you out there in a minute or two." He picked up the pen and focused on the papers.

She took pictures of the rocking chairs and the old stone walls. Walking out to the sidewalk, she took a wide shot of the entire porch, making sure to include the colorful bikes leaning in front. The scene felt like a moment of summer captured.

Chapter Thirty-three

The door creaked as Travis pushed it open and stepped out onto the porch. "Let me grab the bags, then we'll head up."

She wrapped her arms around him before he opened the trunk. "Thank you for this. It's beautiful and very romantic."

His heart beat so loudly, he feared she'd know something was up. "I can't wait until you see the room."

Inside, they followed the hotel owner up the steps and down a short hall. "Ma'am, this is your room." He handed Mari a key as the door swung open.

She walked into the room, and a wide smile pulled at her cheeks. "This room is huge. I don't need this much space." Facing Travis, she shook her head. "It's beautiful. I don't even know what to say."

All the work that went into his surprise had been worth it, every email, the long phone calls. He couldn't wait to see her reaction. "Look behind you."

Mari whipped around.

"Surprise!" Remi and Charlie waved their arms in the air.

Mari spun back around. "You did this?"

He dropped the bags and brushed a tear off her cheek. "Aren't you going to say hello?"

She hugged her friends. "You're still coming next month, right??"

"Of course, but there was no way we could pass up a chance to surprise you." Remi spun in a circle. "This is such a great place."

Travis leaned back against the wall and watched Mari with her friends. As much as he wanted to spend time with her, she needed her friends around. He'd spend a quiet weekend reading or walking through town, enjoying glimpses of her smiling face.

Mari blinked away tears and smiled, fanning her face.

Charlie pulled Mari in for another hug. "And he's a great catch."

Travis hadn't expected such a declaration, but he had no complaints.

"Remi, Charlie, I'd like you to meet Travis." Mari slid her arms around his waist.

The look she gave him sent his heart soaring.

He pulled his gaze away from her. "Hello. It's so good to finally meet you both."

"Now, how did you pull this off? How did you coordinate?" Mari scanned their faces.

"His contact info was on the page you sent us. The one with his photo." Charlie grinned. "Remember how I emailed him the night you were at the hospital."

"And I emailed her back asking for ideas to surprise you." Travis picked up his bag. "Ladies, it was a pleasure meeting you. I'm going to go get settled in my room."

"You better come right back." Remi put her hands on her hips. "You're one of us this weekend."

"She's right." Charlie waggled her finger. "Don't be gone too long."

Mari giggled at him, which probably meant his shock was written all over his face. He'd planned on letting them visit during the weekend.

"I shall return. Shortly." He bowed before sauntering out of the room.

Chapter Thirty-four

Mari hugged her friends again before curling up on the sofa.

"Mari, he's delicious." Remi always had a flare for words.

"If I had any doubts about the man, I don't now." Charlie dropped into an overstuffed chair.

Mari kicked off her shoes. "What did you message him?"

Charlie waved her hand. "I hardly remember now. I was so worried about you that night. He called me as soon as he saw the email. Even over the phone, his concern for you was abundantly clear. Then, like he said, he messaged me back."

Remi grinned. "When they messaged me, they'd already hatched this plan. Does Travis have any single friends, brothers?"

Mari shook her head. "Well, consider me surprised. When he asked if I wanted to spend the weekend in Comfort—"

"You thought romance and candlelight, but you got us!" Remi flopped down into the bed, and her tone sobered. "I'm not going to ask about Carlos and the move right now, so I have to ask about Travis. Is it serious?"

"We've been dating two weeks." Mari perched at the edge of the sofa. "Lots of romance, but no kisses."

Charlie raised an eyebrow. "You didn't answer the question."

Mari glanced at the door. "It could be. Maybe."

Her friends sat quietly, waiting for more.

"We haven't talked about it, but—I don't know."

Remi sighed. "It's more than a summer fling."

"It was never a summer fling." Mari rolled her eyes. "I've known the man for seven years. I know his favorite brand of pen, what direction his shirts face on a hanger. I know how he takes his coffee. I know his favorite restaurants and what he likes to order. It was part of my job to know all that."

"I bet that made the whole first date less awkward." Charlie stood up and started unpacking her bag.

"But I didn't know that he'd like to race cars or that he could flirt with a look. I haven't felt cared for—not like this—in a very long time."

A knock sounded, and Remi jumped up. "He has good timing. I was about to cry."

Travis walked in, his smile betrayed by his tense shoulders. Chitchatting with women who had been friends for years fell way outside his comfort zone.

"Were your ears ringing?" Mari grinned as he made his way to the couch.

"Only a little." He leaned against the side rather than sitting down.

Charlie piped up. "What do you say we go out and walk through the town? We've got time before dinner."

"Great idea." Mari slipped on her shoes.

Remi opened her bag. "Give me just a minute or two to change."

"I'll be in the hall." He bolted out of the room.

Mari followed him. "I'm trying not to say 'thank you' every two seconds. This means so much to me."

"This morning was like closing a well-loved book, a book you can never read for the first time again. You needed a distraction."

"What exactly did you plan to do? You seemed surprised when they asked you to hang out in the room."

"I brought a book. Figured I'd walk through town."

She stepped closer him. "I don't want to keep it a secret anymore—at work, I mean, or anywhere. Starting Monday, I mean Tuesday"—she swallowed back the sob holding back her words—"I'll be working as Roger's personal assistant."

He slipped his arms around her. Her words carried a meaning she hoped he'd understand.

"That news is bittersweet." He scanned her face, and his gaze settled on her lips. But before his lips touched hers, the door opened.

Realization struck. *He's been waiting on me.* Letting go of the secret told him she wasn't afraid, told him that she trusted him. She trailed her hand down his arm and clasped his hand.

Remi backed into the hotel room, bumping into Charlie. "Sorry. We'll uh—I think I forgot my ..."

Mari shook her head. "It's all good."

Travis kissed her hand, which felt like a promise of more to come. "Let's go." He led the short parade down the stairs and out to the sidewalk.

Once outside, he hung behind as the ladies strolled along, deciding on their first destination.

When Charlie spotted the knitting shop, her eyes widened. "Please." Her two loves in life were numbers and yarn.

Mari glanced at Remi. "What do you think?"

"As long as I get wine later, I'm game." Remi pointed to the wine-tasting room down the block.

"I think we can manage that." Mari paused until Travis was

next to her and caught his hand. "You don't have to be the caboose."

Inside the knitting store, a rainbow of choices lined the walls and covered tables. Mari didn't crochet or knit, but the lure of the yarn almost made her want to learn. Travis settled on a couch tucked in a side room and was joined by a large cat, who seemed eager for attention.

After only a few minutes in the store, it became clear that Charlie would either be checking an extra bag to go home or Mari would be shipping a box of yarn.

She settled next to Travis on the sofa, trying not to disturb the cat. "Are you okay with my decision?"

"I am. Don't get me wrong, I don't exactly *like* it. It won't be the same, but I'd choose this over having you as my personal assistant." He kissed her forehead. "I'm sorry you have to work with Roger, but I think he'll be okay with your choice. He all but hinted to me—"

"He straight up asked me if I could just hire a personal assistant for you."

"But will you call it temporary, please? And keep the job posting up."

"Why?"

"We will need someone to fill your spot, and I want you to be able to leave the position if it's not a good fit." He brushed his thumb on the back of her hand. "You're making a huge sacrifice. I get that, but if it doesn't work, we'll figure something else out. Okay?"

Mari appreciated that he was trying to protect her, so she didn't argue. "Temporary is fine. I just didn't want it to sound like I'd be back working for you as soon as someone else came along."

"Good point."

"Maybe on a trial basis? He might not like working with me, either."

"That works." Travis pulled out his phone. "I'll text him."

"Word it however you want. And you'll need to decide if you want me to hire someone or fill my position with Fran or Erika and then fill that spot."

Travis tapped away on his phone then tucked it back in his pocket. "That can wait until Monday, but now that Roger has been informed, I'd say that you are no longer my direct report. I told him you'd start Tuesday morning."

Mari kissed his cheek. "No more sneaking?"

"No more sneaking."

An hour later, Charlie was all smiles as she stepped out of the store, carrying multiple bags. "One of you can choose the next stop."

Poking through antique and collectible stores filled the next couple of hours.

In one store with glass cabinets lining every walkway, Remi discovered a hat. The brim covered in flowers, it looked as if it had been designed for her. She left the shop with her treasure.

As they walked out to the sidewalk, Mari let go of his hand when she spotted Lucy from the office, the same Lucy that had shared photos from the wedding. "Travis, look."

Remi figured out what was going on and looped her arm through Travis's. "It's so fun having you in town."

Giggling, she hung on him, which clearly left Lucy confused. Without letting go of Remi, Travis tucked his arm around Mari.

Lucy waved from across the street and glanced both directions before crossing. "Hey, y'all. What a surprise to see you both here."

Mari spoke up before Remi said something embarrassing. "Hi. What brings you to Comfort?"

"Came for the craft market and decided to hang around." Lucy looked from Remi to Travis's other hand. "It's such a … romantic little town."

"I totally agree." Charlie poked her head over Travis's shoulder, sounding like she was imitating Remi.

Travis squeezed Mari's hand. "Are you here often? Any restaurant recommendations?"

"The small place next to the hotel on the next street over is supposed to be wonderful." Lucy pointed toward their hotel.

"Thanks. These are our friends, Charlie and Remi." Travis remembered his manners, which was good because Mari hadn't even thought of introducing her friends.

"Well, I'll let y'all shop. Good to see you." Lucy wasn't two steps away before focusing on her phone.

Once they were around the corner and out of earshot, Remi and Charlie laughed.

Remi patted Travis's arm. "I tried to run interference, but I'm not sure she bought it."

"I can only imagine what she's telling people." Mari hoped the word harem wouldn't be used.

∽

After dinner, which Travis insisted was his treat, all four settled in the hotel room with a bottle of wine and an array of sweets. Conversation flowed until the wee hours of the morning.

"You'd make a great character for a book. Billionaire romances are really in right now." Remi poured herself another glass of wine. "I might have to write you into one of mine."

Mari patted his back when he choked on his wine. She wasn't sure she wanted to share any part of their story with the rest of the world. "I'm not sure I want anyone else swooning over my hero. There's enough of that at the office."

"There are so many things wrong with that idea, Remi. I'm not even sure where to start." Holding Mari's hand, he leaned close and lowered his voice. "Hero? I do like the sound of that."

Charlie stretched. "Sorry to be the fuddy-duddy, but I need sleep."

He pushed up off the sofa. "This has been a blast, ladies. Thanks for letting me hang around."

Mari followed him out and caught his hand. "Can we talk for a minute?"

"Of course." He leaned against the wall.

"In your room?"

"Yes." He gripped her hand.

As soon as the door closed, Mari let loose the apology she'd been mulling all evening. "I sat in that restaurant saying all those things, and you just listened. The whole time you were keeping this massive surprise a secret. I'm so sorry."

"Mari—"

"When I said 'I'm sorry' last night, you tensed. Did you think …?"

"For a moment." He brushed his fingers along her hand. "I wasn't sure how I'd get you up here if you were ending things. From the start, this weekend was about you getting time with your friends."

"It means so much. Seeing them, watching you laughing with them—it makes my heart happy."

Blue eyes, the color of a hot flame, stared through her. He leaned down, and his lips brushed against hers. Mari stretched up on her tiptoes, and he deepened their kiss.

After a lingering, wine-tinged kiss, he squeezed her hand. "I—" Brushing a knuckle across her cheek, he kissed her again. "Let me walk you back to your room."

Mari wanted him to finish the original sentence.

When she walked back into her room, neither Remi or Charlie were in bed.

Charlie put her hands on her hips. "Spill it. Something changed."

Remi hugged a pillow to her chest. "You could totally feel the love in the room. What did you say to him?"

Mari didn't bother denying it. "I won't be working as his personal assistant anymore."

"You quit?" Remi sounded alarmed.

Charlie raised an eyebrow. "So, you are no longer his direct report."

"I didn't quit outright. I'll be working for one of the vice presidents, but it means Travis and I don't have to sneak around in little towns anymore."

Remi clapped. "Yay! I'm so excited for you."

"He seems to understand what that means." Charlie was about to open a can of worms Mari wasn't inclined to discuss.

"That's a conversation for another night." She sucked in a deep breath. "We should sleep."

꣑

When the alarm went off in the morning, no one had gotten enough sleep.

"I'm glad I packed last night." Charlie zipped up her bag. "Sure you don't mind keeping that yarn until next month?"

"It guarantees you'll come." Mari hugged her friends. "This weekend was exactly what I needed."

Remi wiped her eyes. "Don't get me started. This has been so fun. I'm going to miss you guys. I think I laughed more yesterday than I did all of last year."

"We should go. I want to be sure we get to the airport with enough time." Charlie seemed determined not to cry.

Mari opened the door.

Travis stood in the hall, his hand raised to knock. "I wanted to say goodbye and thank you."

Remi threw her arms around him.

Charlie followed suit. "Thank *you*. This has been wonderful, and it was great to meet you."

"Likewise. Let me carry those bags down." He gave Mari a quick kiss before heading down the stairs.

She was in love, but two weeks into a dating relationship seemed way too soon for a declaration of that sort.

On the way back home, Travis took advantage of every opportunity to hold her hand, only letting go to shift gears. "I'm meeting Marisa later today to look at condos. If you're free, maybe you could come along to share your opinion."

"Sure. Do I have time for a nap first?"

"I hope so. That was on my agenda. Have time for breakfast? We could pick up tacos."

"Sounds perfect."

When they got back to the house, he unloaded the bags, and she carried in the tacos.

Quietly and without fanfare Mari returned home to her empty nest, but everything was different. The two of them sat down to tacos, the silent companionship heralding a new phase.

After finishing his food, he stood and threw away his trash. "I'll text when I'm headed back over. I'm meeting her at three, so about two-thirty."

"I'll be ready." She walked him to the front door.

Before he left the porch, he pulled her close. Lips pressed to hers, and she closed her eyes. The man did everything well.

Chapter Thirty-five

After his much-needed nap, Travis showered and dressed, happy that Mari agreed to visit condos with him.

Travis texted that he was on his way and pulled up to the house at 2:30. He didn't even have time to get out of the car before Mari ran out and climbed in. Before buckling her seatbelt, she leaned across the cab and kissed him.

He loved the change in the relationship. "Hi. Feel better?"

"Yes. Naps are wonderful things." She buckled her seatbelt. "Did you get one?"

"I did." He shifted and pulled away from the curb.

"Have you had much interest in the house?"

"It's under contract."

"Wow. That was fast." She turned to face him. "Does Marisa know ... about us?"

"If she doesn't, she will. But I'm guessing Kate mentioned it. She's a tad excited that we're dating."

"I thought you wanted a house. A place big enough to host family dinners and space for grandkids to wander."

"I do, but ... in the short term, I'm going to get a condo." Long-term decisions needed to wait until other changes had been set into motion.

When they parked, Travis checked his phone.

Carlos had messaged: *Is my mom okay? Has she stopped crying?*

Travis tapped out a reply: *She's doing okay. I made sure she was well distracted this weekend.*

"Who needs your attention?" Mari raised her eyebrows.

"Carlos was asking about you." He reached over and clasped her hand. "He's excited about his new place, but he misses you."

"He told you that?"

"We've talked a bit." He kissed her fingers. "It was just the two of you for several years."

She leaned over and kissed him. "I'm glad he talked to you. Really glad. Now, I need to get out of the car before I cry."

He grinned. "Marisa just pulled up."

As Travis helped Mari out of the car, Marisa waved. Her expression said that Kate had shared the news.

For more than an hour, they toured condos, commenting on what they liked and didn't like.

The second stop was easily Travis's favorite. A wall of floor-to-ceiling windows in the spacious, open living room overlooked the Hill Country. The master bedroom faced the same direction, and French doors opened to a balcony. The ginormous bathroom had his and her sinks, a shower with a glass surround, and a large copper tub that would easily fit two.

Mari gasped when she stepped into the kitchen, and he guessed that she loved the place, too. The office held the real treasure. A large window seat, closed off with drapes, took up only a small chunk of the room, two walls of which were lined with shelves. Unfurnished, it was easy to picture his things in the space and Mari in the window seat.

While he walked through a second time asking Marisa questions, Mari snuggled into that special space.

They looked at three other places that day: one was much larger but farther from the office, another was closer to the office but had very little storage, and the last looked more fitted for royalty. None of them had a window seat overlooking the Hill County.

Back in the car, after the last stop, as he drove her home, he prodded for her opinion. "What did you think? Which did you like?"

"They were all nice, but I didn't care for the last one. It was too fussy."

"Have a favorite?" He knew she did.

"Yes, but this is about you. Which one seemed most suited to you?"

"I need to sleep on it." He parked in front of her house. "I had a fabulous time this weekend."

"I've probably already said it a hundred times but thank you. I loved every minute. Want to come in?"

"I should get home." He smiled and brushed a finger along her hand. "But I will walk you to the door."

Mari shook her head as she stepped out of the car. "If someone had told me six months ago that we—that this—I wouldn't have believed them."

"And why is that?"

"You're my boss—*were* my boss."

"I'll miss working with you." Wrapping his arms around her, he met her lips. "But, the timing was good. I have tickets to the symphony this coming Friday. I've had them a while but hadn't mentioned anything because I couldn't guarantee that we wouldn't be seen there together."

"The tickets in the envelope?"

"You've been snooping?"

"No, but I saw them. You had those before the wedding. Those were on your desk right after Carlos's accident."

"I bought them about the time Kate settled on a wedding date. And I was joking about the snooping."

"I don't understand. You hadn't—we hadn't …"

He stepped closer, her back to the front door. "I'd planned to ask you out sooner. I'd hoped things would be less complicated." He paused, not ready to tell her everything he'd been working on. "When we were on our way to Kate's, I started to, but the call interrupted me. After the accident, I decided to wait. Working together made it hard to know what to do."

"You are very good at keeping secrets."

He reached into his pocket and handed her a small pouch. "I need you to help me pick out a chain for it, but I had this made for you." He dropped a pendant into her hand.

Shaped like an empty nest with a bird perched on the edge, ready to fly away, the gift hit its mark.

"Travis, it's beautiful. Where did you …? It's perfect."

"Kate's friend, Becca, made it."

"I love it. You spoil me, surprise me. I'm not even sure what to expect next."

He tilted her head, leaning in close. "This."

When he lifted his head, she sighed and leaned her head on his chest. "See you in the morning."

"We'll meet first thing, and I'll have boxes for you to move stuff."

"I imagine it'll be an interesting day."

"I probably won't make an announcement tomorrow, but sometime this week, we'll let the secret out."

Mari patted his chest. "I'll leave the when and how up to you."

He snuck one more kiss before leaving.

At home, Travis texted Kate before he launched into packing: *We had a great weekend. And it's not a secret anymore.*

I'm so happy for you. I like her, Dad. A LOT. Any other secrets I should know about? Kate had the ability to read him in an almost unnerving way, which amazed him since she'd only known him a relatively short time.

Have a great evening. Love you. He wasn't going to say anything more just yet.

Boxes open all around him, he started the big job of packing up the house. Years of memories, waiting to be relived, were tucked on every shelf and in every drawer.

His planned changes were well underway, and the biggest still remained a secret.

Chapter Thirty-six

Monday morning, Mari spent the entire drive to work holding back tears. The morning would be busy.

She hurried into her office, glad that Fran and Erika hadn't yet arrived.

Boxes, already taped together, sat next to her desk, and the door to Travis's office stood open. His car was in its spot, and she wondered how early he'd gotten to work.

Mari took a deep breath, ready to finalize all the changes, but stopped when footsteps sounded behind her.

"Oh, great. You're ready to pack." Roger's eagerness should've been flattering.

"I need to arrange a few details with Travis, but I should be down in a while."

"I'm happy to help you carry boxes. This is a great solution. Thank you." He grinned like a kid with a new toy.

Mari nodded and knocked as she stepped into Travis's office. He wasn't at his desk, and she scanned the room.

He leaned out of the sunny spot and held out a mug of coffee. "Thought we could meet in here."

"Perfect." She sat down on the sofa. "Roger had already been up to see me. He's a little bit excited."

Travis closed the door and dropped down next to her. "This is harder than I thought it would be." Tangling his fingers in her curls, he kissed her.

"That makes it totally worth it." She smiled and meant it. "Totally."

"So, what do I need to know? What do I need to decide?"

Mari didn't need to look at a list. She'd gone through the questions multiple times since last night. "Who do you want to replace me?"

"Let's have Fran fill your spot, but we'll call it temporary for now. And keep the position open like we discussed."

"I'll meet with her this morning and carve out time each day this week to bring her up to speed. I'll let her know she can message me whenever she needs anything." Mari imagined there would be lots of questions.

"If you want to take her to lunch, it'll be my treat. I'm guessing she'll have a few questions that she might not want me to hear."

"Then she may not want to ask me." Mari winked. She didn't ask about why he didn't choose Erika but wondered if had anything to do with her running her mouth after the wedding.

Mari sipped her coffee. "As far as projects and contracts that I've been working on, I'd rather just finish them rather than try and explain it all to Fran, if that's okay. I can stay late a few nights this week and get most of it completed."

"I hate that you have to do that."

"It will save me so much time."

"That's fine, but record your hours." He gave her a look that said not to argue.

"Yes, *sir.*" Her teasing was rewarded with a lopsided grin. "I need to write up a job description and then pack up my office. Do you want to tell Fran, or should I?"

"Once you have the job description written, bring it to me, and I'll talk to her." He brushed his knuckles on her cheek. "If you don't like working with Roger, we'll figure something else out."

Mari nodded, determined not to complain to Travis if she didn't like working for Roger.

"Promise me, Mari." Travis's deep blue gaze made her heart race.

Mari shifted. "Travis, this is why dating the big boss is a bad idea. I'm not going to run to you any time I don't like something Roger does."

"That's not what I mean. If you find yourself hating your job, I will find you a different one. I need you to be honest with me. Please."

"I'm not the one keeping secrets." She immediately regretted her jab. "Forgive me. I'm not handling it all as well as I should."

"Thank you for giving up a job you love so that—" Travis scrubbed his face. "I think I need a third cup of coffee."

She pressed a quick kiss to his cheek and rushed out of the room. She gave up the job she loved because of the man she loved. She tried not to think about any of that while she scribbled down a job description.

Erika and Fran arrived, and gossip started as soon as they walked into the kitchen.

"Have you heard?" Erika had no idea how to whisper.

"Do you mean about Lucy seeing Travis with three women in Comfort?" Fran needed to quit talking about Travis's life outside the office if she had any hopes of being his personal assistant more than a few weeks.

"*What?*" Erika's surprise made Mari laugh. "I was talking about Mari going to work for Roger. I heard him talking about it downstairs."

"I hadn't heard that." Fran sounded shocked; she'd be even more shocked when Travis asked her to fill the position.

"Back to what Lucy saw. Tell me more." Erika had to be in the know.

Fran cleared her throat. "Lucy wasn't sure which one he was dating, but he had his arm around Mari. The lady hanging on his other arm was younger. She had on this hat covered in flowers. Lucy said that one looked smitten."

"Interesting. Who do you think Travis will hire to fill Mari's spot?" Erika had her sights set on the job it seemed.

Fran giggled. "I'd happily be his *personal* assistant."

Mari was glad that the choice was temporary and marveled at the completely unprofessional things these women said at the office. Since she'd been kissing the boss in a side room, she decided not to bring it up.

She walked the job description into Travis's office. "Here you go."

"Thanks." He glanced up. "I'll talk to her in a bit. Need any help packing?"

"I'll let you know." Mari leaned on the edge of his desk. "I keep thinking about what you said about change—about it bringing new opportunities. That's how I'm viewing this job change."

"Maybe tonight, we can drink to new opportunities." He stood up and gazed down at her. "If you are free for dinner?"

She touched his hand. "Yeah."

What took seven years to accumulate only took an hour to get into boxes. As she taped the last box closed, Travis asked her to join him in the conference room. Erika, who sat with her arms crossed and a scowl on her face, and Fran, who looked like someone was shining a bright light in her eyes, were both already seated at the long table.

"Mari, I let Fran and Erika know that you decided to work

as Roger's personal assistant. Until we hire a replacement for you, Fran agreed to step in. I'm sure she has a list of questions for you."

"I'll be one floor down, and you have my number. I'm happy to answer questions." Mari smiled, trying not to let them see how much she wanted to curl up and cry.

"Travis mentioned lunch. I'd like that if you have the time." Fran looked a bit overwhelmed.

Mari nodded. "Of course, let me grab my purse. We can go now and be there before the crowds."

While Mari was at lunch with Fran, answering question after question, Travis and Roger shuffled Mari's boxes downstairs. When Mari walked back into the bare office after lunch, the finality hit her, but she couldn't disappear into the sunny spot and pretend everything was okay. She had a job to do—a new job with a new boss.

Mari walked out to the elevator.

"Good luck. Working for Roger, you'll need it." Erika flashed a smile and glanced toward Travis's door. "Seems so cruel to demote you after seven years. I'm so sorry."

"She wasn't demoted." Travis's normally blue eyes were steel grey. He'd been down the hall, within earshot.

The elevator opened, and Mari stepped inside. Travis followed.

When the doors closed, he clutched her hand. "I told Roger that you'd already scheduled leave for Friday—all day. He has that on his calendar now."

"Thanks." Mari clutched his hand as the elevator descended one floor. "I'm okay."

She stepped off and waved as he stayed on, continuing down to the first floor. She walked into her new windowless office and sighed. It was time to unpack.

For the next couple days Mari hardly saw Travis at the office. When she did, it was across a crowded room, but quiet dinners each night often accompanied by cheesecake assured her that changing jobs was the right thing to do.

∿

Thursday afternoon, after skipping lunch, Mari wanted a snack and needed a few minutes away from her office. With change in hand, she slipped on her heels to head downstairs.

Travis texted before she stepped onto the elevator: *Have a few minutes?*

She tapped out a reply: *I'm headed to the breakroom to grab a snack. Can come up after.*

After hitting send, she took the elevator down to the second floor, preparing for the stares and whispers. They'd increased in the last week; she was sure of it. There were rumors about why she'd switched jobs, rumors about Travis dumping her for her younger friend. What seemed most common was that people thought she was gunning for the boss but that he didn't return the affection.

On the second floor, she stepped into the break room, and a momentary hush settled in the room. She beelined for the snack machine, and the murmurs of conversation started again. She put in her money, then punched in the code. The coil holding her snack turned but stopped just before the cookies dropped free, and she'd only grabbed exact change. *Perfect.*

All chattering stopped. Stuck cookies couldn't be that interesting. Mari glanced toward the door. Sparkling blue eyes and a bright smile greeted her. She couldn't remember the last time Travis had wandered into the break room.

She was pretty sure it wasn't professionalism written all over his face and wondered what he had planned. Whatever he planned to do, she liked him. A lot. There was another L word that was more fitting, but she wasn't quite ready to venture there, not in a crowded break room.

He wove his way through the tables, smiling and greeting employees by name. As he approached the snack machine, the quiet got somehow quieter.

Glancing from Mari to the machine, he asked, "Is there a problem?"

"My cookies didn't fall." She pointed at the dangling package.

Coins jingled as he reached into his pocket. With one hand on her waist, he leaned around her and inserted the coins. After punching in a code, two packages of cookies fell.

"I made our reservations for dinner tomorrow night." He added more money to the machine and selected a candy bar.

"What time?" She loved how naturally he transformed into the Travis she spent time with outside the office, and she especially loved the way he'd let the secret out.

"Five-thirty. Gives us plenty of time for dinner before the symphony starts. I'll be by about five, if that works."

"Perfectly. And thank you for the cookies."

He winked. Once they were in the hall, he brushed his hand against hers. "That was kinda fun."

She waited until they were alone in the elevator. "I'm not worried about where this is going. Even if this doesn't—"

He leaned down and brushed his lips against hers. "Doesn't what?"

"Hmm?" Anticipating a deeper kiss, she closed her eyes.

The elevator dinged, and he stepped back. "My office?"

"Yes, please." Running would be a bad idea, but it took self-control not to.

Travis paused near the reception desk. "Flowers will be arriving soon. Let me know when they get here."

"Yes, sir." Erika covered the phone in her lap.

News spread fast in the office.

When Travis closed the door, Mari stepped into his open arms, and they picked up right where they'd been when the elevator dinged. His soft gentle kiss became hungrier and more passionate.

Interrupted by a knock at the door, he squeezed her hand. "Hold that thought." He strode to his desk. "Come in."

Mari dropped onto the sofa, watching the door. It swung open and a huge bouquet of flowers preceded Erika into the office.

"Flowers arrived. For Mari. Should I send them to the sixth floor?"

"Just put them there by the sofa." Travis leaned on the edge of his desk, eyes focused on Mari.

Erika set them on the table and smiled. "Oh, I didn't realize you were in here. Beautiful flowers."

Mari pulled the card out of the holder. "Thank you."

Faster than Mari had ever seen Erika move, she clicked out of the room. Because she had news to share, time was of the essence.

Travis sat down on the sofa as Mari slipped the card out of the envelope.

To someone amazing.

She ran her finger over the words, remembering when he'd used that phrase sitting on her couch, when she thought he had someone else in mind. "You meant me that day, and I had no idea. Well, when you showed up with flowers the next morning, I should have realized."

Lifting her chin, he kissed her again, a long lingering kiss that awakened desires that had been dormant for years.

"Now that we can be seen together, what about the gala on Saturday?"

"New opportunities."

"If you recall, I asked you to get two tickets. Will you accompany me?"

"The symphony and the gala? All in one weekend?"

"Unless you have other plans."

Showing up on his arm to either event would make ripples. Showing up to both would be an announcement. "Yes. But I can't promise to be nice to the sharks."

"With you, I'm no longer chum." He pulled her close and left little doubt how he felt.

"I need to go." She hugged him one more time, wanting to say more but reining in her impatience. Letting him drive seemed to be working well. "I should get back downstairs." She kissed him again.

"See you tonight."

After a productive hour, where she'd channeled her excitement and nervousness into getting things done, Mari stretched.

Fran knocked at her office door. "Have time for a few questions?"

"Sure. Come in." Mari shifted a box out of the extra chair.

"You've really lit up the gossip chain today."

"Oh?" Mari's cheeks warmed.

"He's a catch. That's for sure." Fran lowered her voice. "I think it's great. Just be aware that some aren't being kind. You'll have to ignore them."

"I expected as much."

"When you stepped off the elevator, the way he looked at you." She sighed. "I remember when my husband looked at me that way."

As tempting as it was to explain what had happened on the elevator, Mari wasn't going to add to the rumor mill. Some things were best kept secret. "What questions did you have for me?"

Chapter Thirty-seven

Since she'd spent every evening with Travis, Friday was all about shopping and trying to find the perfect dress. Two, actually. She wanted to look amazing at the symphony and at the gala.

Shopping in stores she never frequented, feeling like the oldest person in the building, Mari scoured racks for something special. When she and Travis were sneaking around, it was only about the two of them. Dating for all the world to see brought her into his world, and that made her nervous. Would his feelings change if she didn't fit in?

Brushing aside those thoughts, she grabbed several dresses and headed to the dressing room. The black dress she'd picked up looked better on the hanger. On her, it looked like a bedazzled bag. Eliminating outfits proved easier than choosing one. She tried on the next one.

Smiling at her reflection, she smoothed the vibrant blue fabric. More form fitted than anything she'd worn in a long while, the dress hugged her curves. She snapped a photo and sent it to her friends.

Beautiful! Remi lived to encourage people. *You look amazing!!!*

Charlie's response was just as encouraging. *Remi is right. That color is perfect on you. He'll be drooling.*

Mari anticipated the gleam in those blue eyes.

Glancing at the time, she changed back into her clothes and headed to the register. She needed another dress, and the clock kept ticking.

⌇

When Travis knocked, she ran down the stairs, carrying her heels, but she slipped them on before opening the door. "Hi."

"Wow." He wore her favorite blue shirt, and it almost perfectly matched her dress. "I guess I should have sent notice of what I was wearing."

"That's my favorite shirt." Mari snatched up her purse. "I'm ready."

Travis held her hand as they walked to the car. "Nervous?"

"Can you feel me shaking?" She stopped when she spotted the limousine. "Oh, wow."

"Wow is right. You look amazing." He pulled her close before opening the car door. "Why are you nervous?"

"Travis, we run in very different circles. Tonight, I feel like I'm stepping into yours." She kept her voice low, so the driver wouldn't hear her.

Travis slid in next to her. "Our worlds aren't so different, but I'll be by your side all evening."

"I'm counting on that." She kissed him.

"I love not having to sneak around."

Once they were on the road, Mari felt her nerves knotting. "What's it like? I've never been to a symphony there. Are we going to a restaurant first?"

"I made reservations for us at a restaurant close to the center.

The limo will drop us off and pick us up. I didn't want you to have to walk in heels."

The more he talked about the evening, the more excited she got.

"For the symphony, we have box seats on the Grand Tier level. We can visit the Founder's Lounge for drinks."

"It's like I'm living someone else's life." Mari clutched his hand.

The limo dropped them off, and Travis led her through a gate and into the small restaurant. Twelve tables were covered in white linens. Wrought-iron fixtures dangled glass bowls holding candle-style lights. Tiny, flickering candles added a warmth and charm to the space.

Seated at a table overlooking the river, Mari couldn't imagine a better start to the evening. "This place is so quaint and charming."

"Everything in the kitchen is done by hand, not by mixer or chopper. They don't use anything that plugs in. They only cook what's available locally."

"Well, I love it." She glanced at the menu, too overwhelmed to make sense of it. "Just order for me."

He nodded. She loved that he was as comfortable in an out-of-the-way barbeque joint as he was in an upscale dining establishment.

Not long after Travis ordered, the waiter brought out an *amuse bouche* for each of them. Mari had only ever heard the term on the food channel.

With each course, she relaxed a little more.

After the course the waiter called the *entremezzo* and before the entrée was served, Travis cocked his head, giving her an amused look. "It's fun watching you."

"Like I told you before, it's a different world."

"Did you forget about the raccoon in the pillowcase?" He chuckled.

"Also a different world. You are an extremely interesting man, Travis Bentley."

"I'm glad you think so—very, very glad."

"Did anyone say anything to you—you know—after our encounter in the break room?" Mari tasted the lamb and sighed. "This is *so* good."

"No one said anything *to* me. I've caught a few whispers *about* me."

"And working at the same company won't cause you trouble?" The last thing she wanted was to mar his reputation.

"It should be fine. I probably won't carry you down the halls or make out with you in the break room."

"What about in the sunny spot?" She rubbed her foot along his.

He only grinned.

⁓

When they left the restaurant and slipped into the limo, Travis whispered, "And now, we're off to the symphony."

It took longer to get in and out of the limousine than it did to drive from the restaurant to the performing arts center. Travis helped her out onto the sidewalk, and she paused.

She'd been by the building but never in it. On his arm, she made her way up the steps, under the arches, and into the building. Mari drank in the surroundings, wanting to remember every detail.

He eyed her, delight adding a sparkle to the vivid blue. "I love your smile."

"I seem to do that a lot these days. You're spoiling me."

"Should I stop?"

"You know you don't have to, right?"

"Mari, I haven't done any of this because I have to, only because I want to." He led her into their luxury box.

"These seats are amazing." She squeezed his hand and scanned the horseshoe-shaped room.

Seating covered the first level, and five levels of seating surrounded the orchestra level.

He shifted the chairs, then sat down next to her. "Mari, I'm so glad it worked out that you could come with me tonight."

"You could've said something. I might've made my decision sooner."

"It had to be your decision."

"Do you know who has tickets for those other two seats?"

That lopsided grin appeared, and he pointed at the doorway.

In walked Roger with a stunning blonde on his arm. "Good evening. Mari, Travis, I'd like for you to meet my wife, Jessica."

Mari knew Roger was married but never expected that his wife looked like a model. "It's nice to meet you."

"Mari? So, are you the one who is helping out my Roger?"

"Yes." Mari appreciated the warm hand that pressed against the small of her back.

Jessica held out her hand. "It is so nice to meet you. And Travis, it's good to see you again."

"Likewise, Jessica." Travis shook her hand.

The conductor stepped onto the stage, and the foursome took their seats. After a brief introduction, the conductor lifted his hands, and music that pulled Mari to the edge of her chair and brought her close to tears filled the room, Travis holding her hand the entire time.

When it stopped for the intermission, her cheeks almost hurt from smiling. Travis escorted her into the lounge.

They sipped wine and mingled.

Lacking notoriety, Mari blended in as a way of life, but it felt like half the city recognized Travis. She didn't miss the double-takes followed by whispers, but true to his promise, he stayed by her side.

"Travis!" Tall, curvy, and younger than Mari, a brunette slipped her arm through his. "Aren't you just full of surprises. I didn't expect to see *you* with a date."

Mari felt his hand press into her back, but before he could say anything, she piped up. "Surprises are his specialty."

Travis moved away from the brunette. "This is Mari."

"Paula. So nice to meet you." The woman didn't come across as condescending or haughty. "Perhaps we'll see each other again sometime." But she was definitely fishing for information.

"I'm sure you will." He glanced at Mari. "You ready to go back in?"

"Whenever you are." She slipped her hand in his as Paula strolled away. "It's as if *everyone* knows who you are."

Concern etched in his brow. "I hope that's not a problem."

Mari shook her head. "Not at all."

⤸

The next morning, Mari laughed when Travis sent a picture of his tux with a message: *This is what I'm wearing. Trying to avoid the Twinkie thing.*

She tapped out a response, deleted it, and decided to call him.

"Hello." His greeting was tinged with laughter.

"My outfit looks just different enough that no one will call us Twinkies."

"Are you going to send me a picture?"

She did enjoy a good tease. "Nope."

"It'll be a long day." He sighed.

"I'm free for lunch."

"I'll be there at noon."

She stared at the red evening gown hanging on her closet door. Remi and Charlie had given advice based on pictures Mari sent from dressing rooms. When she sent the photo of the red one, the decision was unanimous. It won.

She opened a new message. *I so wish y'all were here. Remi, you could do my makeup. Charlie could give me an honest assessment of how I look.*

Charlie responded quickly. *You'll look fantastic!*

Remi chimed in: *We can video chat while you get all prettied up.*

I'd like that. I gotta go. Travis is picking me up for lunch, and I'm still in my jammies. Bye! Mari slid off the bed and flipped through the clothes in her closet.

After grabbing capris and a flowy tank, she pulled a sandal off the top shelf. The other had to be up there. Reaching up, flailing around for the other shoe, she smiled as a thought formed. *Things couldn't be any more perfect.* She winced when the other shoe fell off the shelf and hit her on the head.

Chapter Thirty-eight

Travis wasn't sure Mari could look any more beautiful than she had the night before, but she proved him wrong.

"You're stunning. I can't take my eyes off you." He patted her hand on his arm. "You look great in red."

"Thank you." She inhaled as the doors to the ballroom swung open. Once inside, she turned to face him. "This is amazing."

"I *really* like this dress." He trailed his fingers along her bare back. "Tonight, I want you to enjoy yourself."

Nearly backless, the dress hugged her in all the right places.

She took hold of his arm again. "I thought I was here to keep the sharks away, even fight them off if it comes to that."

"I might be the one having to fight people off."

Moving through the lavishly decorated ballroom, he watched as she took in every detail. Over and over, they were greeted by people they'd seen the night before, including Paula, and he introduced Mari to others he knew. The entire evening, she engaged with the waitstaff with the same smile and warmth as when she met Travis's acquaintances and friends.

She loosened her grip on his arm, hopefully relaxing. "Will Roger and Jessica be here?"

"He didn't mention it."

He touched her back, and a smile lit up her face. Every touch and glance from him garnered the same result. Travis marveled at how effortlessly their friendship had blossomed into so much more.

After sampling food and sipping champagne, he asked her to dance. With Mari smiling up at him, he knew what he wanted. He didn't yet know when to tell her. Hoping he'd be able to tell her everything soon, he waited. Offering her his heart but withholding information didn't feel right.

Living in the spotlight had been so much a part of his life. He stayed out of it when he could and used it to fund the charity when he couldn't. Mari handled the spotlight with grace and calm, as if she were born into the role.

He leaned down. "In the kitchen that morning, when you talked about chum in the water, I hoped that you'd be on my arm tonight. I want you to know that this evening has exceeded all my expectations."

She kissed his cheek. "You've exceeded all my expectations."

Travis bit his tongue. She needed more than three weeks before he sprang more on her.

As he led her off the dance floor, he slipped an arm around her waist. "I think I'm ready to head out, but I was thinking we could stop off for cheesecake on the way home. What do you think?"

"Like this?" Mari pointed at her dress.

He let his gaze sweep over the vivid red fabric. "Absolutely."

"Travis, just the man I needed to see." Kip Snyder, a straight-shooting businessman who enjoyed a good laugh, stuck out his hand to Mari. "Good evening."

"Kip, Good to see you. This is Mari Gonzales. Mari, Kip Snyder." Travis kept one arm around Mari.

"Well, Mari Gonzales, it's very nice to meet you." Kip glanced across the room. "I'm not the only one who was curious."

Travis liked Kip. "What can I do for you?"

"I do need to ask you about something, but after my wife commented a third time, wondering about your date, I decided to come introduce myself. Easiest way to get answers."

Mari grinned, clearly appreciating the forthcoming way Kip stated his motives.

"Can't argue with that." Travis trailed his fingers along her back, ready to be away from the crowded gala. "What's the other thing?"

The man waved at his wife across the room. "The golf tournament next year. Will your company be sponsoring again? I'm hoping I can count on you."

Travis tensed, not ready to make commitments for next year. "I'll have to get back to you."

The company had sponsored that tournament every year for almost a decade.

"Alrighty. I'm being beckoned, but it was very nice to meet you, Mari."

"You too, Kip." She waited until the man walked away before she stretched up and whispered, "I don't think I can learn anymore names tonight."

"With everyone you met tonight and knowing how some of them are … everyone in San Antonio will know that we're dating by mid-afternoon tomorrow."

She traced a finger along his jawline. "I'm not sure why I ever wanted to keep it a secret."

"It's definitely time to get out of here." Travis led her out of the hotel.

◡

Tucked into the same side of a booth, Mari fed him a bite of double chocolate cheesecake. "Maybe tomorrow we can spend a little time together before you have to leave town."

His flight left on Monday, and he'd have to wait until Saturday to see her again.

"Maybe we should spend another day by the pool. I haven't closed on the house yet."

She wiped chocolate off his lip. "I like that idea."

"Mari."

"Hmmm?"

"About my trip." He sipped his coffee, deciding what he wanted to say.

She scooped up another bite and offered it to him. "You leave on Monday. Land in Los Angeles, and then fly back here on Saturday. Fran only knows that you'll be out of the office."

"I'll miss you."

Hand on the side of his face, she pressed a quick kiss to his lips. He hadn't told her what business he had in California, and she hadn't asked. He hoped that meant she trusted him.

Chapter Thirty-nine

When Mari woke up to thunder and lightning, she wanted to cry. As her coffee brewed, she texted Travis: *Looks like our date has been rained out.*

His reply popped up a minute later: *I still want to see you. Come whenever.*

She smiled at her phone. Cautious didn't describe her behavior the last few weeks. She'd free-fallen into a new normal. *Putting shoes on. Will be over soon.*

Shoes are optional. He followed the text with a wink.

When she arrived, Mari waved at the neighbor before knocking, but the man just stared without acknowledging her.

Travis opened the door. Boxes, taped closed and labeled, lined one wall. A stack of flattened boxes leaned against the opposite wall.

"Excuse the mess. I've been packing." He glanced at her feet as he stepped aside.

She stopped inside the door and kicked off her shoes. "Better?"

He laughed. "I was going to suggest we go grab breakfast."

She slipped them back on. "Sounds good to me."

"I like this." He caught her around the waist.

"This?"

"Seeing you every day. It's not the same as when we were working together."

Unexpected but greatly desired, his kiss took her breath away. She slid her arms around his neck, happy to delay breakfast until lunchtime, or even dinner.

He pulled back, his eyes like blue flames. "This isn't about not being alone for me."

"Travis—"

"I just want you to know that. Because before, when I toasted to friends and not being alone—"

"Travis, I'm not here because my house is empty. I'm here because you are."

He pressed a kiss to her forehead. "Let's go get breakfast."

"Then, I can help you pack. If you want my help."

"Sounds like a plan. I'm not even sure where to start in the kitchen."

"We can stop and get packing paper while we're out. Looks like you have plenty of boxes."

After a quick breakfast, they tackled the task of packing the kitchen. Mari opened cabinets, seeing what was tucked away. The kitchen held more stuff than he'd be able to fit in the any of the condos he visited.

"Do you want to separate what you want to keep from what you want to give away?" She stacked packing paper on the island counter.

"No. Not for the kitchen. I'll decide when I unpack." He taped boxes together, getting them ready to fill.

She pulled a stack of plates out of the cabinet and set him to work wrapping and packing. While he did that, she packed cups and saucers.

She wanted to ask about his travel plans but didn't, determined to trust him. The longer she didn't know what he was up to, the harder it was.

"I know it's only been a few days, but how's it going with Roger?"

"Fine. He's just more … direct and curt than you are. I'm getting used to it."

He put down the plate he'd been wrapping and pulled her close. "It bothers me to think that you aren't happy. Maybe, if you'd let me, you could—"

She wasn't sure what he was about to offer but wasn't about to accept his help until they'd moved beyond the dating stage, if they moved beyond the dating stage. "I'm okay. Really."

Thrilled to spend time with him, she found herself less satisfied with kisses and togetherness, hoping for something more long-term and intimate. Were they on the same page?

By the time all the cabinets were empty, the sun had long set.

"I'll stop and get you disposable plates and utensils this week. Not that you can cook anything here now."

"I can't believe how much we got done."

"If you want—and I understand if you'd rather not—I can pack some while you're out of town."

He strolled away, leaving her standing in the kitchen, then stopped and turned around. "Can I show you something in here?"

She followed him into a massive office, which looked more like a library. Bookshelves lined one wall. Floor-to-ceiling windows over-looked the lawn and pool. "This room is amazing. It's like an art gallery and library combination." She gazed at the framed art hung around the room.

"I used to love this room, but this is where the incident happened."

"Oh, with Kate and that woman with the gun?"

He nodded as he dug around in a drawer. "Found it. I knew I had an extra key." Grinning, he dangled it in front of her. "This room will require a bit of time. I could hire movers to pack stuff, but …"

"I don't mind at all. Besides, you dug through my stuff. It's my turn." She giggled at his look of alarm and tucked the key behind her back. "Any other rooms?"

"Let me show you around upstairs. Just please don't hurt yourself trying to lift heavy boxes." He turned left at the top of the stairs. "Master is off to the right. I think I can manage to pack what's in there." Stopping, he pushed open a door. "This guest room doesn't have much in it, but I haven't packed anything in here. And the next room was the room we had set up for Claire—Kate."

Mari eased up beside him. "Did she ever see it?"

He shook his head.

"Does she know you're moving?"

"I should tell her."

"Why haven't you? Poor Marisa."

"Now you're making me feel bad. I just don't want Kate to feel like what happened to her is the reason I'm selling the house. It's only a small part."

"Then tell her that." Mari kissed his cheek. "I'll wait downstairs."

He shook his head as he pulled out his phone. "Stay. *Please.*"

She wrapped her arm around his waist and leaned into his back while he made his call. Snuggled against him, she listened as he explained to Kate he was selling the house and why.

"It's not just because of what happened. That's part of the reason, but I'm making some changes. … She's standing next to me. … I wanted you to know, but I also wondered if you wanted to see your room before we pack it up."

Mari hugged him tighter, both because he'd used the word *we* and because choosing to tell Kate about the room left him open to being hurt, not that she would intentionally wound him. Hearing him speak of changes only stirred Mari's curiosity, but knowing Kate associated any change with Mari affirmed her feelings about him and about their relationship. She was quite happy with the idea of *we*.

"You would?" His shoulders relaxed. "I'll be in California all this week for meetings. Sunday? … Great. And thank you. … Love you too, sweetheart." He ended the call and stuck the phone in his pocket.

"I'll leave her room untouched." Mari moved in front of him. "Want me to drive you to the airport?"

"I'd love that. Oh, I forgot to tell you. I chose a place."

"Was it one of the places I visited?"

"Yes. It was your favorite."

"I didn't tell you which one I liked best."

"You were so taken with the window seat, I wasn't sure if you noticed the hot tub on the balcony."

"I did not notice that."

"I get the keys on the first."

Mari scanned the calendar in her head. Her friends arrived the second. "I guess I know what I'm doing Thursday night, then."

She caught a glimpse of that lopsided grin before he kissed her again.

Mari navigated traffic, trying not to think about the approaching goodbye.

When she pulled up to the curb outside his departure gate, he leaned across the seat. "Don't get out. I'll call when I land, and anything you need this week, just call or text. If I'm in a meeting, I'll call as soon as I can."

"All right." She avoided his gaze.

His hand cupped her cheek. "Mari." His goodbye pressed to her lips.

"Hurry back"—she stole one last kiss—"to me."

He grabbed his bag and waved as he walked through the sliding doors. Mari didn't linger. After pulling away from the curb, she dialed Charlie on speaker and headed to the office.

"Hi, Mari. Don't usually hear from you this early."

"Remi probably isn't up yet. I need to talk."

"Everything okay?" Concern weighed in her voice.

Mari laughed at herself. "Yes. I just dropped off Travis at the airport. He'll be in Los Angeles all week."

"What takes him out that way?"

"He didn't say."

Charlie hesitated. "Is that unusual?"

Mari sighed. "Very. I booked the flights. He just didn't say what it was about, which is unusual—very unusual."

"But?"

"He's given me no reason not to trust him. I'm trying to remember that."

"What will you do all week? Sounds like you two have been seeing a lot of each other."

"If Remi had said that, the question would've meant something entirely different."

Charlie laughed. "I know you, Mari. But don't avoid my question."

"Working, and in the evenings, I'll be at Travis's, packing. He's getting ready to move. You should see the place he's moving into. It's amazing."

"What are you not telling me?"

Mari wasn't ready to say it out loud. "Same thing I'm not telling him, but I will, when the time is right. It's just—and please don't repeat this—he's holding back about something, and it's needling me. I need to know he feels the same way."

"Mari, I think he does."

"What happened to proceed with caution?"

"It's a bit late for that, I think." Charlie laughed.

"Maybe. I just pulled into the parking lot. Thanks for keeping me company this morning and cheering me up."

"Anytime. Call Remi. She'll want to be in on the news. Maybe she'll meet up with him while he's in town."

"That's a scary thought." Mari giggled, trying to imagine Travis at lunch with Remi, being sized up as a character. "I might suggest it to him. Bye."

Later than normal, she arrived at an already busy office.

Roger poked his head into her office as she sat down at her desk. "Oh, hi. I wondered where you were."

"I'm sorry I'm a few minutes late. I dropped Travis at the airport."

Roger dropped papers onto her desk. "If you could go over these and get them back to me before lunch, that'd be great." He left without another word.

Mari set to work, glad to be busy. She jumped when her phone buzzed a half hour later.

Mr. Bentley hasn't shown up. Fran's text surprised Mari.

Mari picked up the phone. "Hello, Fran. He's out of the office. All week."

"Oh. That's why his calendar is greyed out, and I can't add any meetings."

"Yes. That's why."

"So, I should just work on the stuff we talked about last week?"

"Yes. It's usually pretty quiet when he's out."

"Thanks, Mari."

She laid her phone down, and it buzzed again. This time it wasn't Fran.

About to board. Intentional in all that he did, with three little words, Travis let Mari know she was on his mind.

I miss you already. Have a safe flight. She wasn't sure when caution up and disappeared, but it was entirely possible that it evaporated that day by the pool, like those water droplets in the summer heat.

〜

Mari dialed Remi and taped a box together while waiting for her to answer.

"Hello." Remi sounded out of breath.

"It's me."

"How's the hottie?"

Mari shook her head. "Travis is in LA this week."

"Really? Give him my number. Maybe we can meet. That's okay with you, isn't it?"

"Yes, Remi."

"What are you doing since your boyfriend is out of town?"

"Packing up Travis's guest room."

"You're in his house? Alone?"

"His guest room is in his house, and he's in LA, so yeah."

"What's his bedroom like? Have you poked through his drawers?" Remi giggled. "Get it, drawers?"

"I get it, Remi. And no, I haven't. That feels a bit intrusive."

"True, but still. What a wasted opportunity. Why is he in LA?"

"I don't know. Business of some kind."

"Secret meetings? I'd definitely be snooping."

"How's the book coming?" Mari wanted to move on to another topic.

Remi sighed. "Behind schedule. Having people fall in love should be easy, but I need them to argue. Haven't yet figured out the reason."

"I'm all ears if you want to bounce ideas."

"Maybe he is taking a trip somewhere and won't tell her where or why."

"What an original idea! How would that start an argument?"

"She'd doubt him, question what he was up to. Wouldn't she?"

"Possibly." Mari couldn't call the idea silly.

"I could make it a love triangle, and then she'd be wondering if he chose the other woman."

"Really, Remi?"

"I just need a wisp of inspiration. Maybe I'll go hang out in a florist shop and ask guys why they are buying flowers."

"You'd get several argument ideas from that."

"I gotta go. My date is here." Remi hadn't said anything about dating.

"A date? Message me later."

"Maybe!" She laughed as she ended the call.

Mari spent the rest of the evening packing the guest room. By the end of the night, the entire room was boxed up. She labeled the boxes but left them for Travis to carry down the stairs.

As she locked the front door, a man shouted. "That's not your house."

"Hello. I'm helping Travis while he's out of town." Mari recognized the neighbor from the other day.

"Sounds fishy to me. Travis didn't say anything about that." He waved his cane, emphasizing his point.

"I'm Mari." She stuck out her hand. "I'm helping him get ready for the move."

He ignored her hand. "I saw the sign. Sad to see him go." He pointed the cane at her. "You wait there, Mari—if that's your real name. I'm going to call him."

Mari whipped her phone out of her pocket and shot off a text to Travis: *Please answer your phone. The neighbor has me pegged as a prowler or worse.*

The man put the phone on speaker and held it out, almost as if he anticipated hearing Travis deny any knowledge of her. "Travis, this is Avery Duncan. I found a woman leaving your house."

"You must have met Mari, my girlfriend." Travis seemed to be enjoying the conversation.

The man stared. "Describe her."

She resisted the urge to roll her eyes. The neighbor was unbelievable.

Travis chuckled before responding. "Brown hair, beautiful, is holding keys to my house. She may or may not be wearing shoes."

"She has shoes on." Mr. Duncan looked a bit embarrassed. "Sorry to bother you."

Travis behaved like a gentleman. "Thanks for checking, Avery. Have a nice evening. I expect you'll see her at my place several nights this week."

"Goodnight." Mr. Duncan nodded, mumbling as he marched away, his cane more of an accessory than a need.

She texted: *Thank you.*

The kissing emoji was not what she expected in response, but it put a smile on her face.

She sent another message: *Remi wants to meet up while you're in town if you have the time or inclination.*

That could be interesting. Send me her number. Travis was a brave man.

Mari climbed into her car. *Guest room is all packed. Left the boxes in there, but they are labeled.*

Thank you. Call me when you get home?

I will. She dropped the phone and pulled out of the driveway.

Chapter Forty

After paying the cabbie, Travis stepped into the store.

"May I help you?" A young woman in a tailored dress walked around the counter.

He nodded, excitement making it hard to speak. "I've been working with Zelenka. She designed a ring for me, and I'm here to pick it up."

"What's the name?"

"Bentley. Travis Bentley."

"Let me get her." The woman picked up the phone, punched a few numbers, and whispered into the receiver. After putting the phone down, she smiled. "She'll be here in a moment."

Travis couldn't wait to see the ring.

"Mr. Bentley!" Another woman, older, with hair the color of fresh winter snow kissed him on each cheek. "I know you will love the final result." She motioned toward the counter.

"I'm excited to see it."

From somewhere behind the counter, she pulled out a small box and pushed it toward Travis. "Have a look."

He lifted the lid. The platinum ring looked even more beautiful than the sketches and photos he'd seen. "You did a great job."

"I think she will love it."

"I hope so." He slipped the platinum ring out of the box. The flawless princess cut diamond was surrounded by a halo of smaller diamonds. The ring's twisted split shank was also set with diamonds. "And I can get a matching eternity ring for a wedding band?"

"Absolutely."

"Thank you." Travis made his purchase and glanced at the time.

He had just enough time to get across town in time for his meeting, and he'd spend the rest of the afternoon answering questions and hoping the men on the other side of the table liked the answers.

As for the ring, it would accompany him everywhere until he made it home.

He pulled out his phone and texted Mari: *Miss you.* He followed that with a kissing emoji. With the little box in his pocket, he thought of her often.

⌒

That night, he couldn't wait to talk to her. Their late-night calls were the highlight of his day.

"Hi." Travis tried not to let his exhaustion show in his voice.

Mari didn't miss it. "You sound worn out."

"I'll be okay." He stifled a yawn. "I have a huge favor to ask of you."

"What do you need?"

"You met Gram at the wedding. She's the friend of my mom's that still lives in Schatzenburg."

"I remember. Her grandson is Becca's husband?"

"Yes. She wants to take you to lunch."

Mari was quiet for a few seconds. "Okay. When?"

"Tomorrow." He needed to give Mari at least a little warning. "She says unexpected things sometimes, so I'm—"

"Consider me warned. This should be interesting."

"I'm having lunch with Remi tomorrow, so we can swap stories." He leaned back on the bed.

"What prompted this lunch?"

He hoped she caught his attempt at humor. "You gave me Remi's number and said she wanted me to call her."

"Travis."

"I talk to Gram regularly. She was in many ways like a second mother, a close aunt, especially after Mom died and all that happened after. Your name came up in our conversation. She remembers you from the wedding and wants to have lunch." He couldn't imagine Gram not loving Mari.

"Does she know we are dating?"

"Yes. Mr. Duncan give you any trouble tonight?"

"Walked right by without a word." Mari yawned.

Travis yawned in response. "I should let you sleep. Hearing your voice is a nice way to end my day."

"Goodnight." Mari ended the call.

Travis closed his eyes, imagining the look on Mari's face when she saw the ring.

Chapter Forty-one

Mari paced in the downstairs lobby, nervous about lunch. Two minutes before noon, the doors opened and in stepped Gram. Dressed in slacks, a pale blue twinset, and the requisite pearls, she seemed much younger than her age. Mari didn't know exactly what it was, but based on what she'd been able to piece together, the woman had to be approaching ninety. As an interrogator, she was frightening.

"Hello, Mari. Thank you so much for accepting my invitation." Gram smoothed the hairs that had slipped out of her bun.

Mari breathed in deep and clutched her purse. "It was a surprise, but I'm looking forward to it." *Surprise? That might not have been the best choice of word.* Mari's nervousness showed, and that bothered her.

Taller than Mari, Gram made eye contact. "Travis is important to me. Since you are important to him, I want to know you as well."

Mari hoped she'd be able to eat and that the butterflies in her stomach were on board with that plan. "Shall we go?"

"I hope you don't mind my candor."

"Not at all. I appreciate it." The unstated truth knotted in Mari's stomach. If Gram didn't like her, that could change things. The thought bothered Mari.

Gram was silent while Mari drove. Rather than filling the quiet, Mari focused on the road, concentrating on each breath. *Am I what she expected? Why am I so nervous?*

At the restaurant, once they settled at their table, Gram eyed Mari over the tops of her readers. "How long have you known him?"

Small talk wasn't on the menu with Gram. Mari guessed that chitchat and talking about the weather wouldn't make the questions any less awkward.

"Seven years." Mari squinted at the menu, then pulled the readers off the top of her head. Able to see, she scanned the menu, her mind on the conversation more than the menu choices.

Gram closed her menu and set it aside. "You work together?"

Mari glanced up, preparing herself for disapproval. "We did. I was his personal assistant."

"So, you worked *closely* together?"

Gram's questions pulled Mari down a blind path. Answering honestly, she didn't know what to expect next. "Yes."

Flashes of Travis unbuttoning his shirt were not welcome but showed up nonetheless.

Eyes on the menu, Gram kept an even tone. "Good-looking, he has always been one that ladies chase after. Owning a company makes him even more of a target. Now that Emma is gone, I'd hate to see someone try to take advantage of that."

Mari felt the stab, intended or otherwise. Words on the menu blurred as her thoughts spiraled. *How do I respond to that?*

"What you said is true. Good-looking and, by all appearances, wealthy, he does get quite a bit of attention from the ladies, though I'm not sure he always notices. Travis is a remarkable man, and I would *never* do anything to intentionally hurt him or take advantage of him." She glanced around, wishing the waiter would bring the drinks. Sipping tea would give her something to do while being grilled. She closed her menu and dropped her hands into her lap. Clenching her fists, she willed her heartbeat to slow down.

"I make you nervous?" Gram seemed to enjoy her role. The CIA could've used her in the field.

"I shouldn't be, but you do."

"Why is that?"

Mari crossed her arms. "Travis thinks the world of you. Your opinion is important to him."

"You are important to him." Gram dropped bold statements as fact, statements that Mari hoped were true.

What has Travis said to her?

She fought the urge to pick up the menu again, something to use as a shield. "It would be better if those of us that are important to him all liked each other. That's what I think."

"He's different now." Gram straightened her silverware.

Mari appreciated that they'd moved on, but her thoughts raced, trying to understand the meaning behind Gram's words. "You mean since Kate returned?"

Gram grinned, her brown eyes twinkling in a way that made Mari curious. "I like you, Mari. Let's order some food."

On cue, the waiter set drinks on the table and asked what they wanted to order, leaving Mari to wonder what magical powers Gram possessed that Travis failed to mention. Somehow, Mari had passed a hurdle, but she wasn't sure what about her last answer accomplished that.

After ordering, she couldn't let it go. "What about my answer swayed you?" Being content with the fact that she was liked would've been the better option, but she needed to know.

The twinkle returned. "You didn't assume I meant it was because of you, *and* you are right. He has changed since Kate's return. It shows me that you notice him, the little things." Gram sipped her tea. "At the wedding, I noticed you. You care for him."

"I do." Mari thought back to the day of the wedding, wondering what else had been noticed.

Caught up in the emotion of that day, Mari hadn't cared what others thought. Well, she cared, but short of any awkwardness, she simply enjoyed being by his side, chatting with his family and friends. Gram had sat on the other side of him at the table.

"What do you want, Mari?"

A lump formed in Mari's throat. Breathing required focus. Gram wasn't asking about Thai food. The question was blatantly about intentions.

Mari couldn't say what she hadn't even admitted to Travis; what she'd barely said to herself, though the thought was never far away. "I want the waiter to show up on cue when I need him."

Gram reached across the table. "I'm sorry for getting ahead of you. We should have lunch again in a few weeks." The woman must've been a nightmare on the road. She changed direction faster than lightning.

"What do you mean?" Mari hadn't followed her jump in logic.

"I've made assumptions based on our conversation. I was perhaps a bit hasty, and I apologize." Without any hint of accusation, Gram exuded a warmth that eased the tension. A little.

Risking embarrassment, Mari responded with what she hoped would be taken as humor. "So, you don't like me?"

"On the contrary. I like you even more. Let's eat." Gram winked.

The waiter appeared with plates of food, and Mari wondered what parts of the conversations she'd share with Travis over the phone or at all. Hopefully his lunch with Remi was entertaining. One thing Mari had learned—she wanted Gram's approval. It mattered. But even being at lunch with Gram mattered.

"May I call you Gram?" Mari poked at her food.

"Please."

"I want you to know how much I appreciate you inviting me to lunch, Gram."

A smile was the only answer.

Chapter Forty-two

Travis stood as Remi approached the table. "Good to see you again."

She hugged him. "I wasn't sure you'd call."

"Why? Because I'm afraid that you'll do nothing but grill me over lunch?"

"Exactly. I'll let you decide what you want to order before I start the questioning."

He had no idea what to expect in the way of questions. "How's your book coming along?"

"I finished. Seeing you and Mari was the final inspiration I needed. Now I'm just waiting on the cover designer."

"So glad we could be helpful."

"Oh, you were. I've already started the next book. It's the first of a series called Texas Billionaires."

He only shook his head. Trying to convince her he wasn't in that economic bracket didn't seem worth his time.

The waiter took their order, and Remi raised her eyebrows. The questions were about to start.

"Mari deserves the best. You better not break her heart."

He'd expected a question, not that. "She does deserve the best. I would never hurt her, not intentionally."

Remi sipped her strawberry lemonade. "She doesn't need to be rescued from loneliness, you know."

"She does not. I'm hoping she likes having me around."

"Don't tell her I said so—and she hasn't *said* this—but I think she loves you." She eyed him over the rim of her glass.

Travis fought the urge to reach into his pocket, just to feel the small box. "What makes you think that?" Careful with his response, he didn't want to give away too much with his reaction.

"Intuition. You going to marry her?"

"Have you considered moving to Texas? It would help your research on Texas Billionaires."

"Know any?"

"One or two."

"Would you introduce me?"

"Possibly."

"You trying to distract me from my questions?"

"Yes." Travis wondered how Mari's lunch with Gram fared, and if Mari was back at the office.

"Because you are so adorable and honest, I'll let that slide." Remi slid a business card across the table. "This jeweler in town has a wonderful designer. Here's her card. If you were in the market for jewelry of any sort, I'd recommend this place."

He accepted the card with Zelenka's name on it. "I'll keep that in mind, if I find myself in need of jewelry of any sort."

"You are impossibly hard to read."

The waiter set plates on the table.

"Let's eat." Travis would leave an extra tip for the waiter's impeccable timing.

⌇

Back at the hotel, hoping Mari wasn't working late, he called her. "Hello, beautiful."

"Travis." She almost sighed his name.

"I couldn't wait any longer. I'm almost afraid to ask how it went. Are you home from work?"

"I just pulled in your driveway. Lunch was interesting. Gram said that she likes me, so that's good. There were questions. She wants to have lunch again in a few weeks."

"Oh, good. I'm so glad. Have you ever heard Kate tell the story of when she first met Gram?"

"No. But I'm guessing it's entertaining."

"The way Kate tells it, Gram had her engaged to Alex before Kate knew her true identity." He chuckled. "And Gram wasn't too far off. She likes to instigate when she sees romantic potential."

"Is that what we have? Romantic potential?" Mari's question surprised him.

Travis missed her more every day that he was away. "I wish we were snuggled next to each other right now. As for what we have? I'd say romantic potential was sometime back in June, maybe even May. Am I wrong?"

"I miss you." Mari made him want to hop on a plane. "Tell me about Remi."

"She's nutty and crazy, and I got grilled."

"I'm sorry." Mari giggled. "But you had a nice time?"

"I did. And I think I passed. If you hear differently, let me know."

"She's been messaging me hearts on and off all afternoon. I think you scored an A plus."

"Don't pack boxes tonight. Go home. Read. Maybe have a piece of cheesecake. There is some in my freezer. I stocked up for you."

"Make that an A plus plus."

"Text me when you get home or call if you want to chat more."
He grinned as he heard the freezer open.
"I will."

Chapter Forty-three

Mari woke up early, prepped dinner, and changed three times. Wearing capris and a t-shirt, she tucked the premixed margarita in the refrigerator, so it would be chilled by that evening.

Three hours. She had three hours before she needed to leave. Grabbing keys, she ran out to the car. Packing would hopefully be enough of a distraction. There wasn't much left to pack in that office.

Back at Travis's, she waved at Mr. Duncan, who stood appraising his lawn. He nodded in response. By the time he graduated to greeting her, Travis would be ready to move out.

Inside, she kicked off her shoes and headed to the office. The few books left on the shelves fit into a box. Mari moved onto the desk. She assembled file boxes and arranged the files in the same order they'd been in the drawer. Several boxes later, the file drawers and the file cabinet were empty.

She moved back to the desk and opened the center drawer, ready to pack pens and other office supplies. A letter with her name scrawled on the front stopped her short. She'd opened every other drawer, just not that one. Hand shaking, she picked up the letter. *Did he intend for me to read it? Or had he forgotten it was here?*

She dropped back into the chair, staring at the envelope.

If it was important, it never would have been tucked away unseen in a drawer.

Or would it?

She had no idea what could be inside. She wouldn't know unless she opened it, but maybe he never intended for her to open it.

Her phone rang, pulling her attention away from the dilemma. Carlos was calling.

"Hi, sweetheart. How are you?"

"Doing great. You and Travis want to come see the place tomorrow?"

She loved that he invited Travis also. "I think that would work. Can I get back to you? I'm picking him up at the airport in—I'm leaving to go get him now."

"Just let me know. If not, next weekend works." He inhaled. "How are things, you know, with him? Still good?"

"Yes. He's been out of town this week." She prayed Carlos wouldn't make her explain that she had no idea why.

"I like him, Mom. Seems like he treats you right."

"He buys me cheesecake. I think he's a keeper."

Carlos laughed. "I'll let you go, so you can drive. Love you."

"Love you too. I'll text you about tomorrow." Mari slid the letter in her pocket and ran out the door, wondering what time Kate planned to come see the room. Even though Mari really wanted to see Carlos and his new place, allowing Travis that time with Kate ranked a higher priority, and Mari wanted to be there.

At the airport, she parked in the short-term lot. Welcoming him back, while trying not to block traffic wasn't how she pictured his return. After getting out of the car, she slid the letter into her purse. She'd think about it later. Maybe he'd bring it up.

Cool air greeted her as the doors slid open. She found a spot near the wall in sight of the ramp into baggage claim. She hadn't told him that she'd be waiting inside.

He texted: *Just landed. Will pick up bags then meet you by the curb. I'll text again when I'm headed outside.*

Her heart thudded with anticipation. *Can't wait to see you.*

Passengers trickled in a few at a time, then more followed. Mari scanned the throng that made their way into baggage claim. Travis came into view. Worn and tired, he trudged down the ramp. She waited until he drew closer before calling out to him, hoping he'd look her way.

He glanced up, and when he spotted her, a wide smile cut across his weary features. He closed the distance quickly and shifted the laptop bag on his shoulder as he hurried up to her.

"Travis." That was all she managed to say.

Without a word, he folded her into his arms and kissed her, greeting her in a way that made people stop and stare.

Mari ignored the audience. She had what she wanted. "You're home."

"I am now." He snuck another kiss. "There is so much I want to tell you—about my trip—and other things, but I can't just yet."

Mari laid her hand on his cheek. "Tell me when you're ready."

If the letter was old or held any hint that he'd ever felt differently than how they were together in that moment, she wasn't sure she ever wanted to read it. She should never have taken it. If he wanted her to read it, he'd have given it to her. She needed to figure out a way to put it back or give it back, but later.

He clutched her hand as bags started down the carousel. "I missed you."

"You passed with flying colors. Remi asked if you had a twin."

Travis raised an eyebrow.

Mari knew enough of Travis's life story to know that he had a brother, now deceased, who was nothing like Travis.

Mari kissed his hand. "I assured her that you are one of a kind. Let me hold that bag for you."

He handed it to her. "Gram called me. Gushing might be the word I'd use for how she talked about you."

"I was so nervous."

"Of Gram?"

"Have you *met* her, Travis? The woman looks into your soul and asks questions like '*What do you want?*' How am I supposed to answer that?"

His bag passed him by as he turned around and stared. "What did you say?"

"I didn't." Baggage claim was not where she wanted to have that conversation. "That's your bag, isn't it?"

He grabbed his bag and clutched her hand as they strolled to her car. "Dinner plans tonight?"

"I figured we'd eat at my house. Dinner's prepped, waiting to be cooked." She loved how he read her cues and changed topics without question.

"Mind stopping by my house? I'll drop off my bags."

"Sure." She unlocked the car and dangled the keys in front of him. "I'm going to let you drive."

He reached for the keys. "I can do that."

While he loaded his bags, she tossed her purse into the car, spilling its contents. After shoving in the makeup bag, wallet, and other odd and ends, she buckled into the seat.

Before backing out of the space, he leaned across and unbuckled her seatbelt. Hand on her neck, he pressed his mouth to hers. Feeling like a love-starved teenager, she parted her lips, and he deepened their kiss.

When he pulled back, she grabbed his shirt, tugging him close for another kiss. "Travis."

His name escaped as a breath.

Even as worn as he seemed, he lit up. "I know. Me too."

They'd both hinted at so much but said little. Suspended in a free-falling position, Mari deemed the waiting important. All that she wanted to say, all she expected him to say needed to wait. On what, she wasn't sure. But just like he'd waited on her cue to be kissed, she'd wait on him. The trip to California fit in somehow. Not knowing was frustrating, but trusting him was easy. Most of the time.

"Carlos wants us to come visit tomorrow. I know Kate is coming. If we can't make both work, we can go see him next weekend."

"I'm so sorry. I forgot to tell you what we planned." He shot Mari an apologetic look. "They are coming to the house about ten thirty, then we were going to grab lunch. I expected you'd be there."

"I'll be there. So then would tomorrow evening work?"

"Absolutely. Tell Carlos we'll see his place, then take him to dinner."

Mari rubbed his arm. "Thank you."

He nodded.

Back at her house, after dinner, they curled up on Mari's couch, sipped margaritas and, watched Netflix. Snuggled next to him, she sighed. *This is what I want.*

Chapter Forty-four

Travis flipped on the office light, thankful and amazed at all Mari had done while he was gone. In just over two weeks, he'd be moving out, and so much was already packed. It eased his stress.

When he spotted the box labeled *Desk —Top Drawer*, he remembered what he'd left in the drawer. She had to have seen it. He tore open the box and rummaged through it, confirming what he thought might be true. She'd found it and taken it.

In the car, when she'd sighed his name, had he misunderstood? Why hadn't she said anything?

Travis sat the little box in the center of the empty desk, questioning everything. He'd spent years being guarded; being betrayed by his brother had only made it worse. Although Travis had tried to be different after Kate's return and succeeded somewhat, the idea that he'd misjudged Mari's feelings fueled that guardedness faster than he could think of any other reason she wouldn't have said anything about the note.

She didn't feel the same way. That would explain why she

didn't bring it up. He had no doubt that she liked him, but perhaps she wasn't ready for more than that.

Since she'd read the note, she knew how he felt. When she felt the same way, she'd bring it up. Until then, he'd try not to act like he was in love, if that was even possible.

❧

Monday, he didn't see Mari at all. When he'd popped into her office to say hi, it was empty. He texted her as he left the office: *Dinner?*

Working late. Can I have a raincheck? She followed her message with a sad face.

Just say when. He drove home, hating that she worked for someone else.

Travis picked up take-out on the way home, and after eating, he packed up the other bedroom, since Kate had been over to see it. He hadn't noticed any shift in Mari's behavior when Kate was around or when Travis and Mari had driven to see Carlos. She'd been just like she was at the airport, but he could feel the shift in himself.

Later than normal, he picked up the phone and called Mari. "Hey, hope you aren't still at work."

"I got home about an hour ago. I'm sorry I didn't call. I ate a slice of cheesecake and took a hot bath."

He bit his tongue, choosing not to say anything about Roger. "Thanks for everything last week. You even managed to get my desk packed." He hoped his mention of the desk would spark a conversation about its contents.

"There's one or two drawers with office supplies that I didn't get to. On the left, the little drawers."

"I took care of that." He listened for signs of a reaction. "Any trouble with anything?"

"Not at all." Mari wasn't making it easy. "I hate to end our call early, but I'm so tired. See you tomorrow?"

He didn't know what to make of her silence on the subject. "I'll make a point of it."

During the next few days, between her working long hours and his schedule, they managed to meet for dinner once. Studying her every word and glance, he didn't notice a difference, but with each passing day that she didn't bring up the note, his walls went up.

Hurt and disappointment surrounded him. How could he have been wrong?

He tucked the little box in a drawer, thinking he wouldn't need it, after all.

Chapter Forty-five

Digging through her purse in search of a much-needed Tylenol, Mari jumped when a hand touched her shoulder. She snapped her purse closed and whipped around. "Hi. It's you. Didn't hear you come in."

After Travis had mentioned the desk, she'd looked for the letter, planning to give it back, but it wasn't in her purse. She'd lost it, and she still didn't know what was inside, which pricked her with guilt each time she saw him.

The sparkle washed out of Travis's blue eyes. "Everything okay?"

"Horrible headache. It's been a day." She wanted to bury her face in the curve of his neck, but since they avoided blatant displays of affection at office, she didn't.

"Anything I can do?"

"Not unless you have pain meds squirreled away in your office."

"I think I do."

That was when Mari noticed the first shift. Instead of extending a hand or waiting to walk next to her, he led the way to his office, paces ahead of her.

She waited until they were alone behind closed doors. "Travis, is anything wrong?"

He shook his head without turning around and searched through a desk drawer. "Here you go. Hope you feel better." He gave her a peck on the cheek. "I can't do dinner tonight, but maybe we can sneak away for lunch tomorrow."

"Okay." She observed the strain in his shoulders, the tightness of his muscles.

Controlled and intentional, he didn't intend to share whatever bothered him.

Mari went back to her office wondering what had changed.

Telling herself that all the long hours she'd worked were clouding her judgment, she tried to remain positive.

Lunch didn't happen on Friday because Roger thought he could plan meetings whenever he wanted and asked Mari at the last minute if she'd sit in. When she'd texted Travis the news, he'd only replied: *Okay.*

Saturday morning, she sipped coffee, trying to decide whether to call him—it was rare that they didn't have plans for the weekend—or wait for him to call her. She had no interest in playing hard to get, so she dialed his number.

"Hello?" Background noise made it hard to hear Travis.

"Hi. I hadn't heard from you. What are you doing this morning?"

"I'm at the golf place with a couple friends. Mind if I call you tonight?" He made it clear they wouldn't be seeing each other.

"Sure." She hung up before he got any sense of her hurt.

Blaring music, Mari grabbed a bucket and rubber gloves. Starting in the pantry, she scrubbed anything that wasn't moving.

Wentworth rubbed against her leg, somewhat confused by her frantic cleaning.

"Oh, Wentworth. I'm not sure this will work out like I hoped."
The cat meowed in response.

"I know you liked him, too. Maybe there's nothing wrong. Maybe working for Roger is making me cranky and overly sensitive."

She didn't think that was true, but Travis had never given any hint of being the kind of guy that would toy with her heart. She took a deep breath and continued her cleaning, determined to give him the benefit of the doubt.

Over the next few days, she watched for differences. Travis had pulled back. No one else at the office would've seen it, but Mari noticed. When he held her hand, his thumb didn't caress her skin. When he smiled, it didn't reach his eyes.

When she tried to guess at what was wrong, she always landed at the same conclusion. His feelings had changed, and he wasn't sure how to end it.

No matter how hard she tried to shake that thought, she couldn't. It stood front and center in her brain every minute she spent with Travis, which were fewer than the weeks before his trip.

⌒

Mari curled up at the end of the sofa with the laptop open. Almost a week had gone by since Mari had promised to give Travis the benefit of the doubt. He'd made a point to stop in her office during the week, but she rarely had time to chat. At night, they still chatted, but the conversations felt stilted and strained.

When they'd gotten together for dinner, he'd kissed her and said all the right things, but she felt the separation, the wall.

The thought that he wanted to end it filled her head, making it nearly impossible to interpret his actions without bias.

She stared at the computer screen and opened a new message: *Something is wrong. I'm not sure what. The day I picked him up from the airport, I thought we—things were so good. But he's changed. I'm not sure if it's something I did. I need to talk to him but can't make myself bring it up. When I do, things will change. I know they will.*

Before hitting send, Mari read over her note. Finger poised over the delete key, she forced herself to hit send.

Talk to him! Charlie lived for pragmatism.

Remi answered as any romance author would: *Romances must have a happy ending.*

Not sure when I'll get a chance, but I'll talk to him. I will. I just need to find my nerve. Mari snapped the laptop closed after sending the message. She also needed to find the nerve to return the note she should never have taken, but she needed to find the note first. Maybe she could go to his house and tuck it into one of the boxes in the office without him noticing.

She wanted to be wrong about the wall. She wanted the same Travis that kissed her at the airport to show up to work on Monday. She wanted to be excited about Thursday and celebrating his new place. She wanted a lot of things, but one person held the spot at the top of the list.

⤾

After two weeks of his guarded behavior, Mari expected Travis to end the relationship. He hadn't mentioned the hot tub night, but neither had he canceled their plans.

She buried herself in work and prayed she could make it through the day without crying. If he didn't bring up their plans for the evening, she'd leave a little early—if she could sneak away without Roger noticing—and pick up cheesecake and wine on the way home.

She started when Travis walked into her office.

He jingled keys. "All the paperwork is signed. The place is mine."

"Congratulations." She wanted to be excited but worried that the day wouldn't end well. Breaking up in the beautiful condo would somehow feel like a double sting.

Travis leaned on her desk. "We still on for tonight?"

"Yes. What should I bring?"

"Your suit and two towels." He grinned, a hint of sparkle in his blue eyes. "The place is empty. It'll just be us and the hot tub."

She jumped up and closed her office door. "Travis, are we okay?" At the office wasn't where she wanted to have the conversation, especially in the middle of the workday, but the question begged to be asked. "I'm worried that—"

His kiss cut her off. "Tonight. Let's talk tonight."

She wrapped her arms around his neck, nodding into his shoulder.

He pressed his lips to her temple, then stepped away. "I need to run. I'll pick you up at six."

The rest of the afternoon was a waste. Mari accomplished nothing, unless worrying counted as something.

Chapter Forty-six

Travis buckled his seat belt before pulling away from the curb. "I said it'd be just the hot tub and us, but I brought wine too."

"Need me to run in and get glasses?"

"I made sure to grab some." He shifted gears before clasping her hand.

Hints of the Mari that kissed him at the airport offered a glimmer of hope.

At the condo, he unlocked the front door, letting it swing open for her to enter. "Still like it?"

"I love this place." She headed straight for the wall of windows. Staring out at the Hill Country, she smiled as he stepped up behind her.

He dropped a kiss on the curve of her neck. "Wait right here. I'll get the hot tub heating." He'd been looking forward to spending time with her all week.

He still wondered why she hadn't mentioned the note, but he also felt guilty that Roger demanded so much of her time.

As he walked away, he glanced back. Mari stared after him, her brow furrowed.

After attending to the hot tub, he uncorked the wine. "It shouldn't take long to warm up."

She rolled her shoulders, the tightness evident from across the room. Facing the window, she kept her back to him.

When he wrapped his arms around her, she stepped away from him. Travis's heart sank. That wasn't like her at all.

"Let's talk now." She took a deep breath and glanced at the door.

"We can. You asked if we were okay." He handed her a glass of wine.

"You just—it seems like you've been more—I don't know— guarded."

He stared at the hardwood floor, deciding what to say, how much to admit. He didn't want her to feel cornered into loving him. "You aren't imagining that."

Mari's lip quivered.

She made her way to the counter. After setting her glass down, she turned and faced him. "I'm sorry." Darting across the room, she grabbed her purse, stopping only to slide her flipflop back on that had flown off in her haste to get out of the room.

"Mari? Where are you going? Wait!" Travis's pulse beat on his eardrums.

She ignored his pleas.

He chased her down the stairs. "Please talk to me." His world was collapsing, and he didn't know why.

She stood on the sidewalk, blinking away tears. "Please take me home."

Travis wasn't going to tell her no. "I'll get my keys."

Silent, he drove to her house. The short drive seemed like a cross-country trek. When he parked by the curb, he clasped her hand. "Please talk to me."

She shook her head. "I'm not mad at you, but I can't. It's hard enough just—" Swinging open the car door, she ran to her house, leaving her flipflops halfway up the walk.

He ran toward her but stopped.

She slammed the door, but it swung back open just enough for him to see her run up the stairs.

Travis stood on the walkway, trying to make sense of what happened. He anticipated the possibility that the conversation about the note would be uncomfortable and maybe awkward, but he hadn't expected her to run out on him. It didn't make sense.

As he wallowed in heartache, Wentworth strolled out the open front door, flicking his tail.

"You aren't supposed to be outside, sir." Travis hurried up the walk.

The cat acted as if he hadn't heard but stayed just out of Travis's reach. He darted under bushes, slinking along the edge of the house.

"Come here. It's really not a good time for this, Wentworth." Travis raked his fingers through his hair.

Dropping to his hands and knees, he reached under the bushes. Wentworth moved away.

Someone was going to see Travis crawling around in the bushes and call the police. *That wouldn't be awkward at all.*

Wet food might lure that cat back into the house, but leaving him risked losing sight of him.

Travis dropped Mari's shoes inside and sat on the front step. He wanted to chase Mari up the stairs and beg her to talk to him. Instead, he was chasing a stupid cat. It was just as well. The letter was gone, and she hadn't mentioned it. In the car, she'd said enough for him to piece together her feelings.

She didn't feel the same way, and it was too hard to tell him.

Face buried in his hands, he pictured the ring. In love, he'd raced ahead, thinking she felt what he felt. If he'd taken things slower, would she still be in his arms, smiling up at him?

Fur brushed against his hands, and Travis grabbed the wayward cat.

"Time for you to go inside. Look after her for me, okay?" Talking to a cat was stupid, but it didn't stop Travis from continuing. "Go curl up next to her. She doesn't need to be alone right now. And tell her I'll be in my car, waiting, in case she wants to talk."

He set the cat inside, twisted the bottom lock, and pulled the door closed.

In the car, Travis waited.

Chapter Forty-seven

After what felt like forever, Mari sat up. Wentworth, curled up next to her, butted his head against her hand.

"I love you, too." She stroked the soft, grey fur.

After padding down the stairs, she stopped. The front door was closed, and the knob was locked. Her flipflops lay beside the door. Mari knew enough to know she hadn't left them there, hadn't even locked the door. His actions—making sure she was safely locked inside her house—only added salt to the wound.

She glanced out the front window. His red Porsche was still parked along the curb at the end of the walkway. *Why?*

After turning off the lights and bolting the door, she ran upstairs, changed into jammies, and slid under the covers. A text from Travis popped on the screen: *I hope one day our friendship will be what it once was.*

Sobs started anew as she envisioned walking into the building. Friendship. She hated that word. If she'd ignored her romantic notions and continued working for him, she wouldn't be working for a man that irritated her and cradling a broken heart.

She opened her laptop and sent off an email to Roger.

I'm sorry. Please accept my resignation.

Consider this my two-weeks' notice.

She stared at the words for more than a minute before hitting send. Somehow, she'd make it work, but she couldn't stay at the company.

Staring at the ceiling, she thought about the last few days and weeks. What had changed and when? She might've over-reacted to what he wanted to tell her, but having him pull away hurt in ways she couldn't explain. Having him end things after she'd given up her job only made it worse.

She pulled the covers up to her chin and closed her eyes. She cried and may have drifted off to sleep. But when an image of the letter in the drawer popped into her head, she launched out of bed. Finding it was imperative. Without hesitation, she dumped the contents of her purse onto the floor. Had she missed it?

The letter wasn't there.

Remembering the day when stuff from her purse had spilled onto her floorboard, she slipped on her shoes and tore outside. Why hadn't she thought of that before?

She hoped the neighbors wouldn't call the police. Someone digging through a car in the middle of the night would be suspicious if anyone was awake to see it. Under her seat, she found it.

Walking back inside, she stared at the white rectangle, running her finger across her name scrawled on the front. She could give it back, or she could read it. With nothing to lose, she tore it open.

Of all the changes I'm making, you are

the best of the best. <u>I love you</u>.

She read it a second time. And then a third.

The world paused on its axis, and the sun giggled somewhere below the skyline. She'd carried that bit of sunshine with her, hidden in an envelope, thinking it could bring storm clouds. The last few hours replayed in an instant. She'd been the storm cloud.

Her stomach soured, and her heart sank. Tears, the kind that erupt from a broken heart, poured out. Fueled by regret and pain, hope and desire, she shoved stuff back into her purse, grabbed the letter, and ran to her car. She only stopped long enough to check the time. *4 am.* She'd wake him up if she had to.

Where had Travis spent the night? He hadn't moved anything into the condo, so she drove to his house. It was dark. Hoping the nosey neighbor was sleeping, she knocked on Travis's door. No one answered.

She rang the bell and waited.

After all that happened, she doubted he'd be sleeping soundly, if at all. She drove to the office. He worked when stressed. Why hadn't she gone there first?

She spotted the red Porsche in his reserved spot and tried not to cry. The security guards didn't need to see her coming apart. It wasn't until she got to the door that she realized she hadn't grabbed her badge. Standing at the glass doors, she knocked and waved, hoping the guard on duty would recognize her.

He sauntered toward the door, a quizzical look on his face. "It's early even for you, Mari. Everything okay?"

"Thanks, Miguel. I forgot my badge."

"You the reason the boss has been at work all night?" Miguel swiped his badge so that she could access the elevator.

Mari nodded. "Yeah. Could you—maybe not—"

"My lips are sealed." He winked. "I hope y'all get it worked out."

More than anything, she wanted things to work out with Travis.

"Me too." She yanked the letter out of her purse, praying his feelings hadn't changed since he'd written it, wondering when he'd written it.

When the door opened at the top floor, she barged into Travis's office, waving the piece of paper. "Is this true?" Sobs followed the last word, and she struggled to maintain any hint of composure.

"What are you—" Alarm registered on Travis's face, and he bolted out of his chair. Concern spiraled in his sad blue eyes. "What? Is *what* true?"

"This!" She crossed the room and slapped the note down in front of him. "I need to know. Was it? *Is* it?"

He stared at the slip of paper and raked his fingers through his hair. "Yes, it's true, Mari. But I understand that you don't feel the same way, and I can live with that. It'll be—"

Mari grabbed his wrinkled shirt and pressed her lips to his. He put a hand on her waist but didn't pull her close.

She pulled back but slipped her arms around him. "I'm so sorry."

"But I thought—" He blinked, confusion evident in every line on his face.

"You thought I'd read the letter?"

Travis dropped into his chair, still pensive. "Didn't you?"

"You thought I didn't—that can wait—please say it out loud. I want to hear you say it. I need to hear the words." She squeezed his hand.

"You want me to say it?" Still confused, he wrinkled his brow. "But if—why?"

"Let me explain. You thought I'd read it but didn't feel the same way. I hadn't read it, not until moments ago. I felt bad for taking it, so I didn't read it. I should never have done that. Please forgive me. I couldn't figure out how to give the letter back, but then it fell out of my purse, and I couldn't find it." She was giving way too much detail. "While I was crying, I thought of it and looked for it again. I found it under the seat of my car."

That lopsided grin cut across his face, and he pulled her into his lap. "I love you, Mari." He glanced down, and his brow furrowed. "If you do feel differently, I'll understand."

"You think I'm here at this hour in my pajamas acting like this because I feel differently?" She leaned her forehead against his. "That's what I wouldn't say to Gram because I hadn't even told you. I wouldn't even let myself think it too loudly, but I might've let it slip to Wentworth."

"What do you want, Mari?" The glimmer of a tease that she'd come to love danced in his eyes.

"I want *you*." She pressed her hands to his chest. "And I love you too."

A laugh rumbled inside him, and he cocked an eyebrow.

"You know what I mean." She kissed him again.

"Last night, earlier, whenever it was—what happened? I was going to ask about the letter."

"You locked up my house and put my shoes inside?"

"And I chased Wentworth, who seemed very pleased about escaping. But I was worried about you, so I stayed outside. But when you peeked out the window, saw that I was still there, but didn't come out, I decided you didn't know how to tell me it was over. That's when I left."

"What time was that?"

"I don't know. Midnight?"

"When you said that I wasn't imagining that you were more guarded, I thought you were going to end it, break it off. Hearing the words would've hurt too much, so I left."

Travis shook his head. "Really, Mari? How could you think I would break it off? I thought my feelings were obvious; guess I was wrong."

She sighed and pulled his arms around her.

He kissed her. "I like that Carlos and Kate seem excited about the idea of us dating; although, Carlos probably hates me about now."

"No one knows."

"You didn't even tell Remi and Charlie?"

Mari shook her head. "Besides the fact that almost everyone I know is asleep, if I couldn't bear to hear you say it, you think *I* was going to be able to say it, type it, or whatever?"

"How much sleep did you get last night?" His soft voice soothed her.

"Depends on what counts as sleep. Crying with my eyes closed count?"

"No."

"An hour probably. Not sure."

"I spent the night here at the office. Might as well tell you because you'll just check timestamps anyway."

"That's what Miguel said."

"Mari, when you ran out—"

"You'd been so guarded, and I'd fallen for you so hard."

Travis stole a quick kiss, his smile reflecting in his eyes. "When I saw that the envelope had disappeared and you didn't say anything, I wondered if maybe I'd let things move too quickly."

"Will you say it again?"

He flashed that grin. "I love you."—he kissed her cheek—"I love you."—and then her lips—"I love you."

"I love you too. When are the movers scheduled?"

He laughed. "Sometimes, I can hardly keep up with you."

"I want to be there to help you. I need to mark myself out of the office on the calendar that day." She didn't wait for an invitation. "Roger will have to understand. Besides, with all the late hours I've worked, he shouldn't complain.

"Wednesday."

"Oh, no!" Mari remembered her hasty email. "I emailed Roger my two-weeks' notice."

"Why? When? Mari you didn't—"

"I can email him again, maybe change my mind, but I don't know." She wasn't even sure what she'd say to Roger.

"You don't like working for him, do you?"

"It's very different than working for you." She almost felt bad for Roger.

"Mari, don't worry about it. Roger will be back in the office on Wednesday, and you can talk to him then. Whatever you choose is okay with me. But this weekend, just enjoy your friends."

"You were going to let me find that letter when you were way out in LA?" She poked him in the ribs. "Really?"

He brushed the last few tears off her cheek. "After Emma wrote those letters, watching Kate read all the things that Emma never got the chance to tell her gave me a new perspective. If I have something that needs to be said but the time isn't right, I write it down. That way, if anything ever happened, my feelings would be known."

"Why didn't you just say it?"

His fingers traced the seam along the side of her pajama top. "I wrote that before I'd even kissed you. Having you find it while I was out of town wasn't part of the plan. I wanted to tell you myself."

"You told me I could pack up your office."

"I promise that wasn't why."

"Why have we been dancing around it?" She thought back to the day at the airport when she'd picked him up.

"I'm not used to easy."

Mari understood what he meant, but the way he said it made her want to laugh. Stifling her giggle proved unsuccessful.

Travis paled. "That came out all wrong. I wasn't trying to imply—"

She kissed him. "I know. Finish your thought."

Arms wrapped around her, he rested his chin on her head. "You know some of it, but so much in my life has been difficult, in my personal life. Emma and I were happy together; I loved her, but life was hard for both of us. Business was a success when everything else barely held together."

"But then Kate came back."

"I felt like it gave me permission to be happy, to enjoy life."

Mari stayed still, waiting to hear more.

He tilted her chin so that she met his gaze. "I found myself looking forward to Monday mornings, more than most people look forward to Friday afternoons. Then the time we spent helping Kate with the wedding—I worried it was too good to be true, so I tried to take it slow. I wrote down what I couldn't yet say out loud for fear of running you off."

"And then I carried it around, feeling guilty for taking it and thinking it might shatter what I thought we had. Probably because it seemed too easy. Then I made assumptions and took a hammer to everything."

He sighed. "I'm pretty sure Gram guessed my feelings, and that's why she took you to lunch."

"I am sorry I ran out last night." Mari rubbed her temples.

"I'm just glad you ran in this morning."

She kissed his cheek. "I know you are still working on some things you can't talk about yet, and I'm okay with that. But what other changes? Any you *can* talk about?"

"That's another reason, I hesitated to tell you. Saying 'I love you' and keeping secrets don't always go well together."

She kissed him. "True."

"Some you know—selling the house, buying a condo. I'm thinking about expanding the charity, spending more time with it. I also renewed my passport and switched to boxer briefs."

"Wild man."

"Take off next week and spend it with me."

"Monday's a holiday. Remi and Charlie leave that morning. Tuesday, I have a pile of stuff to do, but I can take off Wednesday through Friday."

"I'd like that." He ran his hands down her sides, his gaze riveted to her face. "Are you okay?"

"My head feels like it's about to explode. Other than that, I'm wonderful."

He opened his desk drawer and handed her the bottle of pills. "Let me grab you water. Be right back."

As he dashed off to the kitchen, Mari sat in his chair, shocked and amazed at all that had changed.

"Your water, Ms. Gonzales."

"Thank you." She jumped up, so he could sit down.

"What time do you pick up Remi and Charlie?"

"Two." Glancing down at her outfit, she chuckled. "I need to change out of my jammies."

Travis wrapped his arms around her. "You need to get some sleep."

"But—"

"Either I can drive you home or you can sleep on my couch while I run to your house and get whatever you need."

"You haven't slept either." She poked him in the arm.

"True."

"You sleep on your couch, and I'll go home. I'd already planned to take off the afternoon, I'll just take off the whole day."

"I figure you have about a half hour before the early birds start showing up for work."

"Then I should go. Miguel was kind enough not to mention my jammies. Others might not be so polite."

"Go sleep. I'll be at your place about five."

She closed her eyes and rested her head on his shoulder. "I'll leave in a minute. Keep talking." Being in his arms ranked more important than sleep at the moment.

"I'm looking forward to seeing your friends again. Although, I'm a bit nervous about what Remi will ask."

"She'll ask to meet your billionaire friends."

He kissed her on the temple. "After tonight, it's just the three of you. I promise."

"You aren't crashing our evening. They specifically asked that you come. And I want you there. Mostly, I want you everywhere."

"Remi is probably just gathering ideas for her book."

Mari sat up and cradled his face with her hands. "I'd read it."

"That's why I love you."

She slipped her arms around his neck. After a kiss, she tried to fake a scolding tone. "You better sleep."

He nodded. "Yes, ma'am."

She rested her head on his shoulder. "I love you, Travis." The words sounded fuller and richer each time she uttered them.

His response came out in a whisper. "I wasn't sure I'd ever hear that from you. Those words are music to my ears."

Mari kissed him before running to the elevator, hoping to make it to her car without bumping into anyone else.

At home, even as excited as she was, once her head hit the pillow, she fell asleep and slept soundly until her phone buzzed.

"This is your courtesy wake-up call." Travis cut off the last word with a yawn.

"Did you sleep?"

"Just woke up."

"Can't wait to see you." Mari rolled out of bed and threw on jeans and a t-shirt.

She made it to the airport in record time and sat in the cell lot until Charlie texted: *Walking into baggage claim.*

Mari drove to their gate. Charlie waved from the sidewalk, and Mari found a gap in traffic, pulled along the curb, and popped the trunk. Her friends tossed in their bags before climbing into the car.

Remi squealed. "I have been looking forward to this for weeks! Pretty much since I flew home last time."

"Same here." Charlie grinned, studying Mari.

"Maybe y'all should move here."

If anyone would spot a change in her demeanor, Charlie would, not that Mari's bed head and lack of make-up weren't obvious. "You okay? I thought Travis was coming."

"He's meeting us at the house in a bit." Mari blended into traffic. "Although, I think he feels like he's intruding."

"You told him that wasn't true, right?" Remi leaned forward, her head between the seats.

"I did, and he's coming. But I doubt we'll see him much the rest of the weekend. He wants us to have time to visit."

Charlie cocked her head. "Did you go to work?"

"I woke up just before your flight arrived." Mari didn't want to recount what happened.

Remi gasped. "Did you—"

"No!" Mari wasn't even exactly sure what Remi was going to ask.

Charlie grinned. "You can explain later. I like him a lot."

"Me too." Mari wanted to hold his declaration close to her heart a little longer before sharing it with her friends. Besides, talking about it would make her cry, and she didn't want to do that while driving, not intentionally.

Mari smoothed her dress and checked her makeup. Satisfied with how she looked, she headed toward the living room but stopped when Remi answered the door. An opportunity to listen was too good to pass up. Mari leaned against the wall, listening as Travis entered.

"Long time no see." The way he treated her friends made Mari love him even more. "Mari upstairs?"

"Want me to get her?" Charlie's voice drew closer.

"No, no. Let her finish getting ready."

Mari started down the stairs. When he came into view, she paused.

He slipped past her friends and stood at the bottom. "Since we won't all fit in my car, I opted for other means of transportation."

"Another surprise?"

He held out his hand. "Come see."

Mari eased up beside him.

Remi yanked open the front door. "A limo? Please tell me it has a bar inside. I'm totally going to have a drink on the way to dinner."

Charlie shook her head, laughing as she followed Remi out. "I think I'll have one too."

Travis beamed. Leaning down, he whispered, "Have y'all had time to talk?"

Mari shook her head and smoothed his collar. "I love you."

"I love you too." He pulled her in for a quick kiss.

Gasps and giggles sounded from the porch.

"I guess they heard us." Mari winked.

When she and Travis slipped into the car, Charlie and Remi were already inspecting the bar.

The young driver closed the door and smoothed his dark hair. Once he got behind the wheel, he turned to face the group. "Good evening. My name's Art, and I'll have you at the restaurant soon." The glass between his seat and the back started to rise.

"Don't do that." Remi tapped the glass. "We want to talk to you."

Travis laughed. "Working on a Billionaire Chauffeur Romance?"

"Oooh! That's not a bad idea. He could be posing as a driver to get near the woman he loves." Remi leaned close to the driver. "What's the craziest night you've ever had driving people around?"

The chauffer laughed. "I'm not sure there is a craziest, but there's been a lot of crazy. Once, I picked up a guy who was incredibly nervous. From a mile away, you could tell he had big plans for the evening, and butterflies were dancing the conga in his stomach."

"Was he going to propose?" Remi typed a note into her phone as he recounted the story.

"That's what I assumed. He gave me the address of where to pick up his girlfriend, and the closer we got to the house, the more he sweated. He kept wiping his forehead as I drove. I was starting to worry that he might have a heart attack."

"That would be horrible. Has that ever happened?" She leaned over the seat.

"No. Anyway, when we were a block from her house, he shouted for me to pull over, so I did—just in time."

"What happened?" Charlie's eyes were wide.

"The poor guy threw up on the side of the road. I appreciated that he hadn't done it in my cab. He wouldn't have been the first, but that's a much less interesting story. Once he'd finished and climbed back in the car, it was clear the man needed at least a mint, but preferably toothpaste and a toothbrush" The chauffer paused as he navigated heavy traffic.

"Don't stop. I need to know what happened." Remi ignored a look from Charlie.

"I drove him to a pharmacy. He bought what he needed and ran into the bathroom to get cleaned up. When he came back out, blue spatter covered the front of his sweat-soaked shirt. I made the mistake of mentioning it. In the parking lot, this grown man started crying. We were late to pick up his girlfriend, and if she texted, he didn't know because his phone had fallen out of his pocket when he jumped out to be sick."

"This story better have a happy ending." Remi looked concerned.

"So right there in the middle of the parking lot, I started taking off my shirt—"

Remi clapped. "I'm liking this story better already."

Charlie swatted Remi's arm.

"Since we were about the same size, I took off my shirt and told him to put it on. We drove back to the girlfriend's house, but she wouldn't answer the door for him. After begging at the door, he trudged back to the limo but wouldn't say anything. With him in the backseat, ready to throw up a second time, *I* went to the door."

"But you didn't ruin her surprise, did you?" Remi's expression changed, more caught up with hearing the end of the story and less concerned with writing it down.

"I knocked until she answered. Her face covered in tears, she didn't say a word. I didn't want to ruin the surprise, but I had to get her into the car before he ruined *my* shirt. Anyway, I explained that I'd had a rough night and—oh what was that guy's name? I think it was Bert or Brent—no Bill. I explained that Bill had been delayed because of me. Technically I did drive him to the pharmacy which made him late. Turns out, because he had been kinda sneaking around, she thought he was cheating or about to break it off or something."

Travis nudged Mari, but she didn't dare look at him. Squeezing his hand, she leaned closer.

Remi downed the last of her wine. "So, what happened?"

"When I opened the door for her to climb in, he was on one knee in the backseat. She almost tackled him, shouting 'yes.' And I paced the sidewalk for twenty minutes, waiting until they were ready to go to dinner."

"Aww." Remi clutched her hands to her chest.

Charlie asked, "Did you ever get your shirt back?"

"I did not." The guy laughed as he pulled along the curb at their destination. "Not sure I wanted it back." He jumped out and opened the door. "Here you go. I'll be back to get you later."

After everyone climbed out, Remi stopped in front of him. "I like you. What's your name again?"

"Arturo, but you can call me Art." He rolled both Rs, which delighted Remi.

She giggled as she was being dragged away by Charlie. "Bye!"

Travis laughed. "Have enough for another book?"

"Maybe. At least a short story." Remi looped her arm through his and tugged until he stopped, then whispered in his ear.

Travis glanced at Mari and tightened his grip on her hand. Looking back at Remi, he nodded. "Thanks for the suggestion."

Charlie pointed at the tower. "Is that where we're eating?"

"It has a great view." He led the way to the entrance.

"It's spinning!" Mari added.

Travis held open the door. "A three-hundred-and-sixty-degree view."

⤳

Mari refilled the margarita glasses while Remi and Charlie changed into pajamas. The conversation would last long into the night, and comfort was a requirement. After carrying the glasses back to the living room, Mari ran up the stairs.

Her phone buzzed, and she smiled at the text from Travis: *I'll be out of pocket tomorrow. I hope you have a fantastic day. Love you.*

Mari tapped out a reply: *Mystery plans? Keep in touch.* She followed that with a kissing emoji. *We we're planning to go dancing tomorrow night.*

Send me the details, and I'll try to be there. He followed that with a wink and a kiss.

"Mari, are you coming? I'm going to need another refill before you get back down." Remi's shouts dissolved into giggles.

Mari changed quickly, then ran back down to the living room. "Sorry. Travis texted."

Charlie eyed Mari as she curled up at the end of the sofa. "Dinner was a real treat. He's perfect for you. Now tell us what's going on!"

"What?" She sipped her margarita, feigning ignorance. "You know we're dating."

Remi slapped the couch. "We didn't know you were using the L word. Love?" She squealed. "I was so right. It's not just a summer fling!"

"It never was!" Mari rolled her eyes.

Charlie leaned forward. "Wedding bells?"

"Marriage hasn't come up at all." Mari hugged a pillow.

Charlie raised her eyebrows, unsatisfied with the answer. "But?"

"There's no 'but.' We've only been dating since July."

Remi wagged a finger at Charlie. "They probably haven't even had their first fight. That always has to happen first."

Mari could feel the blood pooling in her toes.

"They have. Look at her. She's holding out." Charlie leaned forward. "That's why your eyes were red and puffy, wasn't it? Talk."

Tears slipped out before Mari could put words together. "We're okay now, and I'd rather not talk about it. I hope you don't mind."

"You'll invite us to the wedding, right?" Remi refilled her glass. "I told Travis that he should have an extra shirt, toothpaste, and an extra toothbrush around when he proposes, just in case he gets nervous."

Mari laughed, understanding the look from Travis outside the limo. "Seriously, Remi?"

Giggles were the only response.

Chapter Forty-eight

With the doors of the saloon open, country music poured out into the night. As Travis walked past the guys at the door, nods were exchanged. No one asked to see his ID, which wasn't at all a surprise.

Inside, he scanned the room. The deejay was playing tunes Travis remembered hearing on the radio in the nineties, and the band tuned up, getting ready to play. Remi was being twirled around the dancefloor by a guy who was probably the inspiration for her next book. A gentleman cowboy was dancing with Charlie, whose grin was bigger than Travis had ever seen from her.

Alone at a bar-height table near the sound booth, Mari sat watching the dancefloor. The toe of her boot bounced in time to the music. She slid her phone out of her boot, glanced at it, then tucked it back in.

She was waiting on Travis.

In her short red dress and turquoise boots, she made his heart race. He loved her.

Dance with me? He hit send on the text and watched for her reaction.

She jumped a half-second later and bobbled her phone yanking it out of her boot. After seeing the message, she looked around until she spotted him.

He hurried over as she hopped off the barstool.

"You made it!" She slipped her arms around him as she stretched up and kissed him.

"I did." Travis led her to the hardwood floor. "I wasn't about to miss the chance to dance with you again."

"And now, it doesn't matter who is snapping pictures."

"Remi and Charlie look like they are enjoying the evening."

"Do you recognize who Remi is dancing with?"

Travis tried to spot Remi in the crowd. "No—wait. Is that the limo driver?"

"Yes. Art. He told Remi he'd share his stories with her, maybe introduce her to a few people."

"He's going to set her up?"

"I'm not sure about that. He looks pretty interested. She'll be moving here before we know it." Mari giggled as Travis twirled her.

When the song ended, they made their way back to the table. Travis was glad he'd left a certain tiny box at home, otherwise he'd be tempted to drop to one knee in the middle of the dancefloor.

That had to wait.

Chapter Forty-nine

Mari waved as Charlie backed out of the driveway with Remi in the passenger seat. Being abandoned during their girls' weekend wasn't what Mari had anticipated.

Feeling blue, she called Travis. "Hi. You free? Charlie wanted to meet a friend to celebrate something, and Remi wanted to see that chauffeur. Apparently, he has a handful of wealthy clients and was going to give Remi story ideas. So, anyway, I let them borrow my car, and I'm all alone."

"I can remedy that. Want to grab lunch in Comfort?"

"That'd be great. I love that café on High Street."

"I'll be at your house in ten minutes."

Mari bolted up the stairs. She didn't have long to change and put on makeup. Even though Travis wouldn't care, she wanted to look nice.

He arrived when promised, and they spent a few minutes letting their lips say hello before getting into the car.

"You okay? You sounded"—he wrinkled his nose—"frustrated. Hurt maybe."

"Don't say anything, but I am. They both scheduled other stuff on the last day here. They leave in the morning."

"I'll distract you." Travis pulled her fingers to his lips. "I'm all yours."

Mari wanted that to be true. "I like the sound of that."

While they drove out of town, they talked about the move. Thankfully, Travis didn't bring up Mari's job. She didn't like working for Roger and wanted to quit. Spewing that news on the weekend would only throw a wet blanket on their time together, so she waited. She could tell Travis on Tuesday.

Travis parked in front of the boutique hotel that held such fond memories for Mari.

"I love you, Travis."

He leaned across the cab, and with his hand on her cheek, his lips brushed against hers. Soft at first, his kiss deepened. "I love you, too, but I have a confession."

"Uh oh." She laughed, unsure about what he might say but no longer afraid that the relationship was on the brink of disaster.

"I planned a surprise. Every detail is covered except for one part that I could not figure out."

"Okay?" Mari glanced around, waiting for she wasn't sure what.

"So, I'm going to ask you to close your eyes and count to—oh I don't know—sixty-three before you open them. You'll know where to find me. Just in case, here's a hint." He reached into the back seat and handed her a single red rose. After a quick peck, he hopped out of the car. "Close 'em."

Excitement danced on Mari's skin as she counted. One, two, three … They'd only just admitted they loved each other days ago. Would he—no. That was too much to hope. Three, four, five … Maybe he invited Carlos to lunch. That would be a surprise. *Counting. I need to keep counting.* Where was I? Six, seven, eight, nine, ten …

She brushed the rose against her nose. Had he gone into the hotel? Rather than chase rabbit trails of what might be, she focused on counting. As soon as she hit sixty-three, she opened her eyes. At first glance, everything looked the same.

She climbed out of the car, rose in hand. In front of the Porsche, rose petals dotted the sidewalk. Mari followed the trail, which led away from the hotel. The petals led her up a couple steps into what looked like a courtyard, but it was the hollowed-out shell of a building. The follow-me trail led around a koi pond in the center of the room. As tempting as it was to admire the remains of the building, she didn't linger because the petals kept going.

Mari stepped through a doorway into a large room. Even in the daylight, it wasn't bright. The petals stopped just inside the door. She scanned the room. The counter from an old general store dominated one wall. To her right, besides a few tables, the room was empty.

Where was he?

A soft scrape on the concrete drew her attention to the left, and a gasp caught in her throat.

Travis, on one knee, waited beside a sofa. Tears glistened in his eyes. "Before our first date, I said that it was nice not to be alone."

She nearly tripped on her own feet hurrying toward him. "I remember."

"It's more than that. It's about being with you." He stuck his hand in his pocket.

Mari held her breath.

Travis pulled out a small velvet box and snapped it open. "Will you marry me?"

She threw her arms around him. "Yes."

He stood, and his embrace tightened as he lifted her off the floor and kissed her.

"You are one surprise after another." She cradled his face in her hands. "I love you, but I love you even when you don't spoil and surprise me. Please know that."

"I do, but I enjoy your reaction."

"Oh! The ring. I want to see it."

He pulled it out of the box and slipped it on her finger.

"Oh, Travis! It's stunning." Blinking didn't ward off her tears, it only spilled them onto her cheeks. "When? How?"

"I worked with a designer and picked it up when I was out in LA."

"You had it all this time?"

"It's been a hard secret to keep."

Cheers sounded from behind her. Mari whipped around but didn't step out of Travis's arms. "Y'all are all here!"

Carlos hurried over and hugged her. "Travis came by and asked for my blessing yesterday. I'm happy for you, Mom. Is it okay if I walk you down the aisle?"

She wiped a tear off his cheek. "I'd love that."

Kate fanned her face. "I'm trying not to cry."

"She's not succeeding." Alex laughed. "Let's head downstairs."

Remi and Charlie took turns giving Mari a squeeze.

"We sort of fibbed. Travis called, and we had to find a way to sneak out." Remi grinned.

Charlie put her hands on her hips. "I did not fib. I said I wanted to celebrate with a friend. That is exactly what I'm doing."

Mari kissed Travis again. "What's downstairs?"

"A celebratory lunch." He tucked her hair behind her ear. "I was counting on you saying yes, so I had food catered from across the street."

All their friends and family went downstairs, and Mari tugged Travis to the sofa.

"You okay?' He glanced behind him and then at her.

She fingered the pillows that read Mr. & Mrs. and met Travis's gaze. "I'm better than okay."

He sat down next to her. "After your friends go home, we'll discuss dates and venues. Today is about celebrating."

She rested her head on his shoulder. "I love that you had everyone here, but I can't wait to spend time with you—just you."

He answered with a lopsided grin and a wink.

Hand in hand, they descended the stairs to the friends and family waiting down below.

⌒

Monday morning, Mari wasn't ready to say goodbye to her friends, but she was ready to spend some time alone with Travis.

A knock sounded at the door, and she wondered who it could be. The airport shuttle wasn't expected for another few minutes.

Travis flashed a grin and held up a bag. "Breakfast tacos. They haven't left yet, have they? I wanted to say goodbye."

"They're about to." Mari hugged him. "And it makes me sad."

"Hurry up, Remi. Travis is here." Charlie dropped her suitcase at the bottom of the stairs. "Thanks for all the fun and for proposing while we were here."

"I'm glad it all worked out." Travis hugged her.

Remi squealed and ran down the stairs. "I promise not to name my billionaire Travis, but he'll totally be you."

"Aren't most romances about younger guys?" Charlie turned toward Travis. "No offense."

His blue eyes danced. "None taken."

"Young or old, he'll be inspired by Travis." Remi threw her arms around him. "Don't forget your promise."

"I said I'd introduce you if you *moved* here." He winked.

The shuttle arrived, ending the conversation. Once the bags were loaded, Remi and Charlie climbed inside.

Mari waved.

As the airport shuttle pulled away from the curb, Travis wrapped his arms around Mari. "I like your friends."

"I'm glad. Also glad that they feel the same way. Though the limo ride and fancy dinner Friday might have swayed them."

"I do what I can. Kate called me a bit ago. She and Alex are hosting a barbeque today." He pulled Mari close. "I was hoping we'd have the rest of the day to ourselves, but—"

"Let's go to the barbeque." Mari had hoped for the same but felt selfish keeping Travis away from his daughter.

The rest of the day was spent with other people around.

Close to midnight, Travis pulled up to the curb at Mari's. "I'd love to come in, but you said yourself that tomorrow would be busy. I want to hear about your weekend, though." He walked her to the door. "And we have a lot to talk about."

She slipped her arms around his neck. "Tomorrow evening, we can ignore the rest of the world. We'll hide away, have dinner, and just talk."

"Just talk?" He had other plans for the evening.

Chapter Fifty

Tuesday turned out to be twice as busy as a normal Monday. Lost in thought and buried in work, Travis sat at the desk, which was scattered with papers.

A soft knock snapped him out of his thoughts.

Mari slipped into the room and kicked off her shoes. "Long day?"

"Very." Standing up, he opened his arms. "How are you?"

She shrugged. "I haven't decided what I'm going to do about the job."

He didn't want her to stay in a job she didn't love. "What's the hesitation?"

"Money. How was your day?"

"Mari, don't let that be the reason. Please."

"We'll talk about it." She perched on the edge of his desk.

"I wanted to take you to lunch, but I had a meeting and was out of the office for a while."

She loosened his tie. "I heard. Fran called me, wondering if I knew why."

"I want to tell you about my meeting, *and* I want to hear about your weekend, the parts I missed."

"We had so much fun."

"I promise to spend more time with them when they're in town again."

Mari slipped her arms around his waist. "Is everything okay?"

"Yes. The day was busy, but now that you're here, it's perfect." He leaned down and danced his lips on hers.

She nestled closer.

He pressed his lips to her forehead then led her to the sunny spot. The room sparkled with a golden light, the rays of a setting sun warming the small space.

Sharing a sofa, they resumed their kisses.

"I love you, Mari." Gripping her hand, he gazed at her, trying to choose the right wording. "Are there any resumes that meet Roger's criteria? I don't want you to stay in a job you don't like. Especially because you only took the job to date me." He stared at their joined hands. "We are engaged. Please don't let money be the reason you don't quit. Let me help you. Please."

"There are two strong candidates. They are coming in tomorrow." She stood and crossed the room. "I have enough saved up to make it through a couple months, but if we wait longer than that…"

Travis joined her next to the window. "You'll let me help?"

She nodded.

"Mari, I'm not quite done with the surprises yet. You might want to sit down for this next one."

"Now you have me curious and a little concerned." She followed him to the sofa.

"The meeting today, the unscheduled calls, and the business trip I haven't said much about—It's not that I didn't want you to know, but it was a decision I needed to make alone." He hoped she'd be excited. "And I didn't want to get your hopes up and then have it fall through."

She squeezed his hand, encouraging him to continue.

"I've arranged to sell the company. We'll be signing papers soon. The transition will take some time, maybe a year or so. I found someone who won't strip it for parts. They want to keep it going, but it'll be a bit before we make an announcement. So, for now, this has to stay between us." Even saying it out loud, it still didn't seem real. The business had been so much of his life for so long.

Mari blinked, staring at him.

"Back when I stayed up all night working on that contract—it was all related. That account helped the company's position, made it look better on paper." He brushed his thumb along her hand.

Her eyes widened, and she shook her head. "When I said those things at dinner, I didn't mean for you—"

He cut her off with a kiss. "The negotiations were already underway. I'd started the process earlier in the year, said no to a few offers, had one fall through. It's been a long process. And you should never apologize for being right. I went home that night and spent half the night looking at rings."

"I went home and worried that running my mouth changed things."

"It did." He winked.

"What will you do?"

"What will *we* do? Selling the company won't make me a billionaire—I hate to disappoint Remi—but we can retire quite comfortably. Does me selling the company change your answer?"

"No. Are you kidding? I'm just—I don't know what to say. What will we do if we aren't working?"

"Travel, chase grandbabies—though I can't guarantee that part, obviously—visit friends, scratch a few more things off our bucket lists. I'll have more time for the charity foundation. But as I said, things won't change too much for me right away, work-wise."

"When were you thinking of getting married?" Her flushed cheeks and eager smile made his heart race.

He clutched her hands in his. "That's mostly up to you, but hopefully before Thanksgiving because I booked us a trip to Ireland. We fly out that Friday." He kissed her hands. "A honeymoon trip. We'll start in Dublin. Grafton Street will be decorated for Christmas."

"I feel like I'm dreaming. My heart is so full."

He shifted and moved her, so she rested against his chest. "If you want more time, I can reschedule the trip."

"No way. You going to reschedule Christmas too?"

"That's a bit outside my capabilities."

She pulled his arms around her. "Where will we live?"

"We can start house-hunting whenever you want, and we don't have to sell your house. We can live there if you want, or we can live in the condo. I just want to be where you are." He remembered her reaction to the condo and guessed that they might end up living there, at least for a while.

She tilted her head back and tugged him to her lips. "That's what I want, too, and I love the condo. How does the first of October sound?"

"Sounds perfect."

Epilogue

The wood floors in the tiny Schatzenburg church creaked as Mari paced in the side hall, forcing herself to breathe in and out, counting as she did. She hadn't expected to be so nervous.

Carlos stepped in front of her. "You look beautiful, Mom."

"That's only going to make me cry." She straightened his bow tie.

"Sorry." He offered his arm as the music started. "Who is the blonde that's about my age?"

"You're asking me that now? The bridesmaids are walking to the front."

"It's a simple question."

"What about Tori?"

He shrugged. "Apparently I'm not as much fun now that I'm over an hour away. We broke up."

"You are trying to distract me."

"Is it working?"

"Libby. The blonde is Libby, and I'm about to marry her uncle."

"Figures. Think she'll be at Kate's for the reception?"

"Did you miss the part where I said 'uncle'?"

"Just to talk. Sounds like half this town is related to each other. This place is complicated."

"All the interesting ones are." As the double doors opened, she made sure to smile, hoping her nerves didn't show on her face.

Light poured through the stained-glass windows, and colors danced on the floor.

Clutching Carlos's arm, she stepped forward.

Travis winked, and everyone else faded from view. Falling for the boss wasn't how she planned to spend her summer, but she had no complaints.

Stretched out on her stomach, Mari hadn't even opened her eyes but could tell the sun was up and throwing around daylight. She rarely slept in that position, only when she slept hard, which she had. Unsure whether to credit the late-night activities or the fact that she hadn't slept alone, she decided it was the who and not the what.

The bed moved, reminding her that she wasn't alone, as if she even needed the reminder.

Smiling, she turned her head. "How long have you been up?"

Travis trailed a finger along her back. "A little while. I made us coffee, then laid here, enjoying the view."

"Two of my favorite words: us and coffee." She shifted to a sitting position.

A twitch of a grin spoke volumes as he let his gaze sweep over her. "Kate texted, inviting us to join them later this afternoon. Alex is introducing Remi and Charlie to a good ol' Texas brisket."

"What did you tell her?"

"I told her we hadn't even had our coffee yet, but we'd talk about it."

Mari wrinkled her nose. A barbeque wasn't exactly what she'd had in mind for the afternoon. "Maybe?"

Travis set their coffee on the side table. "I have one thing on my agenda for today."

"What's that?" She slid on top of him when he laid back and opened his arms.

"Just you."

Acknowledgments

Special thanks go to Glenda, Michelle, Jessica, Laura, and all the members of the Schatzenburg, TX group on Facebook for reading, listening, and giving feedback when it was needed.

And as always, love and thanks to my husband and boys.

About the Author

Pamela Humphrey is the author of the *Hill Country Secrets* series, *The Chase, Researching Ramirez: On the Trail of the Jesus Ramirez Family,* and *The Blue Rebozo*. She started writing fiction in 2015 after discovering a christening record that revealed a surprising secret. It opened her eyes to the stories around her, real and imagined.

Using the beautiful Texas Hill Country as the setting for most of her books, she looks to the places and people of the region for inspiration. If you've never visited, pick up one her stories and get a glimpse of the landscape and residents. She lives in San Antonio, Texas, with her husband, sons, black cats, and a leopard gecko.

Find out more at **www.phreypress.com**.

Connect Online

Website: **www.phreypress.com**
Facebook: **http://www.facebook.com/phreypress**
Twitter: **@phreypress**

If you want to read more about the town of Schatzenburg, TX, or the characters who frequent that little town, check out the website for extras and short stories.

http://www.phreypress.com

Interested in reading more about Mari's friends?
Subscribe to the newsletter for updates about books 2 and 3 in the *Cheesecake, Margaritas, & Candlelight* series.